What Others Are Saying about This Book...

"Thrilling, thoughtful, elegantly told. So much more than a ghost story." **—Cyrus Webb, CEO, Conversations Book Club**

"The Fabulous Book Babes will definitely read *Mr. Joe* as a selection. After meeting Joseph in *It Started with Dracula: The Count, My Mother, and Me,* our book club is intrigued and eager to read about his remarkable life experiences. We already know the prose will sparkle." **—Fabulous Book Babes**

"There are no lucky breaks, no sudden miracles here, but there is redemption. Love and perseverance can win." **—Jack Rogers, Executive Director (retired), WV Public Defender Services**

"This well-crafted memoir will be a gift to you. *Mr. Joe* tells a powerful story of personal enlightenment and transformation. Its theme of haunting proves irresistible as we follow Joseph through the halls of empty school buildings and the corridors of memory to confront his ghosts. I appreciated that Joe beat unbelievable odds to recover from a lifetime of disappointments, including an illness that left him with total muscular atrophy on his right side. As his personal trainer, I have seen the same determination and positive mindset that enabled him to live with an alcoholic, succeed as a single dad, and become a beloved school custodian." **—Anita Phillips, life coach and certified fitness trainer**

"This is truly inspirational work, a very special book—a gift to any reader." **—Diane Bruno, CISION Media**

D0840240

MR. JOE

Tales from a Haunted Life

Joseph Barnett and Jane Congdon

BETTIE YOUNGS BOOKS

Disclaimer: This is a true story, and the characters and events are real. In some cases, the names, descriptions, and locations have been changed, and some events have been altered, combined, or condensed for storytelling purposes, but the overall chronology is an accurate depiction of the author's experience.

Cover design by Tatomir A. Pitariu
Interior design by Min Gates
Senior editor, Elizabeth Rinaldi
Photos of Joseph Barnett and Jane Congdon by Glamour Shots® portrait studio, Cincinnati

BETTIE YOUNGS BOOK PUBLISHERS
www.BettieYoungsBooks.com

Bettie Youngs Books are distributed worldwide. If you are unable to order this book from your local bookseller or online, or from Espresso, you may order directly from the publisher.

Library of Congress Control Number: 2012944509

1. Barnett, Joseph. 2. Congdon, Jane Barnett. 3. Bettie Youngs Books.
4. Ghosts. 5. Custodians. 6. Addictions. 7. Co-Dependency.
8. Childhood Memories. 9. Alcoholism. 10. Students. 11. Siblings.
12. Alcoholics. 13. Self-esteem.

ISBN: 978-1-936332-78-6
eBook: 978-1-936332-79-3

Printed in the United States of America

"A burnt child dreads the fire." — Middle English proverb

Custodian: keeper; guardian

Contents

Acknowledgments

Many people contributed their time and talents to this book. The authors want to thank the following individuals and groups:

Our amazing publisher, Bettie Youngs of *Bettie Youngs Books*, and her team: cover designer Tatomir Adrian Pitariu, interior designer Min Gates, content editor Mark A. Clements, and copyeditor Elisabeth Rinaldi; and our publicist, Randee Feldman of Get Noticed PR, Jazmin Gomez and the rest of the team bringing this book to print: Your combined talents raised the WOW factor of *Mr. Joe*.

Our early manuscript readers: Laurie Butts, Karen Caldwell, Maggie Moschell, Mary Noschang, Anne Noschang, and Debbie Sebastian. Your suggestions made *Mr. Joe* a better book.

Amy Cole, Assistant on Call, Cincinnati. As always, you expertly formatted the manuscript and found a few typos for us along the way.

Joe's good friend, teacher Karen Mackey: You were a calming influence during Joe's strange experiences at the kindergarten school. You understood and showed him how to talk to "them."

Our personal trainer and good friend, Anita Phillips: You provided fitness and nutrition expertise as well as intangibles too numerous to count.

Jason Barnett, family computer wizard: You did what the pros could not when you recovered Mr. Joe after Jane's hard drive crashed.

We also want to thank Joseph's friends and colleagues who helped with research for *Mr. Joe*, but prefer to remain anonymous.

School custodians have been called unsung heroes. The best ones are like family: caring, flexible, available, and dedicated. They are invested in their schools and communities. The students know their names. That landscape is changing all over America as school districts address budget cuts with layoffs and outsourcing. The traditional custodian is disappearing. We hope this book will shine a light on the value of these unsung heroes. Mr. Joe walked in their shoes.

A Word from the Author

In writing this, I want to acknowledge that some people will not share my beliefs. This book is the truth. When I hear it read back to me, I say, "My God, is that me?" But I know it is. In the years to come I don't want to wish I'd been honest. This is my chance, and I'm taking it.

Ghosts are part of my story. I believe in them; I have no choice. After you've seen one ghost, you can go back and rationalize it. But after you've looked a couple in the eye like I have, you believe. Otherwise, you doubt yourself. I've done that, too—and wondered if I was losing my mind—but I know what I saw and heard.

Here's something else I know: there are many ways to be haunted, and not all of my ghosts were dead. That's the other part of my story. It took almost becoming a ghost myself for me to see my life differently. I believe in ghosts, and I believe in myself. But back when this all started, I was just a guy trying to make a living.

—Joseph Barnett

Prologue
Grandpop

Glen Ferris, West Virginia, 1961

I lingered beside my grandfather's coffin, fascinated by the power of death to take away all signs of personality. Grandpop had been alive when the ambulance came for him; the neighbors said he had waved from the back of the vehicle. Now his hands were folded flat, his eyes closed forever. His face looked empty and old to me, and I cried for the grandfather I had known. It was March, still chilly. I was twelve.

Grandpop had been my special friend. In a world of women talking about dishes, he had played checkers with me. He had come to the house when I was little and had taken me for walks, just the two of us. I was the only grandson.

Grandpop had a gold pocket watch that hung from a chain, and he knew I loved that watch. He would take it out of its special pocket and show it to me, always cupping his other hand underneath it so it wouldn't drop. He had been the same with me: gentle; protective. All of that was over.

Grandpop was the first dead person I had ever seen, and I was shocked at how death had changed him. The body in the casket was, and was not, my grandfather. I recognized him, of course, and there was his suit and there were his wire-rimmed glasses; but the invisible parts of Grandpop—the parts I loved the most—were missing. Those were the traits that had connected us. Until that moment, I hadn't understood. No one had prepared me. I knew Grandpop was dead, but I didn't know he'd be *gone*. Did my good-bye have any meaning? He had left his body, and now I had to leave it and walk on.

"He looks terrible," I whispered to Mom. "Not like himself. I thought dead people were supposed to look like they're asleep."

"Don't ever say that to your grandmother. She's heartbroken. You can't let her know how you feel." It was hard for me to lie, but when I saw the sorrow in my grandmother's eyes, I did it.

A few days after the funeral, I was in front of the bathroom mirror combing my hair. Our bathroom was on the second floor, first right at the top of the stairs. It was small, L-shaped, and lit by a lone bulb in a glass shade. I was standing at the sink, concentrating on my reflection, and then I looked away for a second.

I want to say I had no warning, but that isn't true. No mysterious lights appeared and the room temperature didn't drop, but there's a feeling that precedes seeing a ghost. It's quick; you can hardly separate it from the event; and that feeling is dread. I felt a flash of dread in my gut when I turned back to the mirror, and then I thought I might have a heart attack. I was looking at two faces in the glass: mine and Grandpop's.

He looked alive; only the facts told me I was seeing a ghost. Grandpop wasn't pale the way I'd imagined a ghost would be. His face was in full color and as clear as mine. It floated above my shoulder as though he was standing behind me. He wore no particular expression—no smile, no scowl—but the emptiness I had seen at the funeral home was gone. His eyes were open now and looking straight into mine. He looked real enough to blink.

I was paralyzed. For the first time, I thought my next breath wasn't guaranteed. Seconds passed as my heart raced with fear. I could swear it filled the silence with its pounding. Can you watch a ghost think? That's the way I felt staring at my grandfather's face, helpless to look away. I could imagine him breathing. What was next? My mind sped through the possibilities. Could he turn his head? Would he smile at me? What if he started talking? That would scare me the most. If he moved or made a sound, I knew I would lose it.

Was Grandpop really behind me? I was afraid to turn and look, but what if I did? Would he look solid, or would I see a column of vapor I could put my hand through? I could have seen his head floating in the air, for all I knew. Maybe he wasn't trying to scare me. But I was twelve. Nothing—nothing—could tame the terror I felt at being alone with Grandpop's ghost.

I had to get away before my worst fears came true. I made myself move, hoping he wouldn't follow me. Shutting my eyes, I ducked awkwardly for the bathroom door, praying that Grandpop's image was anchored to the mirror. Even in the hall, even crashing down the stairs, I could feel him behind me. There was no relief until I reached the safety of other rooms and people with beating hearts.

I didn't tell anyone I had seen Grandpop's ghost—they would have thought I'd imagined it—but afterward I was afraid to go upstairs. I especially hated climbing those steps when I was alone. When I reached the top and passed the bathroom door, I focused my eyes straight ahead toward my room at the end of the hall, but I couldn't avoid the bathroom forever. I had to get ready for bed and school.

Every time I looked in the bathroom mirror, I saw Grandpop's face. It never failed to startle me, even after I expected it. I lived in fear. I learned to crouch at the mirror until only my forehead and hair were in the reflection, and then I'd look up to comb my hair. When I brushed my teeth and washed my face, I peeked at myself. I hated to use the toilet; that was the one time I was forced to turn my back on the mirror. My skin would prickle and my heart would pound, even when nothing happened. But then something else did happen.

He always got me alone. I wanted to be ready, but I couldn't keep it up. One day he surprised me downstairs. We had a table by our front door with an oval mirror above it, and that day I looked in the mirror and saw him walking down the stairs behind me. He wore the same neutral expression I had seen before as his eyes found mine in the glass. He had his hand on the banister. It was terrible: the steps and the banister were real, but he wasn't.

It was the first time I had seen his full ghostly body and the first time I had seen him move. He was in full color, dressed in a shirt, a tie, and the vest and pants from his brown suit. The chain to his gold watch hung from a vest pocket. The image was so sharp that I could see the crease in his pants. When he got to the landing, he paused with his hand on the post, still watching me. That was it; I opened the door and ran. I ran until I was on another street. That vision of my sweet Grandpop coming down the stairs all dressed up was the scariest thing I'd ever seen.

Grandpop haunted me for months. What did he want? Why did he pick me? I didn't understand any of it. He didn't try to hurt me, but what is hurt, anyway? He scared me. Just the anticipation of seeing him again wore me down. I had cherished my time alone with Grandpop when he was alive, but not now. Now I only wanted him to leave me alone.

Grandpop was my first ghost, but he wouldn't be my last, and it would have been much too soon to tell me that ghosts would become a metaphor for my whole life.

1
Old Ghosts

Cincinnati, Ohio, 1997

I hadn't been working at the kindergarten school very long when I heard it was haunted. Even though the word *haunted* wasn't spoken, I pieced it together from scraps of conversation. I had been hired as a night shift custodian, and I was still learning the job when one of the maintenance men mentioned that our building had been constructed near a graveyard.

Ours was the oldest building in the district, the heart of it dating back to 1911. Two additions had been put on, one in the 1930s and the other in the '50s. Originally a high school built to serve the surrounding farming community, by 1997 the facility was being used to educate preschool and kindergarten children in a growing city of 20,000 residents. In addition, it housed the offices of the school administrators.

I was assigned to clean the school side. My shift began at two-thirty in the afternoon, while the children were still in the building. Once school was dismissed just after three o'clock, the halls grew quiet. In February, darkness came early. I liked the night, and I didn't mind working alone.

My shift ended at eleven. At ten-thirty my new boss, Dave, arrived to begin his shift on the administrative side, and we always touched base before I went home. One evening I mentioned the maintenance man's remark. I was curious about the graveyard. "Do you think he meant anything in particular?" I asked. Dave and I had been friends for forty years, and I knew he would tell me.

"You might hear stories about weird things happening to people here, Joe. Those stories go around. I try to ignore them."

"What kinds of weird things?"

"People say they've seen things. I never have, but if anything ever happens at night that you want to tell me about, I won't think you're crazy."

"This place has ghosts?"

"I don't know, but sometimes at night when you're by yourself, this old building can be spooky with its creaks and groans. The acoustics are so good that when it's quiet you can hear all kinds of noises. I play music while I clean, and you can do the same if you want to. Anyway, if you ever need me, I'm just on the other side."

"Of the building," I said, being witty.

"Yes, the other side of the building."

I considered my buddy's comments after he'd gone, but I knew I wouldn't let them bother me. I was in training and too busy to worry about a haunted school. Besides, I wanted to keep my job and would have cleaned alongside the Frankenstein monster.

I hadn't planned to be a custodian, but circumstances had led me here like a trail of crumbs from a fairy tale. Weeks earlier I'd been let go from my job as a supervisor in a food plant. The firing was a sudden ending to twenty-seven years with the company. I was shocked, caught off guard. Hurt. Maybe there's never a good time, but the middle of winter was a terrible time for me to be fired. Bills were due, and the holidays had seriously reduced my cash flow.

I was a single dad, forty-eight years old. At twenty-two and nineteen, my sons were grown, but Mike and Jay still lived with me. I had hoped to help Mike, my older boy, with his college expenses, and instead I'd lost my job. My grandfather used to have an expression about rolling a peanut down the railroad track with his nose. Well, that day I would have rolled one down the track in two feet of snow if that was what it took to be employed and have medical insurance.

Dave had come to my rescue, and now I was gainfully employed—in a school built near a graveyard, or over a graveyard; I wasn't sure of the location. Something had spooked a few people in this place, though. I hadn't intended to dwell on the building's history, but I couldn't help thinking about it as I pushed my cleaning cart toward another silent, empty classroom. I'd never been alone in a school building for hours on end, especially at night. There was a creepiness factor that I would have to learn to ignore. It reminded me of the times I'd left school dances or ballgames to find a restroom: the lively noise from the gym would recede, and every sound I made would echo. I would feel vulnerable and suddenly want to hurry. But did I believe in ghosts?

Of course I did.

When you've seen your own grandfather after his passing, you believe. The memories I had successfully stashed in a remote corner of my mind since I was twelve years old came flooding back that night.

The way I remember Grandpop, he could have been Don Knotts's body double. Though he was better looking and taller than the actor, Grandpop weighed only about one hundred forty pounds. He was on the quiet side; when I was little I thought he was the mildest person in the world. I used to hide and then jump out and try to scare him until Grandmama told me he had a bad heart. I didn't understand that; to me, he had a good heart.

My mother's parents lived within walking distance, and when I was a kid Grandpop came to our house a lot. I would look out the dining room window and see him coming down the back walk. Sometimes he'd sit on the couch by himself. Other times I'd show him my toys or we'd play checkers in the living room. I was always glad to see Grandpop, but back then I didn't know the reason for his frequent visits. I didn't know that he was coming over to watch my mother, to try to keep her from drinking that day.

A boy isn't expected to know everything, but that night as I thought about Grandpop for the first time in years, I knew that he had been looking out for me. Had he continued to watch over me after he died? Is that what the ghost appearances were about?

I know one thing: intent doesn't matter when you see a ghost. Chances are, you won't know its purpose, or its limitations, or why it has come to you. The mere fact of being alone with it will scare you half to death; they aren't called *spooks* for nothing. Grandpop's ghostly presence in our house had been a haunting, pure and simple. He had even invaded my last refuge: my bedroom. Mom had hung a picture on the wall facing the doorway, and one night I glanced at that picture from the hall and saw his face in the glass.

When I tried to hang a shirt over that picture, it was just instinct; I'd never heard of the custom of covering mirrors after a death. If Mom and Dad had known about it, maybe they would have covered our mirrors after Grandpop died. But I doubt if the subject of a Jewish custom would have come up in our family. We were Protestants, and not very worldly. I was a grown man before I learned that the practice is based on a belief that spirits are attracted to mirrors, that a dead person's soul can be trapped in a reflection, and that a spirit might linger on earth for a time and might even reach out to the living. No one had to convince me of that.

Now, thirty-five years later, the memory of Grandpop's ghost still had the power to scare me. I could recall all of my feelings from that period; I just didn't want to. As I cleaned my classrooms that evening, I wondered if I was still susceptible to seeing ghosts. The dim halls and deserted rooms of the kindergarten school had pulled at memories I'd managed to put away since childhood. When I vacuumed, I'd remember Grandpop behind me. When I caught one of the dark school windows in my peripheral vision, I'd think of his face watching me in the mirror. I was nearly fifty years old, and I still felt my heart rate accelerate at the thought of Grandpop's ghost.

2
Career Changes

I hadn't wanted to be a custodian. Who aspired to that? When the personnel manager at the meat plant had suggested it the day he fired me, all of my thoughts were negative.

He had spoken without an ounce of empathy in his voice: "We tried to get you back into the union, but unfortunately that cannot be done. Have you talked to Carl lately? Maybe his school district is hiring."

Carl had left the plant to work as a school janitor. Dave had hired him, so maybe I could follow the same path, but did I want to? I was pretty sure I didn't. For most of my career I'd been a factory worker, cleaning the equipment used to process hot dogs and lunchmeat, yet I didn't want to degrade myself by becoming a custodian—or the hated "J" word.

We were called the sanitation crew. Over the years I became very good at cleaning the commercial equipment used in meat production: blenders large enough to process a ten-thousand-pound batch and ovens the meat would pass through on hangers, raw at the beginning and fully cooked at the other end. "Everything but the squeal" was what we used to say about the ingredients.

I was good at my job, and I enjoyed it. The job had been good to me, too. I made a decent wage, I had good friends at work, and in middle age I still had a thirty-two-inch waist; physical labor will do that for you.

After a while it became my job to follow the U.S. Department of Agriculture inspector on his rounds through the plant. Whenever he found equipment that hadn't been cleaned properly, it was my responsibility to bring it up to inspection standards. That led to my becoming a pre-inspector. Every Sunday night—the night before the first shift of the week—two of us would work all night checking the machines. That way they'd be more likely to pass the official inspection.

My subsequent promotion to supervisor had been my downfall. I'd taken it for the money—an additional ten thousand dollars per year—but the job hadn't proved to be a good match for my skills.

Mr. Joe

I was humiliated at being let go. The rejection was devastating, and I still had to tell my boys. How I'd dreaded it. I had no college money for Mike. To make matters worse, my younger boy, Jay, worked at the same plant. I had been his boss.

Upon hearing the news, both of my sons had hugged me and told me not to worry. How could they be so understanding after all I'd put them through? I'd split up our family when they were five and three years old. As the custodial parent, I'd moved us many times in my attempts to give them a proper home. I hadn't wanted to hand my sons a hard life, but I'd struggled. The way I saw it, losing my job at the meat plant was just one more way I'd let my children down.

With the warm memory of their arms around me, I set my course. I may have tripped and stumbled, but I needed to get right back on my feet. I was still stinging from my dismissal and embarrassed at the idea of becoming a janitor, but I swallowed my pride and called Dave. He had helped Carl, and I knew he would help me. The three of us had forged our bonds in the same place: the meat plant. Dave and I were especially close, and we knew each other's work. I found myself hoping he could he get me on as a janitor in his district.

When I was a kid in West Virginia, my dad's company had sponsored a summer camp, Camp Brookside. It was a train ride away, and I started going there when I was seven or eight years old. Each session was two weeks long, and we stayed in rustic cabins furnished with little more than multiple sets of metal bunk beds. We even brought our own linens.

The walls and floors of the cabins were bare wood. Before we were allowed to begin a day's activities—canoeing, archery, crafts, horseback riding—we had to clean the cabin. Each camper made his bed and tidied his own area, and then we swept and mopped the floor. While we were out doing our activities, an adult would inspect all the cabins and give each one a rating. That was all it took to inspire me.

I'd never touched a mop at home, but I filled a clanking pail and carried it to the cabin with two hands, sloshing water on my legs and shorts. At eight years old I slung a mop and didn't think a thing of it. Considering my new career brought back those memories: the outdoor pump; the scent of Pine-Sol on bare boards. Now I could imagine my little self standing in that cabin, holding a string mop as a big voice boomed, "Joe, one day all this will be yours."

Sure enough, Dave set up an interview for me. As soon as I heard, I began to prepare. He'd said I didn't need a suit, just a nice shirt and pants. The point was to look neat. I picked out what I would wear and had it all dry-cleaned. Ordinarily I washed my own clothes, but for this occasion everything but my underwear went to the cleaners.

Dave had told me that smoking wasn't allowed on school premises. The district wanted to hire a non-smoker. I wanted that job, and I knew I could do it, but I smoked. I intended to make sure my habit didn't become an issue. On the day of the interview I took a long, soapy shower and washed my hair thirty minutes before I left the house. I hadn't had a cigarette all day. If I had smoked at all, the interviewing team might have detected the odor and rejected me.

The three people who made up the interview team greeted me: the school superintendent, the head custodian of the building, and the school principal. They began by asking me to tell them a few things about myself. I had no idea what they wanted to hear, but I can talk to people and I had a work history that was relevant. I was glad I'd taken pains to be presentable. From their later questions, I could tell that this group had a keen interest in maintaining a certain image in the community.

After fifteen or twenty minutes they asked me to leave the room. As I waited outside the door, I wished I could smoke. It was hard to tell what impression I'd made, but I was cautiously optimistic about my chances. I felt an edge of excitement. In a few minutes I might be employed; in an hour I might be working! Dave had told me to bring some work clothes with me; if I was hired, I might start that day.

When the three interviewers called me in to congratulate me, I made a point of speaking to Hannah, my new principal. "You've made a good decision," I said. "I take pride in my work, and I will do a great job for you."

"Thank you, Joe. It will take just two or three days to see if that's true." I wanted to call that a vote of confidence.

I was glad to have the job, but I didn't like people calling me a janitor. Shortly after I started at the kindergarten school, a new manager was hired in the district. He got us all together and explained why we were not going to be called janitors. We were going to be called custodians.

"To me, it's a term of respect," he said. "A janitor cleans and does minor repairs; a custodian is entrusted to take care of a property. Custodians typically assume many different duties to carry out that trust. You are already doing that. I'm calling you custodians because you are."

After that, I was pumped to do a good job. I'd always had a strong work ethic, but the fact that our manager appreciated our value made me want to knock myself out for the guy. I began to change my mind about my new career at the kindergarten school. When I thought about all the benefits, it became more inviting than I'd expected.

First of all, I had to be grateful for the opportunity to be employed. The offer had come just when I needed it, and my bonus was the privilege of working for my long-time friend, Dave. He had gone to bat for me in a very big way and I was determined that he would not regret it.

Second, school had always been a safe place for me. When I was small it was safer than home because of my mother's drinking. Now I could help to make the kindergarten school a safe place for those children. I liked the thought that being a custodian would offer me a chance to be a positive influence for kids, even for an hour a day.

There were other benefits. My schedule would allow me to be on my own for most of my shift. I looked forward to developing my own routine. I was used to working nights, so my hours were fine. The district had no budget for overtime, so I could work hard for eight hours and then leave. Best of all, when I got home I could forget all about my job. What would a custodian worry about at home?

The mobility aspect of my job was perfect; I would have the run of the whole school. I'm claustrophobic, so freedom of movement is important. I had never taken a job that confined me to a small area; being stuck in a cubicle or stationed along an assembly line would have done me in. My breathing would change at the thought of the worst job I could imagine: staffing a turnpike tollbooth with traffic streaming by on two sides. The vision also reminded me of the scene in *The Godfather* when Sonny Corleone was blocked in and machine-gunned to death at a tollbooth.

I started work the day of my interview. After I had changed clothes, Earl, the head custodian, had given me a tour. The appearance of the school wasn't impressive on the outside as we walked up to it, so I was surprised when we stepped inside the main entrance. The floor shone. What I could see of the interior looked perfect; everything glistened. I found out it was Dave's work I was admiring. He had been cleaning the administrative side for the past year and a half.

As I walked down the halls for the first time, nothing else stood out to me. The school seemed no different from my memories of schools I'd attended years before. Everything looked small as we passed the rooms I would be cleaning. I guess that was a good thing. There were nineteen classrooms, including two art rooms and a computer room. In addition, I was responsible for cleaning six bathrooms, the principal's office, the nurse's office, the teachers' workroom, and two main halls.

By the time I'd had my tour, I was an hour and a half into my shift. I had roughly six and a half hours left to do my work and no idea exactly how I was supposed to spend that time. There was no instruction book. Earl had left me alone. Did he think I'd automatically know what to do?

I'd had few expectations going into the job, and I certainly hadn't expected that being a custodian would be hard. I thought my experience at the meat plant would help me. It had to. After doing pre-inspections for several years, I'd trained myself to notice even the smallest flaw in the equipment, the smallest piece of meat that should not have been there. As I walked into the first classroom that night, my inner inspector took over. My eyes scanned the room. I was looking for any speck of dust, anything out of line, the way I had been trained to do. Right away I knew my eagle eye would not be required to find the mess.

Instead of desks, the children sat at tables. Those tables were covered with dried glitter, glue, and paint that had built up—over time. That should have been my first clue, but instead the tables became my first challenge. I cleaned every one, and I was just as conscientious about the rest of the room. The next time I paid attention to the clock, three hours had passed. Well over half of my shift was gone.

When Dave came to check on me, I had cleaned a grand total of three rooms. They looked great, but I had just a few hours left and many rooms left to clean. "Am I always going to be up against the clock like this?" I asked.

"You will if you try to do everything; there isn't time. Some things, like emptying the trash, have to be done during every shift; others are done periodically. There are days you wax, days you dust, days you mop, and days you buff. Remember this, Joe: you cannot do everything every day. That is the custodian's creed."

He helped me clean that night, and between the two of us we got it all done, finishing shortly after my shift had officially ended. "You'll get more efficient, Joe. Give yourself a chance to get the hang of it." I would have to; I couldn't keep depending on him to pitch in. Besides being my immediate boss, he had his own work to do. Clearly, I was going to have to streamline my methods in order to finish my work in eight hours.

3
Just Checking

I was learning the layout of the school, night by night. It didn't take long to learn the pattern of the classrooms; most of them were alike.

The floors were carpeted except for a four- to five-foot area of tile across the back. Each classroom had two double closets on the back wall and a sink in the tiled area where the kids could clean up after activities like finger painting.

Space was at a premium in that old building. Each classroom had six or seven of the small, rectangular tables where students sat two to a side. In addition, each room had a few computers lined along one wall and several bookcases placed around the room. The teachers didn't have adequate storage room, so their bookcases were crammed with lesson materials. It seemed to me that teachers had a common trait: they didn't want anything thrown away. They kept items to use over and over, for instance when they taught a particular unit or decorated their classrooms in seasonal themes. I knew their budgets were smaller than most people realized, which was why they reused so many items, but the lack of storage, added to the furniture setup, made for some tricky navigation on my part just to clean the room. I sometimes had to walk sideways to get between the pieces of furniture.

I figured I would have a maximum of fifteen minutes in each classroom because of my other duties. It seemed there were only two things I had to do in order to maintain my areas. The first was to move at warp speed. The second was to forget about taking a lunch break until I had learned how to complete my job in the time I had.

The first thing I did in each classroom was to empty the trash cans. Then I cleaned the sink, swept and mopped the tiled area, and vacuumed the carpet. Initially I had trouble finding electrical outlets for the vacuum cleaner. If they weren't visible, I had to look for them. The problem with that was the impact on my time. More often than not, I would find the outlet I needed behind a heavy bookcase or one filled with breakable objects. If I had to move a bookcase away from an outlet and then back again, that routine would add five minutes to the time it took to clean the room. It doesn't sound like much until you multiply five minutes by the total number of classrooms. Remember, I had nineteen. Just finding outlets could add an hour and a half to my evening schedule. You might wonder why I didn't just plug an extension cord in somewhere and move on. Think about pulling a garden hose down a narrow, winding path between plantings and you'll understand why I didn't even ask for one to use in those crowded classrooms.

Developing my nightly routine was always a race, especially in those early days when I had to factor in my learning curve. The last thing I needed was to see Hannah, my principal, heading toward me, but that's just what happened during my first week.

I had just finished cleaning my fourth classroom. I'd already moved my cleaning cart down the hall and was pulling the vacuum cleaner out of the room when I saw her. I would have preferred to see a ghost.

Hannah had said she would know right away if I was going to work out, and she sure hadn't wasted any time checking on me. I already knew that she had a definite idea of how her school should look, and that most certainly included my contributions as a custodian. I liked her, but she wouldn't accept less than anyone's best work. Everything in the school had to be perfect. It took only one look at Hannah to understand that: she never had a hair out of place or a wrinkle in her clothes. I had noticed it right away.

Once I gave her a compliment, and she told me why she was so particular: "When I was in first grade, I was sitting at my desk one day, and I saw a smudge of dirt on my arm. I licked my finger and wiped it off. The teacher caught me doing it and told me in front of all the other kids, 'From now on, take your baths at home, before you get to school.' I was so embarrassed. That comment stuck with me, and I've never left the house again unless I knew my appearance was perfect."

Now she asked me, "Have you finished cleaning this room?" I said I had.

She smiled. "I've come to help you." Well, it was help of a sort.

She looked around the room, and her attention settled on the windowsill. "Do you see what you missed, Joe? Can you see all that dust on the windowsill? I see a dead fly, too. Do you?"

Sometimes it's all right to speak your mind. There are other times when you should just bite your tongue.

"I didn't see the fly," I said. What I wanted to say was, "No, Hannah, I didn't see the dead fly. I saw the fifteen pounds of elbow macaroni spread across the floor. I saw the dried finger paint in the sink and all over the tile. I even managed to catch the box of confetti that was spilled on the carpet at the other end of the room. But the fly slipped right past me." I had one thought I would never share with her, one universal question I think every custodian would like to ask: where were you when I first started cleaning this room after fifty kindergarteners used it? I doubted Hannah had any idea how much work I'd already done by the time she arrived to "help" me. Some nights it took me an hour just to get a classroom up to what I called "square one": normal dirt.

"I'm glad I could help, Joe."

"I would have loved to see your other school," I said. "As much as you care, it must have been really special."

"No, it was just the opposite. It was dirty. The custodians were nice people, and they meant well, but they weren't that sharp. One of them ran and jumped out a second-story window as a test, to see if it would be safe for the kids to do the same thing in the event of a fire."

"Did he tell you what he learned?"

"No, the last I heard, he was still on medical leave. He broke both of his legs. Joe, I don't ever want anything like that to happen again, or to have a building that isn't clean, because it's a reflection on me. I didn't hire those custodians; you're the first one I've ever hired. That's why I'm training you. This time, I want to get it right."

I was surprised to learn that Hannah was new at this just as I was, but I still felt like a bug under a microscope. I would need a lot of help if she was going to train me. Was it training when Hannah deliberately dreamed up things for me to do? She obviously hadn't heard of the custodian's creed when she suggested I clean the windowsills in every classroom. The windows ran the length of the rooms, twenty or thirty feet, and every inch of sill was covered with plants, art projects, pictures, and stacks of paper. The only way to dust them was to remove everything and then put it back. At a half hour each, cleaning the window sills would take me nine and one-half hours, impossible to do except as a long-term project.

Life was better when Hannah didn't show up. The teachers were nice to me. When I came to work, I'd walk by their rooms to let them know I was in the building. As I got to know them individually, they told me why they had set up their rooms in certain ways, for example to separate activities or to open up more space where the kids could interact. Everything was arranged for the benefit of the children, as it should be. Everything was in its right place and would remain where it was. In other words, the teachers weren't going to rearrange their classrooms to suit me.

The condition of a room at the end of a day depended largely on the teacher. I had already begun to categorize the teachers in our building according to how they left their rooms at night. Some were very considerate, but others didn't seem to care how big a mess they or their students left behind. I was learning to adjust my cleaning schedule to those differences. If I'd just finished cleaning a room that was a total wreck, I needed to go to a room I felt good about and could clean with minimal effort. Otherwise, besides being worn out, I'd start to develop a bad attitude.

The three rooms for preschoolers were the worst. Their teachers wanted the children to experience different textures, so each classroom had a sensory table, which was a plastic half-barrel filled with a substance such as sand, macaroni, Cream of Wheat, confetti, or rice. One teacher mixed Cream of Wheat with water and let the kids play with the wet glop on the carpet. I had to soak and scrape the rug to clean it up.

Try to vacuum up confetti; the wind from the damn vacuum cleaner blows it all around. And try to imagine the rice going *pa-pa-pa-pa* all night, when every grain bounces off the inside of the hose.

One time a preschool teacher filled a bin with chocolate pudding and let the kids do finger painting with it. In order not to mess up the room, they laid their paintings on the floor by the door to dry. They had a fifteen-minute recess while the papers were drying, and when the kids trooped outside they walked over the chocolate pudding and tracked it down the hall.

So, Hannah, sorry if I don't always clean to your perfect standards. I do try . . .

But the smart remarks faded away in light of one fact that wasn't going to change: she was the school principal. I wanted the job, so I needed to adjust my attitude and keep working toward the perfection she and I both hoped to attain for *our* school.

4
Night Music

It's funny how we see things. For weeks, all I worried about during my nights at the school was doing a good job. I rarely thought about the ghost rumors and instead became absorbed with my work. It was hard to forget my encounter with Hannah, and I hadn't noticed anything weird—well, except for the night we heard the footsteps.

My routine before leaving was to take my last load of trash out to the Dumpster. I always cut through the gym. One night on my way through, I heard someone running above me. Whoever it was would run for a few seconds, hesitate, and then run back. Nothing was up there but a ceiling, a roof, and an attic-like space in between.

The running was definitely coming from inside, not outside on the roof—and the steps were too heavy to be made by a squirrel or a raccoon. It had to be a person. After I took the trash out, I found Dave and told him about the noise. He came into the gym and heard it, too.

"Where is it coming from?" I wondered.

"Right above us," Dave said, pointing, "And there's only one way to get up there."

What I'm calling the gym was a combination gymnasium-auditorium; there was a stage on one side of the gym floor and a few rows of theater-style seating on the other side. Because it was old, built to accommodate a small student population, the scale of our gym was nowhere near that of school gyms today.

Up high, between the main sections of seats, was a little projection room accessible by a ladder on the wall. Going through that projection room was the only way I knew that anyone could have gotten into the area where we heard the running, but I didn't see how that was possible. It was kept locked.

"Do you think it's kids?" Dave asked. I had no idea, but I knew he suspected teenagers from a nearby apartment house. Before I started working at the school, vandals had been caught using the building after hours. That was one of the reasons Dave and I checked it so carefully every night.

The police had been over to check the premises before, and we decided to call them. The station was on the next block, but after a certain time of night, calls were routed to a different station. We knew this when we called, but at least there would be a record of the disturbance. The police agreed to send someone, so I climbed the ladder and, with a master key, unlocked the projection room door for them. I didn't open it because I didn't know who I might find in there.

The officer who responded drew his gun and went up the ladder. He checked the projection room, and it was empty. He checked everything he could. There was no sign of anyone, but Dave and I knew what we'd heard. "I still think there was somebody or something up there," he said later. "You could hear it."

Hannah asked me about the incident later, though there wasn't much to say. I understood that she was still keeping an eye on me.

I was on probation. As a new school employee, I would have formal evaluations by my super-picky principal at thirty, sixty, and ninety days. If I passed, my job would be secure, and that's what I was shooting for. I was getting a handle on my duties, and all I wanted was a chance to prove myself. It wasn't my lack of job experience that worried me.

How was Hannah going to evaluate me? Everything she had told me about her previous cleaning staff was negative. Besides Dave's input, what would she use for a yardstick? Her previous school hadn't been well maintained, and one of the custodians had even jumped out of a window. I realized that Hannah had no experience with someone like me. I wanted her to see that I had nothing in common with her previous custodial employees, whom I had no qualms calling *janitors*.

I was determined to excel, and some of the teachers in our school must have felt the same way about their jobs, because they came back to work in the evenings. It wasn't just a matter of staying an hour or two after school; on any given day, three or four teachers could be in the building until eight or nine at night—or later. That was a problem for me, because I couldn't finish my work until they left.

Because every minute counted every night, I couldn't wait for the teachers to clear out, so I tried cleaning the empty classrooms first. I quickly found out that was more time consuming than going straight up the hall from one room to another, because I had to determine which ones were empty. I knew it would eventually catch up to me.

I didn't understand why preschool and kindergarten teachers needed to spend so much time in the classroom after school. At that level, how much paperwork could there be? I'd gotten to know several of the teachers, so one night I asked one of them.

"These students haven't learned to read or write yet," she said. "During class, we can't simply give out work assignments for them to do. We have to lead them through every lesson, and that doesn't leave us any time to prepare for the next day. Some of us have families at home. We have children to feed and put to bed. So, when our husbands get home, they watch the kids for a few hours so that we can come in later, when it's quiet." That made sense, but it didn't help me.

Even if they didn't realize it, those teachers were cutting into my time. Did I walk into a room and start vacuuming during their classes? Of course not, but I couldn't say that out loud. The faculty members were equivalent to my bosses; I was there to serve them, not the other way around. If they had come in to meet with parents or make phone calls, I couldn't disturb them. Some suggested I skip their classrooms in my cleaning rounds. They were trying to help me, and some nights it was tempting, but no way could I comply.

Why was I so particular? Why did I care so much? Part of it was pride, and part was the knowledge that my work would be inspected by a perfectionist. Hannah would notice and complain to Earl about what I'd missed the previous night. She had laid out her expectations in my job interview, and in case I didn't remember, she reminded me all the time: "Joe, the first impression people have of me comes from the appearance of my school, and I'm *entrusting* that to you." There was that word again, and I wanted to live up to it. No pressure; all I had to do was clean an area that in my mind was the size of Vermont, and do it to her exacting standards. It wasn't just a challenge; it was frustrating as hell.

Many nights I worked a little bit past my quitting time, but it was unpaid labor. Even if the school had offered overtime, I was a junior guy. The senior custodians would have been the ones to grab the O.T. if any had been available.

One of my jobs was to mop and condition the floors. I was obsessive about the floors because every employee and visitor would see my work. Most people didn't see the inside of the classrooms, but everybody walked through the common areas.

Waxing was a major project reserved for summertime, but in between I mopped the halls every night, always after everyone had left, and that was for safety reasons; but I also wanted to allow the floors to dry without the surface being disturbed. After mopping, I applied a conditioner that made the surface slicker and added to the drying time. When I finished, those floors would shine like they were wet.

Before I could leave for the night, I had to do a security check of the doors and windows. One night when I was doing my final check, I found a classroom door unlocked. It was nearly eleven, and the teacher was sitting at her desk. "I didn't want to walk on your freshly mopped floor until it was dry," she said. "I kept coming out to look, and it still looked wet, so I came back in and worked some more."

"You can go home," I said. "It's been dry for three hours."

Cleaning Hannah's office was one of my other jobs. I regularly wiped down every surface, including every book on her bookshelf, every object, and every picture frame. Dave knew how conscientious I was, and he had told me a story.

"I'm like you, Joe. I always want to make a great impression. One time just after I started, I was cleaning the superintendent's office. He had a framed photo of his family, and I wanted that glass to shine. There was just one problem: There *was* no glass over the picture, and when I cleaned it I wiped off his wife's face."

My eyes went wide, but I didn't say anything. He went on.

"I had to go in and tell him the next day. He could have chewed me out good, but he was nice about it."

Cleaning Hannah's pictures never failed to bring back that story. Before I took a cleaning cloth to her pictures, I made sure there was glass in every frame.

One night I was surprised to see a big, black spider on Hannah's desk. What would perfect Hannah think of that? Of course I didn't want to leave it there, so the easiest thing was to suck it up with the vacuum cleaner hose, and I did. Before I'd finished cleaning the desk, I saw another spider on the other side. That thing was the size of a silver dollar.

After I saw the second one, I stopped and looked at it for a minute. It wasn't moving. I picked it up and found that it was porcelain, a knick knack. Oops! They were a pair, and I'd sucked the other one into the vacuum cleaner bag. I went downstairs and sliced the bag open, combed through all the dirt, found the spider, and put it back. I didn't tell Hannah that story until much later, when I found out the spiders had sentimental value for her. Fortunately, she laughed.

As for my nightly dilemma—how to get my work done—I finally came up with a solution. I had taken Dave's suggestion to play music while I cleaned. I'd done it to cover up the spooky noises he'd warned me about—the ones I'd said wouldn't bother me—because he was right: there were spooky noises. The footsteps in the gym proved it.

For all my grousing about the teachers, I wasn't used to working alone. I had noticed the wind howling, wood creaking, and the building settling—sounds that could play dark games with my imagination—and I was happy to drown them out with my music. Working to the sounds of the Everly Brothers, Patsy Cline, The Temptations, Buddy Holly, and others gave me the extra push and energy I needed, too. I would put one of my CDs in my boom box and go to town. I had a good selection: country, rock, rap, oldies—you name it. Dave always had a full case with him, too, and sometimes we traded.

I was glad he had given me the idea to bring music in, and I decided to surprise him with a custom tape of his favorite songs. Both of our boom boxes played cassette tapes as well as CDs, so it was possible to tape songs from CDs onto a cassette. That's what I did. I found a blank cassette in a kitchen drawer at home and recorded fast songs on one side and mellow tunes on the other. The process took hours. The music on the second side didn't quite fill the tape, but what was the harm in having a few seconds of silence at the end?

The district big shots often came in to work in the evenings while Dave was cleaning the office area. They didn't mind his music if it wasn't intrusive. They especially liked the mellow side of the tape I'd made, which held such songs as "Harbor Lights." One night Dave was working along to the mellow songs, and a few seconds after the last one ended a male voice began screaming profanity and urging that we "kill the police" and commit other vile acts. I'd already gone home, but I heard about it later.

"Oh, man, Joe! When that gangsta rap came on, I jumped like I was on springs and ran over to turn it off, but I was too late. One of the administrators looked out of her office and said, 'What was *that?*' What did you tape my songs over?"

"Sorry," I said. "The tape must have belonged to one of my sons. I thought it was blank." It was one of those painful stories that would be funny one day.

I made sure I was alone—nobody working late—before I cranked up my music. If teachers were still in the building, they usually shut their classroom doors for privacy, so I could still turn on my songs, but I had to lower the volume. It was on such a night that the idea hit me. Music had been suggested as a way to keep the ghosts at bay, but the same technique should work on live humans.

When teachers were in the building late, I made a point of asking if my music bothered them. Most said no; some even said they were enjoying it. I would ask them what they liked. "I don't care," they might say, "just don't play rap"; or "Anything but country." That was how I learned each teacher's taste—especially what they didn't like.

I had to finish my cleaning before my quitting time in order to complete my security check. When I was desperate for teachers to go home, I'd play whatever they had told me not to play. I didn't do this right outside the classrooms—that would have been too obvious—but I was close enough for them to hear it. Within five minutes, I'd hear the classroom door open and close, and they'd be on their way home. I always told them, "Have a good night." I could get rid of any teacher in the building that way, but I couldn't pull the same thing on our principal.

Hannah was intense with her work, and she often stayed after hours. My problem with that was the same old one, getting the floors finished, but at least it was down to one corridor—the one she used to walk to the parking lot. I got so I would say to her, "I'm getting ready to mop; how long are you going to be?"

"Ten or fifteen minutes," she'd say, so I'd wait. And wait. Time would slip by for her and drag for me. Sometimes she would leave so late that I couldn't even do the floor; yet, if it looked bad in the morning, she'd blame me.

I figured out a conversion formula for Hannah's time. I calculated that her time ran about three and one-half times longer than she said it would. From her estimates and my formula, I knew how long I really had for the floor to dry. If she said, "I'll be right there," the actual time she took would be ten to fifteen minutes, and I could wait until after she'd gone. If she said, "Ten minutes," the reality was thirty-five to forty minutes, and I could set a clock by it. So, even when she said, "Ten minutes," I went ahead. By the time she actually left, the hallway would be dry. It always worked.

I thought Hannah was intense about her work, but was I any different? I think about all the times I grumbled to myself, wanting nothing more than to be alone in that school. It made sense at the time, back when I hadn't seen anything suspicious and had no idea I'd ever be going up and down those halls with my heart pounding, hoping to see a teacher at her desk.

5
Growing Up

Glen Ferris, West Virginia, the 1950s

I grew up in a small West Virginia town mistakenly named Glen Ferris. The mistake had to do with a beautiful feature of our town, the view of the Kanawha River tumbling over the dam that had been built around the turn of the twentieth century. I'd always heard that when the towns along the river were being named, two signs were accidentally switched and Falls View became the name of a town with no view of the falls. Our village became Glen Ferris—the name on the other sign.

Mom, Dad, my older sister, Jane, and I lived in one side of a two-story duplex next door to the Glen Ferris Methodist Church. Our house had been built by EMCO, the metals company that employed many local people at its plant in the nearby village of Alloy. Dad worked there, as had Grandpop. From time to time, Mom would join the ranks as a secretary and ride to work with Dad.

Glen Ferris was a long and narrow village set among mountains. It clung to the path of the river and was accessible at either end by a two-lane road. In the 1930s the company had turned Glen Ferris into a boom town, building new homes and recreational facilities for its employees. By the time I was running around twenty years later, it was a kid's paradise. Besides the gorgeous mountains surrounding our town, we had a ball field, a playground, tennis courts, a bowling alley, and a recreation hall—all within walking distance. Like most of the other kids I hiked, played ball, swam, and even bowled, taking full advantage of the available resources.

Our house was large as company houses went, with a basement; a main floor consisting of a kitchen, a dining room, and a living room; three bedrooms and a bath upstairs; and an unfinished attic above all that. Jane and I played in—or on—nearly every inch of that house, including two sections of the roof. We made clubhouses and hid notes. We used my bedroom window as an escape route, climbing out onto the roof of our little back porch and swinging down. It was all about secrets and the lure of unused spaces.

Mr. Joe

I loved to hide. One time I made a hideout in the linen closet and slept on one of the shelves. Jane once put blankets on two of the bare storage shelves in the basement to make bunk beds for us. The only space we didn't play in was the attic; even in the daytime, it was too dark.

Off my sister's bedroom was a storage room that became whatever we imagined, from a schoolroom to a secret club. The space, though usable, had never been properly finished. The floor was partially covered with linoleum, three walls were open to the studs, and a fourth wall sloped sharply downward under the steepest part of the roof.

Mom hung clothes on rods suspended at one end of the storage room, and I loved to play there. Some of those garments were treasures for a kid exploring a house. I liked Dad's smoking jacket. It was maroon, made of shiny material that bore a subtle pattern, and it had a sash. I'd seen similar jackets in the movies, on rich men who smoked pipes. Dad did smoke a pipe sometimes, but I never saw him wear that smoking jacket.

Mom had a short fur coat and a fox stole. The stole was especially fascinating: you could still see the animals' little heads and feet. One fox's mouth operated like a clip, and the way to fasten the stole was to make the fox bite its own tail. Mom occasionally put her furs on when she went to parties, but really, what kind of life had my parents envisioned for themselves? Our china cabinet was full of beautiful dishes, some on display and others stacked as if waiting for a special occasion. Mom was always redecorating, having workers come in to paint or re-cover furniture or lay down a new rug. I don't mean to give the impression that we were rich. Our kitchen was never remodeled. Its linoleum floor, freestanding sink, and lack of cabinets put us one step above the Kramdens in the old *Honeymooners* TV series.

Mom and Dad had met simply because they both lived in Glen Ferris, a town of a few hundred people. They married in the spring of 1941, Jane came along in 1945, and I was born in 1948. By the time I was in grade school, my parents' marriage had degenerated to open arguing, and Mom had begun to drink inappropriately. Today, those would be sure signs that a split was coming, but back then parents didn't separate. A divorce would have rocked Glen Ferris like an earthquake.

Our house became a scary place. My whole life began to revolve around Mom. What would I find when I came home from school? I never announced myself the way other kids did; I always entered the house as quietly as possible. If Mom was drunk, I wanted to be the one to find her; I didn't want her to pop out on me.

Sometimes when I walked upstairs, the bathroom door would be open and Mom would be standing in front of the sink in her robe, patting her face. "I thought I'd give myself a facial." It could have been a Hitchcock scene. Mom would turn and look at me with bloodshot eyes and globs of white cream hanging off her face, her condition as obvious as if a siren had gone off. Underneath the cream, her skin would have turned blotchy and any previous expression on her face would have gone sliding into history as she lost muscle control. Her cheeks sagged, her eyes were mere slits, and her lips seemed to go their own separate ways. She couldn't disguise the changes with her pathetic version of a facial. By that point, the only thing keeping her upright was the sink.

Liquor dulled all of Mom's body movements. She couldn't walk worth a damn when she was drunk. She was always stumbling and catching herself. She would put both hands on the wall and walk them along for balance. It was both frightening and sickening to watch.

When Mom was drunk, her speech slurred, and she made things worse by talking down to Jane and me. From the time I was a little boy, she called me a son of a bitch. I didn't know how ironic that was, because I didn't even know what *bitch* meant. During those times she was not like a mother at all, but someone with whom I had no connection. I saw no love in her face; instead, she looked at me like she despised me. I wasn't afraid she'd hit me, but why was she angry at me? Sometimes I thought she was mad just because I was there, because I'd been born.

Mom had never been warm the way some mothers are—I don't remember her ever hugging me—so when she drank, it wasn't as if a good person had gone bad. It was more that a cold person had become a walking nightmare. Mom could make my heart hammer with fear. One time I woke up to find her holding a knife over me. She actually cut me with it. What had I done?

The little school I attended from grades one to three was just down the sidewalk from our house, and I walked home for lunch every day. I hated that walk because I didn't know what I would find at the end of it. Even when I was too young to understand why, I didn't like being alone with my mom.

One day it was raining after lunch, and I had to run all the way back to school. When I got there, I stood under the overhang near the door, afraid to go in. My heart was pounding so hard, I thought I was dying. I didn't realize it was just from running. I stood alone outside with the rain dripping around me because if I went into the school and told anyone about my heart, they would take me home — the last place I wanted to go.

When Mom was drunk, I hid or became very still. I wanted to be invisible. That way, I might avoid doing something to make it all worse. But Jane was different. Jane antagonized her. As a result, my sister took the brunt of Mom's drunken behavior. One day after school I witnessed a terrible consequence of Jane's refusal to keep quiet. She was on the telephone with her friend Billie, and Mom had been drinking. Jane said, "Mom's in one of her moods," and Mom snapped. She was on Jane like lightning, grabbing the receiver out of my sister's hand and beating her around the head and shoulders with it. Back then, telephones were heavy. I cried and screamed for Mom to stop, but the beating seemed to go on forever. Jane doesn't remember that day, the day our mother beat the hell out of her, but I can't forget. I still don't know what stopped it.

When I was a boy I thought our house was the only one with such trouble inside, but when I was in grade school I once spent the night at a friend's house. We had been playing in his room, and when we came downstairs his mom was outside running around the yard. Her robe was open, and she was naked underneath it. That night I realized that other kids had screwed-up parents, too. The next morning his mom looked like hell: wild hair, no makeup. I didn't react to any of it because I knew how embarrassed my friend must be. The pattern was all too familiar; I'd lived it.

I had ways to escape my troubles. Mom and Dad didn't pay a lot of attention to what I did, not the way parents do now. Both Jane and I had a great deal of freedom. We roamed Glen Ferris unsupervised, and thus had little appreciation for boundaries. We made tree houses in other people's yards and secret clubs in their backyard storage sheds. Some afternoons she and I went down by the bowling alley and jumped into the gravel pits by the railroad tracks. Sometimes we played in the schoolyard, riding sheets of waxed paper down the slide or hanging onto the big chain links of a swing as we pumped higher and higher. You always hear that some boy or girl went so high on a swing that it went right over the top pole; well, I was that kid. I did it on purpose, and it jarred the hell out of me.

Sometimes I hid in my mind, making up games and pretending to be characters from the movies, like Davy Crockett, "the king of the wild frontier." I also liked to take an umbrella to the top of the stone wall behind the church and use it like a parachute. The wall was much taller than I was, but I'd jump off it over and over to see if the umbrella would slow me down. I loved to climb up onto the roof of the garage behind our house and run back and forth, making a racket on the noisy tin.

I played with a real gun once. Dad kept a pistol on top of the china cabinet in our dining room, and I could stand on a chair and see it. I used to hold it sometimes. Once I showed it to my friend Wade, and we took it up the hill to the railroad tracks and played Russian roulette. We were lucky we didn't kill ourselves.

In addition to playing all sorts of fantasy games, I liked to be *inside* things, to be surrounded by them. I was fascinated by tents and was always making them as a kid. There was a tree on the hill between our house and the church, up by the tracks, where I used to make forts. I would get old blankets and hang them over the tree limbs. Between the blankets and all the vines around the tree, the space was enclosed — with one exception: I always kept a flap open.

I loved my tents as long as they didn't completely close me in. Even as a boy, long before I ever heard the word *claustrophobic*, I always slept with one foot out of the covers. I had to leave an opening, some kind of escape hatch, or I felt trapped and couldn't breathe. I lost control.

In the house I used to back the dining room chairs up to one another and put a blanket over them. Then I'd take comic books into my tent to read. Once I made a tent on our couch. I put a blanket over the back of the couch, draped it down, and tucked it in under the front of the cushions. I took the lampshade off one of our lamps so I could bring the lamp into my tent. When I leaned it against the back of the couch, the bare bulb burned a hole in the material. Mom patched it, and it looked like crap.

I even used to hide under the dirty clothes in the linen closet. We didn't have a hamper; we threw our laundry in the bottom of the closet and shut the door. I bet I got under those clothes a hundred times. No one was even looking for me! I just loved to hide. Even now if I think about it I can smell those sweaty clothes pulled over me. I never felt trapped there, because I always stuck a finger out or left the closet door open just a crack.

If you had asked me, I would have said I hid for fun, and I always thought I was fooling everyone. One time a little girl and I turned her empty plastic swimming pool upside down and played doctor under it. I wasn't even in school yet. Her mom lifted up the pool and found us just as a group of school children were walking by, and they all saw us.

Everybody tells me I was a happy kid, whistling all the time. Well, I was happiest being out of sight.

Once I did want to be found. Dad was going to take Jane and me to the movies to see Elvis Presley in *Love Me Tender*. I was ten or eleven years old, and I wanted to see it, but I hid because I thought Dad would try to find me. It was a game. I was in one of my safe places, the storage room with all the clothes. Dad came upstairs and opened the door, but he didn't come in. After a minute, he shut the door and left. When I came out, I found out he'd taken Jane to the movie, and I was left at home with Mom, so that time the game backfired.

Mine was a childhood spent in an alternate world, one that swung between freedom and fear. Outside our house, I loved playing in the yards and public spaces of Glen Ferris. At home, I found solace in spaces I could make my own. Though it began as a defense against my mother at her worst, hiding stayed with me. It became a solution to life's challenges and affected all of my relationships. I loved to make myself invisible, even when I was safe.

6
A Grand Life

Much sweeter than my childhood memories of my own home were the days I spent with my grandparents during the periods when Mom joined Dad at the EMCO plant. If I wasn't in school, Grandmama and Grandpop became my babysitters. Of course, it was mostly Grandmama; after Grandpop retired from EMCO, he had another job: clerking in the only store in town—the company store, which also housed our post office. My grandfather was the town postmaster. I used to play in the store and the back room where he sorted mail.

In contrast to the effort I put into avoiding my mother, I was content to stay under Grandmama's watchful eye. My happiest days consisted of following her around the house as she did her chores. Instead of giving up her day to watch me play, it was the opposite; I watched her work. Mom wasn't the most domestically talented person, so I was fascinated with Grandmama's routine. Sometimes she read to me or took me outside to watch a train go by, but most days she didn't change a thing for me, and it was a gift.

Grandmama and Grandpop lived in a two-story cinderblock house that seemed to retain the warm scents of delicious food: beef roasting, bread baking, pies cooling. Grandmama was always cooking. Her kitchen had a walk-in pantry equipped with a sink and counters where she prepared food. Many times she lifted me up to one of those counters, where I sat watching her make homemade rolls; apple butter; banana bread; or my favorite dessert, orange cake. Sometimes we sat out on the back porch and I helped her string beans.

When Grandmama did laundry, I followed her down to the basement, a cluttered space with low ceilings and a concrete floor. She would stand at the wringer washer, her model of choice, and load clothes into its big tub for the wash cycle. Next she took each dripping piece from the washtub and fed it through a set of wringers, two moving rollers that drew the garment into the narrow space between them. It was fun to watch the clothes come out flattened on the other side. I had to stand back from the washer, though; those wringers could do a number on a hand, as Grandmama learned the hard way when one of her thumbs was pulled into the device. Fortunately, the washer had a safety switch that caused the wringers to spring apart.

After she dried Grandpop's socks on the line, Grandmama let me match them and roll them together. Grandpop dressed up for work every day, rising early and later walking down the alley to the store. If he ever "chilled out," it was in cuffed trousers and a dress shirt, with a pair of wingtips on his feet. On wash day I liked to put the laundry basket a distance away so I could throw Grandpop's rolled socks and try to hit it. He was so picky about his appearance, and there I was playing basketball with his dark, silky socks.

One room in my grandparents' basement had a door that was kept closed, but I'd seen what was in it. One whole side of the room was dirt. Perhaps it was intended as a root cellar, but to me it was a cave inside a house, and I couldn't resist it. Grandpop didn't want me in there because he kept tools in that room, so I went in when he wasn't home. I'd go in and climb around in that dirt and come out blacker than coal, and then I guess I'd get a bath in Grandmama's deep, claw-foot tub.

My grandmother made many of her own clothes, as well as outfits for Jane and even Jane's dolls. She had a sewing room in the basement where she worked at a treadle machine. Next to it was a big, painted table where she could cut and pin material. I loved to go into the sewing room with Grandmama and play with her button collection or look at her imposing dressmaker's form on its metal stand. My favorite thing was to lie on the wicker couch next to the sewing table and watch Grandmama's foot working the treadle. As her foot moved up and down, the machine would make its noises, and I'd fall asleep on the couch with the rhythm of that treadle singing to me like a lullaby.

Sometimes Grandmama let me walk to the post office to see Grandpop. The building was visible from their kitchen, but houses blocked the view of the alley that led to it, so Grandmama always called Grandpop to tell him I was on my way. It was different, for sure; at home, Mom and Dad seldom knew where I was. I had a warm feeling when I started out for the post office, knowing that I could turn and see Grandmama watching me until I was out of sight.

Even though Grandpop was expecting me, I didn't always stay on the path. I'd get distracted. There was a place I liked to stop, about a third of the way down the alley, where a fire alarm hung from a frame. The alarm was made from a steel ring five feet in diameter, weighing hundreds of pounds and painted red. A huge sledgehammer hung alongside it. If a fire broke out, someone could hit the ring with the sledgehammer and volunteers would come running. Those fire gongs were made from the drive wheels of locomotives.

I loved to lie in the curve of the fire alarm, which was out of Grandmama's sight. There was some reward for me in being inside that ring of steel. I'd climb into it and lie on my back, very still and quiet. Then I'd reach down and rock it with my hand, pushing back and forth on the ground. I'd forget all about the post office, and soon Grandpop would come yelling for me. I ran to him then.

Grandpop usually came home for lunch. He had an easy chair where he'd sit to rest and smoke after he'd eaten. Grandpop's stomach was tighter than a snare drum, but he'd always loosen his belt and sit with his long legs stretched out across his ottoman.

One day I said something mean when Grandpop was home. I don't remember what it was, but he took me downstairs, where he had a section of two-by-four wood nailed to the basement wall. He gave me a few nails and asked me to hammer them far enough into the board that they wouldn't fall out. I had to reach up to do it.

After I'd hammered the nails in, Grandpop said, "Joe, think of each one of those nails as a hurtful thing you say to somebody. Now pull the nails out." I did. "You've taken it all back," he said, pointing to the board, "but the damage is done. When you say something mean, you can take your words back, but the damage is still there. Don't say those words in the first place." When I think of that story, I still cry.

When it was time for Mom and Dad to pick me up, Grandmama would tell me and I'd sit by the dining room window to wait. I guess a lot of kids look forward to their moms and dads coming home from work, but I didn't. Our house was a crazy and frightening place, and my grandparents' home was yet another place to hide—perhaps the safest place of all.

My days with my grandparents fed my dreams of a normal life: Refrigerators were supposed to be clean and full of appetizing foods; clothes were supposed to be folded; fathers came home from work and read the paper; mothers took care of kids. Life lessons were gentle, and secrets were the good kind: where the Easter eggs were hidden; what we were getting for Christmas.

What I didn't learn about families from my grandparents came from watching TV. It would be years before Grandmama broke down and bought a television set—Grandpop would already be gone—but

Jane and I begged Mom and Dad to get one, foolishly promising never to ask to go to the movies again. Thus, we invited the families from *Lassie*, *Leave It to Beaver*, *The Adventures of Ozzie and Harriet*, and *Father Knows Best* into our living room. And when we did, the comparison was brutal.

All I ever wanted was a family, and by that I mean a real family, a functional family, a loving family. I couldn't have that as a boy—not in our house. I wasn't hugged or kissed. My parents never told me they loved me. I'd always thought that once I got away from home, I'd be fine. I'd have a wife and children and a real home, and all of it would last. When you've lived with dysfunctional parents, you want to do better. Even as a boy, I knew that when I grew up I would show my own children I loved them every day of my life.

7
Whodunit?

When I cleaned a classroom, I always vacuumed last. That way, I left every room looking pristine. One night after I'd vacuumed one of the rooms, I took my big trash container outside to dump it. I usually smoked part of a cigarette when I went outside, stretching the trash errand into a mini-break.

When I came back, the vacuum cleaner I'd left in the classroom I'd just cleaned was gone. The first thing I thought was that I'd forgotten where I left it. That would be easy to do; I had a lot of things on my mind.

I went to the room I'd cleaned before that one. Sure enough, it was there. It wasn't plugged in, but it had been when I'd left—at least I thought so. Now the cord was wrapped up, and I was pretty sure I hadn't wrapped it, but I dismissed it.

I brought the sweeper into the room where I needed it. When I started to vacuum, I looked down and saw that the carpet was already vacuumed. At first I thought that possibly the room had been left clean during the school day, but no. With kindergarten students, there is no guesswork as to whether a floor's been vacuumed. I *had* done it; I knew that in my heart.

Once again, I dismissed the incident. Unfortunately, questioning myself in that building wasn't anything new. Sometimes I did get goofy and forget things. But why would I take a vacuum cleaner into a clean room?

After the first time it happened, I had to look for that vacuum cleaner twice more in the same week. Just as I had a pattern to the way I did the rooms, the sweeper seemed to have developed a pattern of its own. It would happen when I left the building. I'd take the trash out to the Dumpster, smoke, and then come back inside and have to look for my vacuum cleaner. It wasn't always in the same place—it could be anywhere—but I'd have to look for it; that part was guaranteed.

The second and third times it happened, I knew something was fishy. It couldn't just be me and my absent-mindedness. How many times in a week could I lose a sweeper? I decided to look at the vacuum cleaner—to *really* look and make sure I knew where it was—before I left a room. I even wrote it down so I would know I wasn't nuts. I kept a log for a couple weeks, noting the location of the vacuum cleaner throughout the evening, and during that time nothing further happened.

One night after I hoped the vacuum cleaner episodes were over, I found my sweeper in a storage room at the other end of the hallway from where I'd been working. I wouldn't have taken it there, first of all because there was no carpet to clean, and second because cleaning the storage room wasn't even on my list of duties.

I picked the sweeper up and went back to where I needed to work. I plugged it in, but nothing happened, so I tried another outlet; still nothing. I plugged it into every socket in the room, but it wouldn't turn on. I flicked the lights on and off; I tried everything. Either the electricity in all the sockets was bad, or I needed a different vacuum cleaner, so I unplugged that one to take it downstairs. Before I could wrap the cord, the sweeper started running.

I plugged it into the wall again and it stopped. I pulled the plug out of the wall and it started. This happened a few times until one time when I pulled the plug and didn't hear the motor turn on. I quickly grabbed the sweeper and went on to the next classroom, wondering if I'd totally lost it—not the vacuum cleaner, but my mind.

Ever since my sweeper had been turning up in strange places, I'd continued to keep records of where it was. I was documenting the whereabouts of a vacuum cleaner: how low was that? I wondered if I was certifiable.

Sometimes strange events have logical explanations, but so far I had nothing to offer that would explain the roving sweeper. I would have been relieved to blame someone else, but I knew I was the only one in the building when my vacuum cleaner—an inanimate object—decided to play tricks on me. Who could I even tell? It would sound ridiculous.

I already knew how it felt to have Dave doubt me. One night he'd told me a story about working in his part of the building, the administrative side, after my shift was over. He was playing his boom box, which he kept on a table in the main hall. The acoustics were so good that he could hear his music anywhere. When he came back to pick out a new set of songs, he found all of his CDs scattered on the floor outside the administrative offices. Someone would have had to mess them up deliberately.

"Joe," he said, "I know I was alone. I'd locked the doors myself."

He brushed the incident off, but I thought about it afterwards. I believed Dave; why would he lie? I thought he must have told me about it to test me, to see if I'd moved his CDs before going home. When weird things happen, you *want* it to be another person. I understood that, but maybe it wasn't a person who'd moved those CDs. Dave knew the history of the school.

Think about how many people have passed through a school building that's eighty-five years old. Whole communities could have been educated there. How many thousands of children had walked those halls, now empty and full of shadows? How many had sat at those little tables or washed up in the old restrooms? How many stories did this former high school hold? How many secrets? If you added in the possibility of something beyond the grave, it was easy to become rattled working alone at night.

Dave didn't like to let on, but he was jumpy. I'd discovered that when I'd inadvertently scared him a few times coming up to ask him a question. He started calling me the Ninja because I was so quiet in my approach. "Rattle your keys, Joe. Shake them *hard*. Let somebody know you're coming!" And I did.

I understood feeling jumpy; I was the same way at night after a few instances of chasing "Poltergeist"—otherwise known as my vacuum cleaner. I got a creepy feeling even when nothing happened. That was because, when nothing happened, I would be relieved and would quit thinking about it. I'd let down my guard, and then the sweeper would move around again.

After one particular episode, my heart was beating fast. I knew something was in that school besides me. I wasn't terrified, but suddenly it was very important for me not to be alone. I had to talk to somebody.

One of the teachers had become a friend. Karen's daughter was in second grade, so she would put the little girl to bed and come back to work on many nights, leaving her husband in charge at home. I always checked in with Karen when she was in the building late. She was credible, so when I got spooked and needed to be around someone, I went to Karen's classroom. She was the person I told about the vacuum cleaner.

"I like my job and don't want to quit," I said, "but I'm not crazy about working in a haunted school. Do you believe in ghosts?"

"Sure," she said. "Some nights they make so much noise in my closets that I can't even work." Karen had two huge storage closets with double doors in her classroom. "Many times when I'm working," she said, "the doors will rattle and shake all by themselves. It's loud. I figure someone is trying to let me know they're here."

I shouldn't have been glad Karen had ghosts, but I was, in a way. Talking to her made me feel better. She understood the eerie quirks of our building and had experienced strange occurrences firsthand. Usually I was guarded about discussing unexplained incidents. I don't think I even told my boys. It isn't something you broadcast.

"I was hoping this was someone playing a joke on me," I said. "I'd like to find a logical explanation. Our head custodian is a practical joker, so I thought it might be him, but Dave says there's no way it was. He was on another shift."

"Could someone else have gotten into the building?"

"No," I said, "we're very guarded with our keys. We have a limited number of sets."

"Well," she said, "I can tell you that electrical appliances do go on and off here at night. It's happened to me. My television sets do that, and my printers sometimes start for no reason. It's weird."

I asked Karen, "What should I do?"

"Just start talking to it. That's what I do. I spend a lot of time here at night, and those noises in my closet unnerve me. I've started announcing myself when I arrive. I'll say, 'I know you're here. Don't bother me; I'm not going to bother you.' Even with my talking, at times my closet doors just freak me out, and I can't stay. Before I go home, I call my husband and tell him I'm on my way. 'If I don't get there,' I say, 'come looking for me.' And I mean it."

Thanks to Karen, my next strategy was talking to it—whatever "it" was. It hadn't tried to hurt me, but it had let me know it was there, so I started talking out loud, even when nothing had happened. "It's just me," I'd say. "How are you doing tonight?" I'd tell it I wasn't there to cause trouble, just to clean the room. I'd say the same things over and over, going from room to room. I talked nonstop, sometimes for five or six hours straight. It was nervous chatter, but it calmed me to let this presence know I was aware of it.

I also told Hannah about the vacuum cleaner incidents. She might have had her faults, but she was the sanest person I knew. I hoped she wouldn't think I'd been drinking on the job when I asked, "Hannah, do you believe in ghosts?" Her answer surprised me.

"I do, Joe. I have to, because my mother saw them all her life. We called them shadow people. Mom would see a crowded room when only she and I were in it. I've never seen a ghost at this school, but I don't think you're crazy."

It was good to have my principal's support. A few days later I brought her a milk shake, my way of saying thanks.

My nightly chatter seemed to be working. The vacuum cleaner stopped messing with me. It took a while to be sure, and I continued to talk out loud to the dark halls and quiet rooms. At least I could still say I hadn't seen a ghost. Yet.

8

Five O'Clock Somewhere

Glen Ferris, the 1950s and '60s

Mine was a five o'clock world when I was a boy, and five o'clock meant one thing: Dad was home. If I looked forward to anything more than Christmas, it was going to our living room window in the waning afternoon and watching my father walk up the sidewalk.

Most days Dad would be wearing a hat and a gabardine overcoat with a suit underneath, looking at least like an imitation of an executive. His title at EMCO was Shipping Supervisor. Was he *a* shipping supervisor, or *the* shipping supervisor? All Jane and I knew about Dad's job was that he worked in an office with three secretaries and could be counted on to come home on time.

When I remember that time, I can picture our row of homes against the mountain, attractive and normal. People all along that row came home to their families at the end of a workday, but for us it was an out-and-out rescue.

For me, Dad's arrival was not just the highlight, but the *point* of every day. My challenge was to get to that point, because Mom and her drinking dominated our lives. To me she was pure evil, and I expended a great deal of energy daily just staying out of her path. When I hid or played outside, I was *surviving* until Dad got home. Sometimes I'd be out in town, playing, and I would see the car pulling into the parking lot of the Glen Ferris Inn, where Dad's carpool gathered and dispersed. If he had driven that day, he'd drive on home and park next to our garage; if not, he walked the quarter-mile home from the inn.

Now, when I picture that scene as a grown man, I think of it from Dad's point of view. What was going through his mind? I looked forward to the very thing he must have dreaded. I know how *I* felt walking up the sidewalk, and I was just a little boy. Our house was a concentration of misery, a black spot on the map. How must Dad have felt, knowing he was the rescuer of the family?

Here's the sad thing about it. My excitement at Dad's arrival wasn't even about him; it was relief that he would take care of Mom for us, make her disappear. Just by being present, Dad stopped Mom's most extreme behavior. She'd be just as drunk as before he arrived, but Dad somehow calmed her down. The two of them would go upstairs to their room, and I knew they would be there a while. I was safe. I could finally relax and sit down to watch TV.

What else do I remember about my father? Not a great deal. He had yellow fingers from smoking. Sometimes he told us jokes he'd heard at the office. When he came home he might have Clark Bars or Tom's Peanut Butter Logs in his overcoat pockets for Jane and me.

Dad was funny. One time Mom asked him if she could get a broom at the A&P, and he said, "No, you have to ride home in the car with the rest of us."

He used to take me to Al's Club when he went to turn in his cards for the football pool. I looked forward to those trips. Al's was a busy bar and restaurant a few miles down the road toward Montgomery. Dad would put his suit on and we'd ride down to Al's on Saturday mornings. I don't remember if Dad drank there, but he always got me a big hamburger. Once he won thirty dollars betting on football, and he was on top of the world.

Dad wasn't athletic. Walking home from work was probably the most exercise he ever got—except for golf. We had a golf club membership through EMCO, but Dad wasn't a good player. He swung like a hack and then swore when he made a mistake. In contrast, our alcoholic mother was a natural athlete who outplayed Dad and often had to calm him down on the golf course.

Our course wasn't easy. It was so hilly that the golfers used to joke that you needed one leg shorter than the other to play there, but Mom was smooth even on those hills. She was sober when she golfed; she took it seriously. Dad looked like a beginner. One guy he played with had a huge bag like the pros used, with "Wilson" written up the side of it. It had built-in dividers, and his clubs had covers—the whole bit. Dad's bag was a flimsy canvas thing that held a few clubs. A golf course is supposed to be a quiet place, but you could hear Dad coming. His clubs would clank against each other in his bag.

I used to hate it when Mom and Dad wanted me to caddy. If Dad muffed a shot, he would get angry and all red in the face and beat his club on the ground. No wonder; he had to hit the ball three or four times to every one of hers. I call his style "the Woody Hayes method," referring to the famous Ohio State football coach's offensive strategy of running instead of passing the ball: "three yards and a cloud of dust."

Dad wasn't handy. I don't remember him ever using power tools. Did we even have any? We had two garages, but neither held a workshop; for that, I went down the street and watched the neighborhood men. One used to fashion lamps on a lathe. Another built a full-sized log cabin for his son. At our house, Mom was the one who took the clippers to our hedge, even though she was allergic to the leaves and would break out in red bumps afterward.

Dad didn't do a lot to help out around the house, either, but he would describe in minute detail every chore he did complete, to make it sound more drawn out and difficult than it was. He'd tell us each step, always in a world-weary voice: "Got up, went to the car, drove to the store, got out, found the milk, stood in line, came home, put the milk away . . ." Later, that kind of routine became a joke between Jane and me.

There was nothing self-conscious about my dad. He didn't teach me about hygiene or show me any kind of grooming techniques, but he sure didn't mind taking a bath in front of us. He had a vertical scar just above the crack of his rear end, about as long and wide as a roll of quarters. After he'd had a bath, Dad would walk right into the front bedroom, naked, and tell us the story of the scar. He told it many times, but to this day I can't remember it; only the tiny wrinkles across the width of the scar, running from the bottom to the top like a little white ladder above Dad's butt. No doubt about it; Dad made himself at home. He would walk around the house or sit and watch TV in his boxer shorts, his legs two feet apart. When you sit like that, you ought to wear briefs — or pants.

Mom once told me that Dad had big appetites. I could verify his passion for food at the supper table, but many years would pass before I understood the other meaning.

You want to love your dad, and I did. You want a good dad, but you love what's there. As a boy, I thought dads were supposed to be like Ward Cleaver on TV, paying attention to their kids, giving advice, and helping their children to solve problems. My dad didn't display much interest in me, and I found him unapproachable.

I saved up and bought Dad a birthday present once so that we could do something together. It was a Daisy BB pistol, and he really liked it. We went up on the railroad tracks and shot at targets.

He never said he loved me. I said it to him once, and afterward I felt awkward, like I shouldn't have. Did he ever hug me? I don't think so. He did draw pictures for us. One time in second grade I had to draw a picture of Santa Claus. Dad drew it, sleigh and all. It was good. I'd give anything to see that picture now. I went to school and tried to tell my teacher I'd drawn it. Of course, she didn't believe me.

Dad was gone so much. During the week he worked, and sometimes he had business meetings in the evenings. Then there were his trips to Cleveland. Dad suffered from hypertension, and every so often he saw a specialist at the Cleveland Clinic. This went on for years. He'd be gone a few weeks at a time, leaving my sister and me alone with Mom and her best friend, the whiskey bottle. Jane and I hated those times.

Mom could get so crazy, so far off the track. One thing she did when Dad was away at the clinic was to get drunk and start talking about how she was going to leave him. Why did she tell me? I was a kid. I would get upset and cry. She wouldn't try to console me; she'd keep talking about it. Once I was lying on the couch and she knelt down and said, "I'm going to divorce your father in the spring." I begged her not to, but she kept saying she was going to leave him. The harder I cried, the more she built it up.

Mom's divorce talk was so ironic: if either of them had felt entitled to leave, it should have been Dad; but even when he and Mom argued, Dad never threatened to leave us. Even though he lived with a drunk and was battered and embattled from it, he never said the word *divorce* around me. It would have broken me if he had.

One time, Dad was due home from the clinic after he'd been gone for several weeks. Mom knew what time he would arrive, and she was drunk. In order to keep a low profile—she would have called it "playing possum"—she got into bed and made me get in with her. I knew I was to pretend to be asleep so that Dad would leave us alone. It was evening when he came to the bedroom door announcing that he was home. Mom kicked me under the covers and grabbed me so I'd stay quiet and wouldn't get up. Dad couldn't understand why I wasn't excited to see him. It was because I was scared to death.

Dad's physical strength surprised me a few times. I saw him knock a guy out of his shoes in Cleveland. I'd gone with Dad on one of his trips to the clinic. We were walking around downtown, and some stranger—maybe a panhandler—grabbed onto Dad. Dad knocked him in the face, and he flew off the sidewalk into the street. His shoes were still there on the sidewalk. Right then, Dad was a hero to me.

I wasn't afraid of him, but I thought twice about crossing him. After I started driving, I bought a Playboy license plate and put it on the front of our car without saying anything to Mom or Dad. Dad drove the car to work one morning unknowingly displaying the distinctive Playboy bunny. When he got home, he was furious. I'd never seen him like that. "I'm a married man, and I was driving around with that on my car!" he said. "All my friends laughed at me." He reached down and grabbed my ankle and pulled me up off the ground, held me up with one hand and hit me with the other, smacking me on my ass. That's the only time Dad ever hit me in anger, but another time I was working out, doing weights and sit-ups to tighten my stomach. Dad was sitting on the front steps, and I came out and stood on the sidewalk in front of him. "Hit me," I said. "I won't even feel it." He did, and I was shocked. I went flying—really airborne. He was sitting down, and he knocked me on my ass. He was something else.

Once he took me on a river trip from Huntington, West Virginia, to Cincinnati. It was just the two of us. We ate our meals and spent the night on the boat. I remember standing on the deck with my father, looking at the lights on shore as we passed town after town. Times like that were so rare.

Mostly I remember broken promises. Dad told me he intended to build a raft. Every time we were in the car together, he'd say he was going to build this raft and we were going to go down the Kanawha River and through the London Locks. He told me that for years. He'd say we were going to make the raft with logs, but that I'd have to be a certain age. The age always moved out from where I was. I never forgot about that raft, and sometimes I'd remind him. "Do you still remember that?" he'd say. Dad couldn't even steer a raft, let alone make one, but I kept bringing it up because I thought he was telling the truth.

I had good relationships with other men who took me under their wing. Our neighbor, Otis, did that. I used to put pennies on the railroad tracks so the trains would smash them, and Otis took me into his workshop one time and showed me how to make a ring from a smashed penny.

Our next-door neighbors had an older uncle who would come to visit. Duane was my friend. In the summertime he would take me out on the river in a sailboat. Sometimes Dad went, too, and sometimes it was just Duane and me. As I tell these stories now, they sound suspicious, but none of those men ever had an ulterior motive. I might not have known it then if they had, but I would now.

Even the neighbors were full of it sometimes. Otis had an old washing machine. He said he was going to take the motor out of it and build me a go-kart. I asked him every time I saw him, but it never happened. I asked him for years. I guess he expected me to forget. I probably would have if my life had been normal, but when I was little I clung to every promise anybody made me.

9
Becoming Mr. Joe

Cincinnati, 1997

I wanted to be a positive role model as a custodian, to be someone the kids could trust and look up to. I wanted them to feel safe at school and have the cleanest environment I could give them. I still remembered even the smallest kindnesses I received when I was young. They seemed so few and far between.

Even after I had worked at the kindergarten school for a few weeks, I didn't look the part. The other custodians wore uniforms with the name and logo of our school district on them. I had turned in my shirt and pant sizes, but it would be weeks before my uniforms were delivered. In the meantime, I felt like an outsider.

Because my shift started before school let out in the afternoon, teachers and students saw me every day. Did they know who I was? Did they have any idea why a middle-aged man wearing jeans and a work shirt kept walking through their building? I assumed they did, because after a while teachers began to introduce themselves. I was sure they'd gone to the office to find out something about me. It's what I would have done.

The students handled the situation differently. When I passed them in the hall, they shied away. I remember seeing kids looking for their classrooms. They might have gone only a few feet to a restroom, but these kids were young, just starting school. They didn't know the building and didn't always pay attention to where they were. Sometimes they'd end up on a completely different floor from their own; but if I offered to help them, they wouldn't answer me. They kept on walking. Their parents probably had told them not to speak to strangers.

It upset me that I didn't fit in and that the kids weren't responding to me. There were even times when I'd get to work and see kids upset and crying. Rather than push myself on them, I would ask a teacher or one of the secretaries to help.

I was one of three custodians in our building. Earl, the head custodian, worked the day shift. He was supposed to attend to the needs of the teachers and students, but he was rarely around. Earl seemed

to prefer fixing things. He spent most of his time on building maintenance.

The other custodian was, of course, Dave, who worked the midnight shift cleaning the offices. Because his shift ended a couple of
hours before school started in the morning, most of the people in my
area had never seen him. That left me as the one direct daily contact
for the kids and teachers. Most of these kids were five years old, and
they needed help all the time. I wanted to gain their trust.

The next time a child ignored me, I decided to ask my principal
what to do. I walked into her office and said, "Hannah, I need your
help. I feel like the kids are afraid of me. They won't let me help them.
They won't even talk to me." Right away I thought, *My God, I've just
told my principal I don't know how to do my job*. At least that was how
it sounded to me—not the best career move.

"Joe," she said, "you need to understand something. You've only
been here a short time. The kids will get to know you, but that takes
time. I'll give it some thought and see if I can come up with a way to
speed things up."

I was noticing a shift in our relationship. Hannah was increasingly
supportive, and I was continually working to earn it. I wanted her to
see that I was doing good work; that I was intelligent. She was no less
a perfectionist than she had been the day I met her, but she had backed
off a bit from her initial zeal to suggest new areas for me to clean.
Maybe it was because, whenever she did, I would say, "I'd be glad
to if you would come with me one day and show me how to do that."
The invitation was sincere; I wanted her to understand what she was
asking, to know what I knew: *you cannot do everything every day*.

We were making progress. I had come to realize that, despite our
different stations in life, Hannah and I were on the same journey. We
were learning together.

A couple days passed before anything happened to help me fit
in with the children. Then one day at the beginning of my shift, a
teacher asked me if I had a few minutes to come to her room. My
first thought was: *What now?* Was she going to show me something
I'd missed when I cleaned? I always thought of the worst that could
happen. Maybe it was because I'd been fired from the meat plant. I
couldn't blow it here.

The teacher took me to the front of the room. We stood together
near her desk, and every eye was on me as she said, "Class, this is

Mister Barnett. He is our new custodian. He is the man who keeps our classrooms and our building clean. If you need someone to help you, you can go to Mister Barnett. And, just so we all remember his name, we will call him Mister Joe."

When I was a little boy, I didn't like my name, Joe. I was named after G. I. Joe, a generic term for U.S. soldiers in World War II. My real first name is Joseph, but of course everyone called me Joe. One of the songs we sang in grade school was "Grumbling Joe." The same girl would always request that song, and then every kid in the class would turn to look at me, as though the song were actually about me. I hated it! I was self-conscious and took the meaning to heart.

Now I felt nothing but pride as the kindergarten children looked at me in wonder. One or two smiled. After that the other teachers, one by one, took me into their classes and introduced me the same way. It felt good, but I still wasn't sure how the kids would react. It took only a day to see some good results. I was cleaning a water fountain at the beginning of my shift when a little girl came up behind me. "Mister Joe," she said, "I can't find my classroom. Can you help me?"

"Sure, I'd be happy to," I said. "Let's go to the office and see who your teacher is." As we started walking, she reached up and grabbed my hand. It was starting to work.

With so many kids getting lost, one of the mothers made cloth flags to hang outside the classrooms. They were silky, and each one had an outline of a different creature on it. After that, if a kid couldn't find the way, I could ask, "What's your room?" and the student would tell me the alligator room, the bear room, or the butterfly room, and we would find it.

There were no male teachers in the building, so I was the only "Mister." Soon I was hearing my new name every day. "Can you help me find my room, Mister Joe?" "My shoes came untied, Mister Joe. Will you tie them for me?"

One day when I came to school, there were Playskool mailboxes in front of the classroom doors. They were red and blue, designed like residential mailboxes, each one on a pedestal and base and complete with a flag. This was a kindergarten. Who was getting mail? I asked a teacher, "Why would kindergarten students have mailboxes when they can't read or write?"

"We want to encourage them to *learn* to read and write," she said.

A couple days later, I saw the flag up on one of the mailboxes. I opened the box, and there was a letter addressed to me, Mr. Joe. It was written with a crayon, obviously by a student. I answered it right then, put it back in the mailbox, and put the flag up. Later I wondered if I'd made a mistake. I wasn't the type to draw hard lines around my duties, but was it wise for a custodian to step into a classroom project? In a few days I saw the teacher and asked her. "No," she said, "what you did was perfect. The student was thrilled that you answered his letter."

The next day when I went in to work, the flag was up on just about every mailbox. Someone was encouraging more kids to write. There were three or four letters in each box, all addressed to Mr. Joe. I was overwhelmed when I opened them. Many had simple drawings of two people, a big person and a little person, both smiling. A few held printed messages: "Dear Mr. Joe. I hope that you like your new job." "Dear Mr. Joe, I hope you have fun." "Dear Mr. Joe, Thank you for cleaning are [sic] room." Every letter was signed with love. That time, I used my lunch break to answer them. After that, it grew to thirty or forty pieces of mail per day. I was trying to answer each one differently, so I had to take them home to do in the evening. Then I'd put them in the mailboxes the next day. I was spending a lot of time on those letters, but I wasn't complaining.

A few weeks earlier, I had been a supervisor directing a crew of twenty people. Now I was cleaning up after nearly four hundred five-year-olds. I was making about half as much money as I had at the meat plant, and I wasn't even sure I could do my new job. None of that mattered so much anymore, now that I was feeling like I fit in. I wasn't a stranger any longer; I was Mr. Joe.

10
Little Extras

I'd started work in winter, a dead time. Now it was March 17, St. Patrick's Day, and I was driving to work. I remembered something I'd been told just after I was hired. The seasoned custodians had said I was lucky to have missed most of the holiday parties. "Boy, those kids can really leave a mess on party days," one said.

As the new guy, I never knew what to believe—people would mess with me sometimes—but I wondered what was waiting for me at school that afternoon. The previous night had already been a nightmare.

Before the Irish holiday, the kids had brought in "leprechaun traps" made from shoe boxes. Each child had left his or her box on the carpet in the classroom, open side down, with one end raised and supported by a stick, like an animal trap. That end was for the leprechaun to enter. When the classroom floor was full of traps, glitter was sprinkled all around to look like gold and lure the leprechaun into the box. Once he was inside, the child could pull a string to jerk the stick out and trap the leprechaun. The traps reminded me of the ones Elmer Fudd set to catch Bugs Bunny in the cartoons.

With leprechaun traps all over the floor, I couldn't take my cart and sweeper through the rooms like I was supposed to, so I gave each room a basic cleaning and hoped the teachers would understand. Along the way, I had an idea. What if some of the children did discover leprechaun tracks the next day?

I found some white flour in one of the classrooms and decided to put my idea into practice there. I made a fist with my right hand and dipped the outside of it in the flour. Next, I carefully went around on all fours and made a few footprints in the glitter by stamping the imprint of my fist for each tiny foot and then using my fingertips to make "toes." When I was done, it looked as though a very small person had walked among the shoe boxes. I told Dave what I'd done.

I finished cleaning the second-floor classrooms and walked back through to make sure I hadn't forgotten something. I checked that every light on the floor was turned off, and then I headed downstairs.

It must have been close to ten o'clock when I started hearing noises coming from the second floor. I knew there weren't any teachers there, so I told myself it was my imagination. Then I thought I heard voices. With a prickle of dread, I decided I'd better check it out. When I got upstairs, it was nearly pitch black, but I could make out two people slowly feeling their way down the hall. Relief rippled through me. "Can I help you?" I asked.

"My son and I are here to try to catch a leprechaun," the man answered. "That was his assignment for tonight." *What?* Had the child misunderstood the assignment? Had a five-year-old really convinced his father to come to school at that time of night to search for a leprechaun? I told the father the children had all left traps in their classrooms that day. There was no reason for him and his son to be at the school at night.

The minute I walked into the first classroom on St. Patrick's Day, my jaw dropped. The children had all packed up their traps and taken them home, so instead of the shoe boxes I'd expected, I was looking at a carpet covered with smashed brownies, spilled popcorn, and an endless river of fruit punch, all resting on a layer of glitter. Now I knew the meaning of "party day."

Should I start cleaning, or should I run to my car and never come back? I'd never seen a mess like that. If my good friend hadn't recommended me for the job, I might have quit right then. Quitting wasn't an option, but I can safely say that was the worst night in terms of cleaning that I ever knew as a custodian. Maybe it was my payback for the tracks I'd made. The teacher had found them and freaked out: something or someone unknown had invaded her room. She immediately went to Dave, who told her what I'd done. She didn't think it was as funny as I had.

One of the kindergarten kids walked up to me later that day. I could tell that all of the holidays had begun to run together in her mind when she said, "I'm sorry our room was so messy, Mister Joe, but it wasn't our fault. The Pilgrims did it."

Besides the seasonal parties, our school hosted many events—concerts, meetings, open houses—that involved inviting the public into the building. People from the community would often have difficulty finding the room where the event was being held, so someone would position two "students" to point the way. The students were actual size, cut out of plywood and painted to look like a little boy and a little girl. Each one had a pointing finger. When I was new, I didn't know this. By the time I arrived at the school, the event might be over, but sometimes the cutout kids hadn't been put away. I'd be cleaning at night, and out of the corner of my eye I'd see a kid pointing at me from thirty feet away. In the unsettling atmosphere of our school after hours, those cutouts scared the hell out of me every time.

I had a few adventures with real creatures. Most of the teachers in our school had plants in their classrooms, and some teachers kept live creatures, such as the ever-popular hamsters and goldfish. None of them were my responsibility unless something unexpected happened or the school was closed.

During school breaks or bad weather, the custodians reported to work as usual, so very often the teachers would come to me individually and ask me whether I'd mind watering their plants or feeding their fish while they were away from the classroom. I said yes, I'd be glad to do those things on my cleaning rounds. It could get to the point where I had seventeen or eighteen goldfish and plants to take care of.

One teacher asked me to water her plants, but said I didn't have to worry about the goldfish. "You have three goldfish," I said. "What if one of them dies because I didn't feed it?"

She said, "Then it'll be time to teach the kids about subtraction."

One night I noticed that something had been digging under the doorway to one of the classrooms., The tile under the door was broken in places. The class had a pet hamster. I don't know how it got out of its cage, but it appeared the animal had dug its way under the door and was getting out at night and running loose in the school.

A few nights later, I was buffing a landing on the stairs. The buffer is a heavy piece of equipment requiring two hands to operate and control it. In the middle of buffing the landing, I looked up to see a pair of little red eyes a couple steps above me. I nearly jumped out of my skin. It was the hamster! Suddenly it jumped off the steps and caught onto my pants. I had to get it off me, but I also had to keep both hands on the buffer. You can't do both.

The way to buff is to have the electrical cord behind you. When the hamster surprised me, I got off balance and the buffer spun around. The cord got all caught in the pad, and the darned thing pulled out of the socket. Sparks went everywhere. I knocked the hamster off my leg and tore up the buffer in the process. It was no fun explaining that one.

Mr. Joe

I looked forward to Dave's arrival each night at ten-thirty. My shift ended at eleven, so he and I always touched base before I went home. Many times I would get so busy that I would completely lose track of time, and then I would hear it: George Thorogood singing "Bad to the Bone." Dave's signature tune was his way of letting me know he was in the building.

He and I often did my security check together, walking through every area of the school. One night as we were doing our walk-through, I noticed a camera I hadn't seen before. It was pointing at the outside entrance to the Latchkey area.

Latchkey was a program that gave students a safe place to stay after school until their parents could pick them up. I hadn't paid much attention to it; I spent most of my time on the other side of the building. "What's the camera for, Dave?"

"It's for the kids' safety. There's one at the kindergarten entrance, too."

"Who monitors these cameras?"

"The head of Latchkey and the principal's secretary rewind the tapes every morning and check to see if there were any problems overnight." I knew Hannah's secretary, but I hadn't gotten to know the woman who ran the Latchkey program.

"Is there ever anything on the tapes?" I asked.

"No, but they still have to check them every day."

We finished our rounds, and it was time for Dave to start cleaning the offices and for me to leave, but I had one more thing I wanted to do. I went to the preschool rooms and searched through the toys. I wasn't sure what I was looking for, but I'd know it when I saw it. I spotted a Bullwinkle Moose hand puppet, and I was in business. As I was leaving the room, I saw another gem, a Mr. Potato Head. I took them both and headed for the Latchkey camera. On the way, I passed the superintendent in the hall. I never knew who would be working late, and there I was with a puppet on one hand and Mr. Potato Head in the other! I managed to hide the toys, relieved that he hadn't noticed my hands behind my back.

Back in the Latchkey area, I made the Bullwinkle puppet dance past the lens of the camera. Once in a while, the puppet would stop to wave.

"Is that you, Joe?" Dave hollered. "I thought you'd already left." As he came down the stairs toward me and saw what I was doing, he just shook his head. He and I had played jokes on people for thirty years. He grabbed a piece of paper and a pencil and began writing. My partner in crime was adding the final touch, the note we left for the Latchkey director, saying we thought we'd heard intruders in the building between ten and ten-thirty p.m. We suggested she should check the tape. I didn't worry about the repercussions because Dave was my immediate boss, but I did hope the Latchkey director had a sense of humor.

The next day after I'd worked a couple of hours, I was told to report to her office. I was busted, and Dave wasn't around to help me. My antics had seemed hilarious the night before, but now I had to look at them in the light of day. Why did I take such chances, especially so close to the end of my probationary period? I did it for comic relief from the nightly tensions of the kindergarten school, but at what price? Was this already the end of Mr. Joe?

I sat down, and the director looked at me across her desk. "Do you know anything about this moose puppet, Joe?"

"Well, I might have had a hand in it, ma'am." That was all it took to make her start laughing. She did have a sense of humor, and my job was still secure, but I knew when to quit. I'd had plans for Mr. Potato Head, too, but I decided to postpone those indefinitely.

11
First Drink

Glen Ferris, the 1960s

Now that I was a custodian, I kept thinking of the way people in my profession were typically portrayed in movies and TV shows. It seemed that they were either of very low intelligence or they would have a whiskey bottle hidden somewhere around the furnace room. Well, that wouldn't be me. I had only a vague idea of where our furnace room was, and I wasn't that fond of whiskey.

I won't say I don't drink—I do—but it was a long time before I was distanced enough from my childhood to enjoy a few beers. I don't like wine, and I rarely drink liquor, although I enjoy a mixed drink now and then. When you grow up in an alcoholic home, the memory of that will turn you off to drinking. For me, it's just another ghost.

I took my first drink with an arrow pointed at my throat. That was ironic considering, first, that my favorite toy as a boy was a bow and arrow set; and, second, that I considered myself "as straight as an arrow" all through high school.

When I was little and we went to the ten-cent store, I got to pick out a toy. Dad, not the most patient of men, would let me make one trip around the toy counter, and I always chose a bow and rubber-tipped arrows. After I got older, I took the tips off and sharpened the points. One day Dad brought home a piece of hickory that someone at his plant had carved into a bow, and he helped me string it. I set up a cardboard box, drew a target on a piece of paper, and stuck it on the box. Every day I stood that box up in the yard and took target practice.

When I graduated from high school I'd never even tasted beer, in spite of it being available in our house. I didn't smoke or drink, but I used to sell Mom's liquor. I was sick of her drinking. When Jane found bottles around the house, she dumped the booze out and filled the bottles with coke or water. I tried the same thing a few times, but I wasn't going to throw it away when I could make two dollars a pint. I told one friend I was pouring it out, and he said, "Don't do that. Sell it to me." So, when I had some to sell, I'd put it under the back porch steps, and he'd get it.

Dad told us to leave Mom's whiskey alone. In my mind, by doing that he enabled her to get drunk. I had to see her that way most of my life. He drank liquor too, for his heart, yet I never saw it change him.

In my teens I liked to go camping. It was fun and a way to get out of the house. My friend Wade and I would camp at the Glen Ferris island. We built fires and slept on the beach. I had a Boy Scout mess kit I'd take, and we ate Vienna sausage or Spam sandwiches. We never drank, but sometimes we'd "borrow" a boat and take a ride.

We would get our food and sleeping bags ready and then break the lock on some old, wooden jon boat that had been abandoned for years and was caked with mud. We'd scrape it out and ride it on the current downstream past the Silver Bridge, a distance of less than a mile. We had no oars, so we couldn't take the boat back to camp. Instead, we'd leave it someplace and walk back.

The summer I graduated from high school, I went camping on the river outside the next town, Gauley Bridge, with another boy. That campout had a different feel to it from the beginning.

Tony had been a couple years ahead of me in high school. I'd liked him all right, but he was a loose cannon. After we set up camp, he wanted to walk into town, to a local business. That was when I found out that one of the owners was a bootlegger. Tony said something to the guy, and he opened a padlocked shed and came back with two bottles that he sold to Tony for four dollars. It was white wine, and it was cheap, cheap, cheap. The sale was illegal, too, because the place wasn't a state store and it was after hours.

We took the wine back to our campsite and sat on the beach. Tony started drinking. I'd never tasted alcohol and had no interest in it at all. He started getting buzzed. Tony was five-foot-nine and very husky — a big boy. He sure outweighed me. Tony wanted me to drink with him, but I didn't want to. He had a bow and arrow with him. The bow was a real hunting bow, and he pulled it all the way back, held the arrow at my neck, and said, "Drink." He wouldn't let me put the bottle down. The stuff tasted like crap, but I was scared. I finally fell over onto my back from drinking. After I got back up, he handed me the bow and said, "Now hold it on me." I couldn't do it. That thing would kill a deer. As I remember it, we both went to sleep on the beach after that.

The first time I drank beer was in college. A group of us went to a night club and got a pitcher for two dollars. I didn't like it, and it hit me hard. I got used to it, though, and would get a pitcher with three or four friends. I didn't like to drink hard liquor, but people had it in the dorms. Eventually I had my first mixed drink, a screwdriver. I made it weak, but I still couldn't stomach it. I just didn't like the taste.

Gradually my resistance fell away and I could even perceive benefits from alcohol. One time I was invited to a party. I was shy around girls, especially, and somebody I was with had a pint of whiskey. I drank some on the way over so as to arrive at the party relaxed. By the time I got there, I went straight to the bathroom. I got sick, fell against the sink, and knocked it off the wall. I hadn't even met anyone yet. On the ride home I sat on somebody's lap, threw up, and was kicked out of the car.

After I was married, I drank wine with my wife on special occasions or if we had company. I didn't really like it—not since my scary experience with the bow and arrow at my throat when I was eighteen. I started drinking beer again after I was divorced because someone told me it was better than milkshakes for gaining weight.

When I worked in the meat plant, the guys would always get a quart of beer on their break. We were working nights. I would get a tall boy, a twenty-four ounce can. We were so good at our jobs on the production line that we'd get ahead and be able to take more time for our breaks. We were setting production records, making our night-shift foreman look good, so management didn't mess with us about what we did on our breaks.

One night I fell on some ice in the freezer. I'd had a twenty-four-ounce beer on break. I didn't fall because I was buzzed, but I was; and I sliced my arm open when I fell. I had to go to my foreman, who was a big deal in his church, a nice guy but as straight as can be. I knew he'd smell the beer on me.

I went to his office. When I showed him my arm, he turned white. The cut wasn't bleeding; but it was wide open. A friend said he'd take me to the hospital. He'd been drinking, too. In fact, he stopped by a U Totem store to get a beer on the way. There I was with my arm laid open, and he stopped for a beer!

I didn't start bleeding for a good while, but when I did, it was a mess. We got to the hospital, and I had to sign a pile of paperwork. That was when my arm finally bled—from the increase in room temperature, no doubt. It bled all over the papers I was signing.

I needed fifteen to twenty stitches that night. As a general rule, nothing good can come from drinking, and that was a lesson I would learn more than once.

12
Teen Years

As a teenager, I had a tame side and a wild side. Maybe lots of guys can say that. In one sense, I was a straight arrow who didn't smoke or drink. Drugs weren't even an issue for the kids in our little town. I was an honor student and shy with girls. At the same time, I was unsupervised and living with an alcoholic. I would take off for days at a time with friends from other towns, friends who were edgy and adventurous. We'd hitchhike hundreds of miles after leaving home with no money and the vaguest of plans. One of those friends ended up dying in prison, where he was serving time for murder. But that was later; back then, we were just boys looking for something new, and I liked anyplace that wasn't home.

My home life was complicated by the natural agonies of growing up. My self-esteem was in the toilet to start with, thanks to a mom who was rarely on my side, and then my body turned against me, too.

Puberty was the worst of times. How long did it last—a year or two? It was hell. I could have used some family support during those awkward times, but I was on my own. Jane was away at college, Mom was usually drunk, and Dad was doing his best, I suppose, but he was like a shadow on the wall. I'd gained some self-confidence preaching and performing magic tricks in front of audiences—more about that later—and that training helped. But between being the "son of a bitch" in our house and the embarrassment of my body changing, life was a constant challenge.

Some things are routine for a boy, but so humiliating. Unwanted erections top the list. They might be part of the process of growing up, but try to live with them. Every time I got up in front of a class to read, I had to hold my papers down in front of my pants. Twenty-four hours a day, I fought "the battle of the bulge." Every boy knows this: you have to read your book report while you're holding the paper over your crotch, just in case. The other guys laughed; they knew what it was like.

I had absolutely no control over my private parts or my voice, which could go high at any moment without notice, even within the same word or sentence. I never knew when it was coming. I used to dread the phone ringing, my voice was so unreliable. I even hated to go into a store to buy something, because I'd have to talk to the clerk. It was really humiliating. Between the voice, the erections, and pimples, oh, man.

The first time my face broke out, one of Jane's friends said, "Oh, you're at *that* age." That was back when Clearasil came out. Dick Clark pushed it on TV, and I tried it. Our bathroom didn't have the best lighting—one lone bulb with a glass shade. I put Clearasil on my pimples and went out. Hell, you could see it. I was polka-dotted! The next day my face was all broken out. I think the Clearasil drew out every blemish that was in me. When I looked in the mirror I was shocked, and things were only going to get worse.

It got so I could feel the pimples coming before they were even visible. It felt like I had a marble inside my face. Most of my breakouts came on my chin or my nose, but I had them everywhere. They were always the worst just before a big event. I used to stand in front of the bathroom mirror and squeeze the blackheads out of my nose, too, always conscious that Grandpop's ghostly face could show up in the mirror. Can you gross out a ghost? If so, I may not have succeeded in clearing up my complexion, but at least I knew how to get rid of Grandpop.

When I wasn't treating my blemishes, I was washing my face to prevent future breakouts. I tried special cleansers and even put toothpaste on my face to dry it up. I became so preoccupied with my bad complexion that my personality changed. My nerves were shot from trying to find a cure. In high school I was so scared of pimples that I went four years without drinking one pop. Mom wasn't any help until I begged her to take me to a dermatologist. Finally she did, and he gave me a prescription, but even that didn't help. I ended up using Noxzema. I was constantly putting Noxzema on my face. When I went out, I used to take it with me in a baggie in my pocket. Sometimes I even carried the whole container, and when I wasn't around other people I had Noxzema on my face, guaranteed.

There was a kid in my health class who had the oiliest skin I'd ever seen. I hate to say it now, but when I felt bad about my complexion, I'd turn around and look at him.

I would not ask a girl out. Between my skin problems, which lasted four or five years, and my even longer reign as persona non grata in our house, low self-esteem was by then a sad and permanent part of me. I remember my first date, but not how I ended up taking a girl named Nancy to a school dance. She was from Glen Ferris; a tomboy until she blossomed into a stunning beauty—but that was later. That night we were young. She took a purse to the dance because that was what girls did, but she had no idea what to put in it. So it would feel heavy the way other girls' purses did, Nancy carried a softball in hers.

I did end up having a girlfriend, but I don't remember how we began dating. I know my friend Rodney helped me talk to her. He lived three doors down from us and was my closest friend.

I was in junior high when I first saw Hope at a basketball game. She was a cheerleader from a rival school. I'd also see her at the Glen Ferris bowling alley, where Rodney and I would go to play the pinball machine. I thought she was cute long before I said anything to her.

When we started going together, I was too young to have a driver's license, so we would do things like go skating at a local rink, or I'd go to her house. I can still picture myself slapping on the Noxzema on the way home. Hope's birthday was in June, a month before mine, so she got her driver's license first. When we went out, one friend would ask, "Did she let you steer?"

Hope's parents weren't crazy about me. It wasn't personal; we were just too young to be as close as we were. We thought we were in love and even talked about getting married. For a while, she wasn't allowed to see me, but one time we both happened to be at the same swimming pool. We spent a couple hours together, talking. By then I could drive, and we left together in separate cars. She was in front of me. The weather had turned bad—heavy rain—and someone ahead of us stopped without warning. Hope slammed on her brakes, and so did I; but I couldn't stop in time, and my car hit hers.

I would have called it a tap, but the accident was enough to bring the police. They called Mom, and she came to the scene. As soon as she got there, she put her hand out for my license. Hope's parents were called to the scene also, and they were hot. Of course, our cover was blown as far as being together.

The police asked me, "Did you hit her before she hit the other car?" I said I thought so; it was so hard to tell. To me, it was an accident. I hadn't done anything wrong; but our insurance man said I'd need to carry high-risk insurance because of the accident. Rather than pay high risk, Mom just kept me from driving for a year. So I had no license and Hope was in trouble for seeing me. It all worked out some-how. We dated on and off for four years and remain friends today.

In school I was up against the ghost of my sister, who'd made straight As in most of her subjects and had finished high school fourth in her class. I was no slouch when it came to grades, but I was always being compared to Jane. I was state vice-president of the Beta Club, an honor society, but no matter how well I did, I was never confident. I was *expected* to excel.

Mom's drinking got worse when I was in my teens. One time it was raining like hell, and I was with my friend Steve outside his fam-ily's apartment. Mom staggered by on the sidewalk wearing nothing but a sheer nightgown. I don't know why she didn't see us; I was al-most close enough to reach out and touch her. Her gown was soaked through and clinging to her. Cars were tooting at her and splashing by her. I was beyond embarrassed. I didn't know if she was going to walk into the damn traffic or what, but I knew she'd fight me right there on the street if I tried to stop her. It's a terrible choice to have to make— either way, you lose—but I turned away from my mother and walked into Steve's house. Later I found out that Mom had been walking to the gas station for cigarettes.

It wasn't the first time Steve had seen Mom in a compromising position. Once after school he and I walked upstairs and saw her lying on her back in bed, naked from the waist up, her arms stretched out like Jesus. She was passed out.

I ran away from home twice in my teens. I couldn't live with the constant pressure; every day was nothing but survival. One time I moved into my friend Hank's parents' house for six weeks and helped them with cleaning, painting, and so on, to pay my way. The second time I ran away, I stayed with another friend for two weeks, but his mom was going through the change of life. I guess my being there didn't help her range of emotions, because she called Mom to come and get me.

After high school, my boundaries expanded. Hank and I hitch-hiked to Myrtle Beach, South Carolina, several times. We would go with ten dollars in our pockets. Once on the way we stopped in Nar-rows, Virginia. We were starving, and we saw a diner along the road. We ordered cheeseburgers with the works, fries, and drinks. We ate until we were ready to pop, and we had no money. They made us sweep and mop the restaurant. More practice for my future career.

We never had a place to stay when we started out. Once we went in the winter during a school break and were surprised by cold weather in South Carolina. We saw an empty police car and got in it to warm up and get some sleep. Then we noticed there were no handles on the inside. We couldn't get out, and we were so hungry. It must have been close to Valentine's Day, because we found a big heart-shaped box of chocolates in the car and ate them all—not the best choice for a kid with pimples.

When the cop discovered us, we were asleep. We took off, but he caught us. He wanted us out of town, so he saw us to the bus station and got us each a ticket for Charleston, West Virginia. We got as far as Conway, South Carolina, cashed in our tickets, and came back.

I thought Mom might send me some money if I called and asked, but she didn't. That night Hank and I didn't have a place to stay. We wanted to be out of sight, and we found some big bushes with soft needles under them. We lay down and slept. When we woke up the next morning, we realized that the bushes were lining the sidewalk to a church. All the people coming to church were pointing at us and stepping over our feet, which were stretched out over the sidewalk. We were bums on the street.

It was raining when we tried to hitchhike home. I was wearing a mohair sweater, and it started stinking. We went to a used-car lot somewhere near the Air Force base outside Myrtle Beach and got in a car to sleep. The next day, after we were chased out of there, a car stopped and picked us up. Two good-looking girls were going home to Raleigh, North Carolina, from Florida. Raleigh was miles and miles out of our way. We didn't get close to home, but we saw Raleigh.

Next, a guy in a Malibu picked us up at two or three in the morning. We rode in front with him. Hank told me to get in first. Just outside some city, the guy turned in at a construction site and grabbed me like a vise you-know-where. It was what Hank had suspected. He got out on his side, went around, and opened the driver's door. I pushed the guy over and Hank shut the door on him. He wasn't big, but he could have stabbed or shot us.

We were stupid, hitchhiking at all hours. After the bars closed, the drunks would mess with us. It was really dangerous. We were five hundred miles from home with no money. Why did I do it? Hank talked me into a lot of it, but I was in my runaway stage—still hiding.

As for my bad complexion, growing up was the only thing that helped it. That whole, terrible episode of pimples lasted until I was nearly a man.

13
Behind the Scenes

Cincinnati, 1997

When the last bell rang, the kindergarten school ceased to be the domain of students and teachers. It was mine. Most of the daytime population went home without a thought as to what a custodian did after school. They might be surprised at all the dramas that played out when their seats were empty.

Hannah's secretary served as a receptionist, and fronting her work station was a large window consisting of two panes of glass that locked together, like the windows in a doctor's office. The secretary could work with the window closed or could slide the panes apart to greet someone. Below the glass was a solid wall to the floor.

One night I was cleaning the glass from the inside—the desk side. I had a key to unlock and separate the two panes, but I hadn't. I must have pushed too hard in the wrong direction with the cleaning cloth, because the unthinkable happened: the whole window popped out the bottom and slid down the wall toward the floor. There was no way I could stop it from where I was standing, so I leaned into the opening and watched, helpless, bracing for the sound of breaking glass.

There's a scene in the movie *Risky Business* in which Tom Cruise as teenager Joel has taken his father's Porsche 928 out for a drive and has parked it on a slope leading to a wooden pier on Lake Michigan. He gets out of the car to plead with his retreating date after a tiff, unaware that she has accidentally disengaged the gear shift before walking away. The empty Porsche begins to roll toward the water.

Joel turns, panics, and grabs desperately at the car, trying in vain to stop it as he bellows "Please, God!" into the night. He finally flops onto the hood, expecting the worst as the car rolls out onto the narrow pier. It miraculously stops just short of the last plank, and Joel's relief is palpable. He cautiously climbs down off the car, which is now sitting still. For a few seconds, all is quiet but for the sounds of lapping water, creaking wood, and the faint squeak of a lamplight on its pole. And then, just when things seem to have settled down, the weight of the car causes the pier to break off and plunge into the lake. My glass pane accident was a little bit like that.

The office carpeting was a flattish industrial weave, yet somehow the huge window caught on its fibers and stopped falling. I looked down to see it resting against the wall, still in one piece. Relief washed over me, but before I could even step around to pick the glass up, it started to move again. That double pane slid the rest of the way to the floor and shattered into a thousand pieces that I had to clean up and explain. Sometimes you can't win for losing.

Hannah and her secretary were both so picky about their office area that they would actually trick us to see how well we were cleaning. One thing they did was to put paper clips the same color as the carpeting under their desks or in a corner and then check the next day to see if they had been vacuumed up.

I'm color blind, so the paper clips didn't stand out to me against the rug. Dave tipped me off. He didn't want me to get caught. The whole thing was petty, but after I knew what to check for, I crawled under the desks at night and felt around for the stupid paper clips. After a bit of that, I asked Dave to order something for me. It was a magnet enclosed in plastic that can be stuck on the front of a sweeper to attract paper clips and such so they won't get sucked into the sweeper. It found them.

I got so busy at one point that Earl was asked to take over vacuuming Hannah's office. He started work early each day and would have time to do it before school began. I don't know that he was any less conscientious about sweeping the offices than I had been, but he did lack the pipeline I had to Dave. One day I heard Earl complaining that Hannah had placed a small wad of paper in a corner behind a door where his sweeper wouldn't reach, and he'd missed it. I felt a twinge of sympathy when I heard him say, "That bitch set me up!"

One night when I was cleaning classrooms, I noticed something new. Every room had a clear plastic cylinder sitting on a table. They were over a foot tall, each one sitting on a base, and each had a lid with something hanging from the inside. I didn't know what it was, so the next day I asked a teacher. The cylinders were science projects, butterfly starter kits that began with caterpillars making their own cocoons. The students could watch the progress of a caterpillar as it became a butterfly. When I cleaned the classrooms, I watched them, too. Every few days I could notice the changes.

One night when I was vacuuming, I noticed that the starter kit in one room wasn't in its place on the table. It was on the floor, open.

Oh, man! I didn't think I'd done it, but the electric cord on my vacuum cleaner could have knocked it off as I was working. Those kits had cost fifty dollars each. My first thought—as usual—was: *I'm in trouble.* I had passed my probationary period; would I ever lighten up?

Whatever was inside that cylinder—including some greenery— had spilled onto the carpet. I swept up the greenery with a whisk broom and started looking for the cocoon. When I turned the lid over, I was praying the cocoon was where it should be, but I already knew it wasn't attached. Finally I spotted it. The cocoon had bounced a couple times and landed a few feet away. This wasn't looking good for the caterpillar.

I panicked. The cocoon was lying on the carpet, and I picked it up. The caterpillar was still inside, but had I killed it? I could always hope it was still alive. I Super-Glued the cocoon back into place and put the whole works back on the table.

As time went on, I heard more talk about the butterfly project. Every few days the classes would discuss the progress of their butterflies—except one teacher, who couldn't understand why hers wasn't doing anything. *Crap.*

Every time I went into that room, I thought again about how that kit might have fallen to the floor. It was a mystery. I remembered that the cylinder had originally contained some dirt, but—strangely—there was no dirt on the floor the night I found it. If anyone asked, I always maintained, and secretly hoped, that I hadn't broken the starter kit. Then I found out that another custodian, who'd since been fired, had wired that classroom for the Internet around the time of "the cocoon incident." That story supported my innocence, but I'd made a mistake in failing to report something that was possibly my fault. So had he.

Then it was spring, near the end of school. The plan for the science project was to release the butterflies into a garden in the schoolyard created especially for them. It was a big deal. The Parent-Teacher Organization had donated a group of plants that were known to attract butterflies. Stone walkways had been installed among the bushes. The teachers were going to release the butterflies together, all at once. Well, minus one.

All the classes came outside to watch the teachers let the butterflies loose in the garden. At the signal they opened the lids, and that was the last anyone saw of the butterflies. Instead of lingering in the garden, they all flew away.

A few weeks later it was summer, and school was finally out. During summer vacation, all of the custodians worked the day shift. In our school, "all" meant Earl, Dave, and me. We did our big cleaning of the year then, when the building was supposedly empty. I say *supposedly* because school personnel were in and out. The office staff worked through the summer, the bigwigs came and went, and we always had a few teachers who couldn't stay away. Did they not have enough to do at home?

Summers were for projects we didn't have time to do during the school year. We cleaned and waxed every classroom, reconditioned the gym floor, and stripped and refinished the halls. Everything was made ready for the next school year. I loved the summertime. It was a time of freedom for me, with the kids and teachers gone, and time to make that school shine.

Dave and I were the same way about floors; we knew how to make them gleam, and we took pride in our work. Earl could fix things, but he didn't know squat about cleaning, particularly when it came to preparing the floors. He wanted to be in charge, but he didn't know what we really did. Besides being practically unknown to the population he "served" every school day, Earl seldom crossed paths with Dave and me. Except for the summers, we rarely saw him, and that was fine with us.

One time a guy came to fix the furnace, and Earl wasn't there. I had to show the repairman where the furnace was, which was funny because I had to find it myself. In my fumbling around, I discovered a little room—or should I say a little hideout? The walls were cinderblock, so it looked like a bunker. In it were a recliner and an ashtray. Had any of the current custodians found this room? Maybe someone was using it. I sure wouldn't!

The lower level of the school wasn't an appealing place. It was creepy, even to grown men. The custodians hated to go downstairs. Two of the guys said they'd felt "cold spots," drops in room temperature linked to paranormal activity. Dave said he'd felt a presence behind him one night: "I wasn't touched, but the hair on my arms and the back of my neck stood up. I turned around real quick, but no one was there." Whenever we had to load salt into the water softener or check the fire extinguisher, we did it quickly and got the heck out.

I was glad Earl was in charge of the basement. He was good at what he did; he just liked being the boss a little too much, and he wanted to be right even if he wasn't.

We all pitched in to strip the floors and rewax them. Unlike cleaning, stripping takes a lot of time, because you're taking layers of wax off a floor. There was one tiled section of a classroom floor that we could not get clean. We all tried using a buffer on it, but that floor had some kind of stain on it that wouldn't come out.

Earl decided to take a screen to it. Screening is done on the wood floor of the gym using a special attachment on the buffer. The screening pad looks something like the screen in a door. The process isn't meant for tile, but we couldn't tell Earl anything. He went right after that attachment.

He didn't wet the floor before he started, which is another no-no, so we had a screen turning around a thousand times a minute on a tile floor. Earl kept repeating the movements of the buffer. He ground the pattern right off the tile. Soon the tile dust had formed a cloud so high that we could barely see each other. We were breathing it in, and that tile was asbestos, but I know of no ill effects from that day.

My favorite job was waxing. A waxed floor starts out slippery and then becomes sticky before it dries. In order not to have anyone hurt or the wax disturbed, I posted signs on the doors in three languages—English, Spanish, and French—that said, "Wet Wax. Do Not Enter." Call me a fanatic, but I taped each doorway like a crime scene; anyone attempting to go in would have to be a contortionist to get around the tape.

One day when I was waxing, Hannah was visited by two parents who wanted to see a preschool classroom. Of the three preschool rooms we had, she took the couple into the room with the wet wax—the one with the warning signs and tape. I had to wonder what went through Hannah's mind sometimes. Why would she choose a room that she and two visitors practically had to climb into? And at what point did they realize the wax was wet? When I came back to check it, I saw three sets of footprints inside, two made by women and the other by a man's shoes. *Thanks a bunch.*

Ghosts apparently didn't take the summer off, and I was surprised to learn that their antics weren't confined to the kindergarten school. One of the custodians in another school, a guy we called Buck, told me about something that happened to him when he was waxing.

In order to wax a classroom floor, the custodian has to strip the room down to the floor and walls. We always start at the ceiling and work downward so that nothing can fall. Pictures, bookcases and their contents, rugs, desks, and all supplies are moved out into the hall. We start at the far end of the room and wax toward the door, and when we go out we lock the room.

Buck's school was empty of people, so he had no worries that anyone would disturb his fresh wax. When he was done with one room, he moved on to another one but came back later to check the wax to see if it was dry. When he unlocked the door to one classroom and turned on the light, there in the dead center of the floor was a pencil. The wax had dried, so Buck walked over to the pencil, the only object in the room. It was lying on top of the wax with a printed message on it, facing upward: "Welcome to my school."

There was no way that pencil had been on the floor when he had waxed it, and the pencil hadn't just rolled to the center like that. No one could have done it; there were no footprints in the wax. Buck knew he was alone in the building, and the pencil had not been in the room before. He knew the message on it was meant for him; it was showing him who was boss.

"Joe," he said, "it shook me up so bad I had to go somewhere and smoke a few cigarettes to calm down." I believed him, but I had to wonder: Who would have pencils made up that said "Welcome to my school"? That wasn't a message anyone would order for kids and teachers.

I couldn't make sense of it. I was just glad I hadn't been the one to find that pencil; I wanted nothing to do with ghosts.

14
Good-bye, Good-bye

Glen Ferris, 1966

I turned eighteen in July of 1966. That was a crazy summer, and mostly terrible, but at the beginning of it I was looking forward to the next chapter of my life. Big changes were coming. Jane and I were both leaving the nest.

Finally, our years of misery in the house by the church would end. Mom and Dad would be left behind to face one another across the supper table as my sister and I took different paths out of our little village. I wouldn't be sentimental in the least. I was excited to be enrolled in West Virginia University for the coming term. Mom and Dad wanted me to study pharmacy. Dad in particular had never been excited about Jane getting a college education, even when she graduated. He believed that girls didn't need to go to college. I was the one they were putting their money on.

For my sister, the summer of 1966 was one of wedding plans. Jane was marrying her college boyfriend, and afterward they would be living in a different county. She had brought him home a few times, and he was a nice guy. I was happy for them.

Dad went to the Cleveland Clinic for one of his checkups that summer, but he would be home in time to give the bride away. As head usher, I was going to wear the first tux of my life and walk my mother in and out of the church. I thought it was pretty cool to be picked, especially since I was younger than the other groomsmen.

On the day of the wedding, reality hit me like a flash flood. What was supposed to be the happiest day of my sister's life became one of the hardest days of mine. The reason was simple: Jane was leaving. She'd already gone to college, but this was different. It was final. I cried so much that my eyes swelled shut.

Dad and I weren't that close, and I was still afraid of Mom, so I'd depended on Jane for a lot. Her marriage underscored the fact that she was grown up. I'd just graduated from high school, so I was no kid, but the thought of her moving out forever was such a big thing to me, so frightening. I cried even though I had a new life coming, too.

Mr. Joe

An older boy who lived down the street had told Mom and Dad and me all about the university, and he'd offered to show me around after I got there—take care of me and let me run around with him. I was glad for John's offer, especially the way I was feeling about the wedding. At least I knew I'd have a friend at college.

In the meantime, I had to get through the wedding. I was in agony standing at the front of the church where everyone could see my swollen face. I had to get out of there, so right after the ceremony I left— alone. I was supposed to walk Mom out before anyone else exited the church, but instead I rushed out right behind the bride and groom. I'd lost it and couldn't wait to get home. It wasn't far to run. I let myself in, sat down in Dad's brown chair, and let loose. I was crying because I realized I was alone.

Just a few minutes later, someone came over to get me. The congregation was still waiting for me to walk Mom down the aisle and out of the church, so I did it. How many times in my life had Mom told me she wanted to choke me? I bet she sure wanted to choke me then!

Mom had been drunk for days. She had left most of the planning and preparation to Jane and Grandmama, instead showing up to each event at the last minute like any other guest. She'd bought new clothes and had been present for the various luncheons and rehearsals, but couldn't she stay sober? That would have been a welcome wedding gift.

Jane's husband was from up North. Several of his relatives had come to town and stayed at the inn. Were they prepared for a Glen Ferris wedding? That was the only kind we knew: a ceremony in the sanctuary followed by a reception of cake and punch in the church basement. In other words, it was dry. Even without Grandmama's religious influence, Jane would not have served booze in the church, so what was left? No one rented a hall or hired a catering service or engaged a band. In hindsight, nothing we did was standard.

After a bit of rice-throwing on the church steps, Jane left for her honeymoon and everyone else eventually went home. Three days after the wedding, I was alone in the house, getting ready to take a bath, when the phone rang. It was Mom. "What are you doing?" she asked.

I said I was going to get cleaned up.

"Well," she said, "don't get in the tub. You need to come down to Grandmama's house right now." I heard my grandmother in the background telling Mom to let me take my bath first. I knew something was really wrong, but Mom didn't say what it was, just for me to come.

Dad was in the hospital. He'd become ill after the wedding. I hadn't noticed anything unusual about him; I sure didn't realize how sick he was.

I had a bad feeling the whole time I was bathing and shaving. When I was ready, I started walking down the street toward my grandmother's. Before I could get there, a car pulled up on the side of the road and let Mom out. She came over to me and told me that Dad had died. *Oh, please, no. Not Dad!* I remember fainting, because I fell into the hedge that ran along the sidewalk.

It was my worst fear. I'd suspected Mom's news might be about Dad, but you can always hope—until you know. From then on, it would be Mom and me. You talk about a lonely time.

Dad had been taking nitroglycerin pills for his hypertension. I remembered him wanting a pill once, and Mom wouldn't give it to him even though she had the container in her hand. She was drunk, and they were both sitting on the floor. He was conscious but struggling to breathe. I told Mom to give him the damn pill, and she laid it on his tongue. I tried to put that whole episode out of my mind, but it haunted me after Dad died. His death certificate said "hypertensive cardiovascular disease," but I wouldn't have put anything past Mom. Whatever the truth of his death was, it would be buried now.

I wore a light-colored suit to Dad's visitation, because that was all I had. Besides, I was in a daze. I didn't realize until somebody mentioned it later that a person should wear dark clothing to a funeral home. Afterward, when people saw me out the same night, I still had my suit on. People would come up and ask me how I was doing, avoiding the elephant in the room. My dad had just died. How did they think I was doing?

I always thought Dad had a rough life, and I was sad for him. One night after he died, I was sleeping on the sofa bed in my room and I saw Dad. He sat down next to me and talked to me. He told me not to worry about him, that he would be fine. I knew he was dead—that I was seeing a ghost—but I wasn't afraid the way I'd been with Grandpop.

People are so quick to dismiss things like that; they'd say it was a dream, and I can't argue. I thought so myself. But the next day when

I woke up, the blanket on my mattress was folded back just the way Dad had folded it so that he could sit down.

After Jane left home, I was sitting in her room one day. Mom came in, sober, and asked me what she was like when she drank. It's the only time that ever happened, and she listened to me when I told her she became another person, one we disliked and feared. She said she hadn't realized that; hadn't known the impact her drinking had made on us. I felt good talking to her, like the conversation would make a difference, but it didn't. Nothing changed.

When Dad died, there was a strike in progress at his plant. Some of the guys he worked with didn't know he had passed away because they hadn't been working. I had a job there that summer, so they heard it from me. That's how I found out how much they'd liked him. My job was swinging a twenty-pound sledgehammer all day in the furnace room. Big slabs of metal would come down a chute, and I had to break up each one to clean the impurities out of it. The pieces I took out were about the size of my fist. It was over one hundred degrees in there, and I wore an asbestos coat because it was so hot. I worked hard in that plant because I wanted to look good to those men. I did it for Dad.

When he died, he left a real void. He wasn't the kind of dad you'd miss for all the things he did, but the potential was there, and that potential died with him. Maybe we would have been friends if he'd lived to see me grow up. Maybe he'd have liked being a grandfather. I didn't have to wonder what Dad would have thought about me becoming a custodian; I think my whole life path would have been different, had he lived. I like to think I would have finished college and become something more, maybe even a pharmacist. But that's not what happened.

At the last minute, my neighbor John changed his mind about going to the university and enrolled in a local college. With my third loss of the summer, my plans meant nothing; they were illusions. I pleaded with Mom to let me attend college closer to home, but she wouldn't budge. She wanted me at West Virginia University, so I went. I was good at taking tests and always tested better than I really was. Because of my high test scores, I was signed up for some crazy classes: intermediate Hebrew, which I dropped; advanced calculus; in all, twenty-two hours of classes. At least I was away from home.

15

The Ghost in the Overcoat

Cincinnati, 1997

Seeing a ghost is scary. What's even scarier is when a ghost sees you.

Autumn came, and the kindergarten school was once again full of students and teachers. It seemed like no time until I felt a chill in the air and seasonal decorations began to appear in the classrooms. The teachers liked to decorate with corn stalks and bales of straw, so I was preoccupied with raking up bits of straw every night. Back then, I thought that straw was my worst nightmare, but I didn't know anything.

It happened one night when I was working alone on the first floor. I was vacuuming a rug in the main hallway near one of the entrances. The door was made largely of glass, and I glanced outside. A man in an overcoat was walking past, which was strange because it was so late.

A little bit later, the same man walked by again. He seemed to stop just past the door and double back, quickly looking in. He didn't look threatening, but why had he gone by twice? Why was he so interested in what a custodian was doing? I was glad the door was locked.

I looked away for a few seconds, and when I turned back toward the door, he was inside. *Inside with me!* I was vacuuming a five-foot rug, and when I looked up he was standing on part of it. This man had magically entered a set of locked doors without a sound, and now he was standing three feet away.

He was probably in his fifties. The overcoat—but not his face— reminded me of Dad, who'd died more than thirty years before. This man's clothes were from an older time, probably the 1940s, and he wasn't in color; he was in subtle shades, like an old photograph, nearly black and white.

He looked me right in the eye, just like Grandpop had so many years before. He wasn't smiling, but he looked completely relaxed. He didn't look mean, or like he intended to hurt me; he just wasn't supposed to be there. That was when I started to get scared—when I realized he wasn't real.

I knew I was seeing a ghost, but that wasn't what turned my legs to water. It was the fact that he had *approached* me. He had looked *at me* through a glass and had come into where I was working. I wasn't just watching something float by; that would have been bad enough, but this ghost was aware of me. He seemed to be waiting, and I didn't have any idea what he was going to do.

I was afraid to run, I was afraid to walk away, I was afraid to do anything—but I had to get away from him. I knew that if I ran down that hall and he wanted to catch me, he would, so I started walking backwards away from him and went around a corner. Then I turned and ran like hell up the stairs to the farthest classroom on the second floor. I don't know which was louder, my feet pounding on the steps or my pounding heart.

I turned on the light, locked myself in, and found the phone. Every classroom had one. I didn't hesitate a second before I called Dave at home and asked him to come and get me. I couldn't leave that room, not by myself.

Dave lived three miles from the school. He was married, and he was usually busy when he was at home, but he said he'd come right away. He knew I was freaking out. While I waited, I hid. It was my natural response to danger, a comfort I had not left behind with my childhood. I turned off the light and sat on the floor under the window. Even though I wasn't on the ground floor, I wanted to be below eye level.

In a few minutes Dave was there with flashlights, and he walked outside with me. I hadn't told him the whole truth, that I'd seen a ghost. Maybe I would later, but that night I said it was a prowler. I told him a man had been walking around the school, and that he'd come up and cupped his hands against the glass of the front door and looked in at me. I didn't say he'd come through the door like it wasn't there and stood on the other end of the rug I was vacuuming.

We checked all around the building and didn't find anybody. Nothing was out of the ordinary. I think Dave knew I'd been scared by more than a prowler, but what could I gain by telling him the truth? I knew that he'd done all he could do for me.

The nightmares started that night, when the ghost in the overcoat haunted my dreams. It was always the same: the whole scene from the school would replay in my sleep like it was the first time. It didn't matter that I'd been through the actual experience; in the dream I didn't know how it would end. I had to go through all of it—seeing him walk by on the sidewalk, turning away, and suddenly coming face to face with him in the hall of the building. I would sweat and shake and finally wake up.

My nights changed dramatically, all because of a few seconds when I'd stared into the empty eyes of a ghost. That ghost hadn't just stolen my sleep; he had cast his dark shadow on my waking moments, too. My evenings, once peaceful, were now filled with terror at what was to come. I hated him for it.. He had taken something that was mine.

I'd always liked the night, at least all my working life. The years of working second and third shifts hadn't just changed my body rhythms; they had taught me the pleasures of quiet time. After I was divorced and the kids were grown, I didn't bother trying to adjust to the rest of the world. Even when I wasn't working I'd stay up and watch TV, write, or even clean, and then sleep late. I might even go somewhere late at night; I had no one to answer to. I liked the small hours best, when most people had settled down and gone to sleep. It became my alone time, and I treasured it. After I saw the ghost, nothing was the same.

It was not easy to go back into that school every afternoon, especially after the students and teachers had left for the day. The last bus would pull out, and before long it would begin to get dark. I wanted to be somewhere else. All night I continued to talk out loud, trying to make friends with things I couldn't see and didn't understand. When you project your voice like that, it's a strain. I talked until my throat went dry. I gained a new appreciation for having teachers in the building, too. I won't say I was never again frustrated when they came back in the evenings, but I was relieved not to be alone.

Whenever I had to be in that hallway, the one where I'd seen him, the glass in the door would tease me. Should I look at it or avoid it? Was he outside? Would my thinking about it cause him to appear again? I was afraid that if I looked, the whole thing would repeat, the way it did in my nightmares. My heart rate would speed up just being in that hallway. Part of me wanted to look and get it over with; I've always wanted to know what I was facing, good or bad. The other part wanted to *hide*, big time. Ordinarily, I'd look forward to ending my shift and going home, but now home had lost its appeal.

If I was scared I'd see the ghost at school, I *knew* I'd see him at home, as soon as I fell asleep. I dreaded it so much that I started staying up as long as possible. That just hurt me; the next day I would be no good at work. I tried drinking beer after work to calm myself, but I always knew what was coming; as soon as I went to bed, the nightmare would start. My dread of sleep got so bad that I started taking NyQuil to knock myself out. It was the only way I could sleep and wake up in any condition to do my job.

I could have quit that job and never looked back, so why didn't I? I had to ask myself why I put up with anything in my life. It was my personality. I looked for the good and wanted to help people. I liked the teachers and kids at school, and I appreciated the chance I'd been given. I didn't want to let Dave and Hannah down, but it was more than that. *I needed to succeed.* It was important to me not to be a quitter.

16
Pool Shark

Morgantown, West Virginia, 1966

West Virginia University was at the other end of the state, eleven miles from Pennsylvania. Going away to college might have been fun under other circumstances, but now I didn't want to be there. I'd had too many losses for my education to matter right then. I started out trying hard, but I was so lost that my efforts at being a good student soon wore off. I didn't want anything to do with it. I had no interest in pursuing pharmacy. At night I went to clubs and danced. I started playing pool for money.

My fascination with pool had started one time when I visited my sister at college, and Jane and I played in her student union. I wasn't any good, but I liked it. At home I began hitchhiking to a club in Montgomery, West Virginia, with a friend who liked to play. I had a good eye, but I didn't know anything about the game. I wanted to be better at it—nobody likes to be humiliated—so I kept practicing and read a couple books. That's how I realized pool was about math, angles, and speed. From that moment, the game of pool had me.

I loved math. As a kid I'd helped my friend Rodney with his math homework. He couldn't go out to play until he had it done. Rodney was a D student, but math came easily to me. He'd write out his multiplication problems and I'd tell him the answers just as fast as he could fill them in. These were high numbers, like 1,700 times 355. I could do them in my head. We knocked it out fast, and then we could go outside. He always got hundreds on his papers.

When I started shooting pool in 1966, I was playing on a snooker table. Snooker tables were made with tight pockets, requiring more precise shots than a regulation pool table would demand. The pockets on early snooker tables, before they were enlarged to make the game more popular, were barely bigger than the ball. If you could make a shot into one of those pockets—as I learned to do—you had it made with the newer tables.

When I first got to the university I continued to play pool, but I kept losing. Pool halls were everywhere, so I started going to the ones in town to watch the games. Word would travel about certain games coming up, and I'd get there early to get a seat. I learned who the great players were, and then I sat and watched how they did it.

In every pool hall there's a "money table" that's reserved for the best players. It's unofficial; the people who shoot know it. That's the table where people are sitting around watching and money is flying as people pay each other off. Sometimes a wire is strung above the table with beads on it like an abacus. In straight pool, such a setup is used to keep score, but it can also be used to keep track of who owes what.

There was one place frequented by a group of older guys who really knew what they were doing. They played on a table that was ten feet long, which meant the ball had to travel farther to its target; thus, shots were more difficult to make. I wanted to learn to play like those men did, but if I asked them anything, they wouldn't tell me. I had to play them and pay for the table time at so much an hour. They played for free that way, and they still wouldn't talk, but I learned about ball control by watching them. Pool is all about controlling the cue ball. I learned to control it so well that I could make it go around the table and roll across a quarter. Every now and then I could even make it stop on the quarter.

I remember an older guy, very thin, who racked balls in that hall for a few cents per game. He looked like the Cryptkeeper on TV. He'd sit inside a telephone booth there in the room with the pool rack around his neck, saying one thing over and over: "Pig's ass is pork." He also used to grab himself in a suggestive way and look right at me, like he was making a proposition. If he had a purpose besides racking balls, maybe it was to serve as a distraction, but his effect on me was the opposite. I ignored him and learned to improve my concentration.

When I came home in the summer to work at the plant, I'd go back to Montgomery and shoot pool. It was ten cents a game and the loser had to pay it. I played with people I knew and people I didn't. Eventually I got to the point when I knew I could win eight out of ten games with the people who frequented those bars. I could take a dollar with me and play all day. My friend Steve and I would go together. I kept getting better and studying the game.

I learned about the diamond system by reading. A lot of people don't know that the decorative diamonds on the side rails of a pool table represent a mathematical system for banking shots. Every table has those inserts, and each insert is assigned a numerical value, but the values are not marked. If a player knows the numerical values of those diamonds, he can calculate the speed and angle of a shot and control the path of the ball. The system is sophisticated, and it took me a while to get it. Once I did, I knew what spot(s) on the rail I had to hit in order to get a ball to a certain place.

I got to a point where I could set my left hand down on the felt and make a shot without looking or thinking. My hand did the work. It was muscle memory. I didn't have to sight down the cue; I could stand straight up and make the shot.

I loved pool because of the math, the precision, and the fact that it was something I could do alone. I practiced all the time. After I got good, I never paid for anything when I went out. I would go to new places and drink for free, because I'd win. Sometimes people would come from another town and ask to play "the best." It was like a Western with people always gunning for the top dog. Sometimes I was the one to beat. If not, I'd watch.

I liked being good at pool and, especially, being *known* for being good. I had my own places where I played. When people know you, you don't hustle; they simply want to play you because you're good. The difference is that when you hustle, it's dishonest. You try to look bad. I don't like to think of myself as a hustler, but that's what I became.

One summer I had a job renting rafts at a campground in Myrtle Beach. The arcade at one of the adjacent beaches had a pool table. A friend and I worked different shifts, and sometimes he'd give me money and say, "Here, see if you can keep the table until I get there."

A guy I thought was a professional would come to the arcade each day at a certain time and hang around the pool table getting up games and taking people's money. He was smart enough to hustle kids, but he looked like an idiot to me. He was so obvious, for instance asking, "Which one do I shoot now?" He'd miss the ball completely or shoot some goofy shot, and then he might make one that would seem like pure luck. But when it came down to an important shot, he'd perform like somebody on TV. He might have fooled the other kids, but not me. In my opinion, real pool players don't go to an arcade.

I did play the guy once. He wanted to play for a lot of money, but I said, "Let's see how I do for five dollars first." I knew he was going to let me win the first game. When he did, I just took the money and left.

You can hustle by not saying anything. If you're good at it, nobody even knows you did it; you just look lucky. I never acted stupid like the guy at the beach, but I had to go to places where no one knew me or they wouldn't even play me for a beer.

I didn't go after other players, exactly; it was always the other person's choice to play me, but I reeled them in. When I went into a pool room, I would find a table to myself and start shooting balls. If I wanted to hustle, I wouldn't make my shots. The idea is to shoot badly when you're playing alone. People are always watching; in a pool hall, they watch everybody who comes in. Before long, somebody would come over to me and ask, "Do you want to play for a dollar?" I was the person being hustled, or so they thought, but it was the other way around.

The term *pool shark* can mean someone who hustles, or it can just mean someone who's good at pool. That's the definition I like. I was interested enough in pool to dig into it when I was young. I liked to use the scientific approach to figure out the shots and then practice until I could make them. For me, the attraction was never the money or the free beer; it was the math.

I didn't finish school, and I sure didn't learn much about pharmacy in my time there. Pool wasn't just my passion; it was my college education.

17
On Dressing

It was the irony of all ironies that every workday I put on a pair of coarse cotton navy-blue slacks and a collared knit shirt with a logo above the pocket. That was my wardrobe five, six, and sometimes seven days a week. My off-duty wardrobe wasn't much different: a few pairs of jeans and some casual shirts; nothing fancy—I didn't need good trousers and dress shirts and ties. My shoes were serviceable, mostly white sneakers.

No one seeing me on the job would have guessed that I, a school custodian and former plant sanitation worker, had a passion for clothes. Sometimes it seemed I'd forgotten it myself, but that passion for clothes was part of the crooked path I took after Dad died, during my so-called college years. When I wasn't playing pool, I worked in a men's clothing store.

I'd grown up fascinated by clothes. I knew fabrics, patterns, fit, and the subtleties of drape—things most boys didn't have a clue about. I loved to dress up and could make a perfect knot in a tie. I knew just how pants should break on a man's shoe, and how long to fade leather oxfords in the sun to give them the best color. I once ordered custom-made Levi's when I was in high school.

What were the chances that a kid like me would grow up to have jobs that never required him to dress up? In my early days at the meat plant, I didn't even have a uniform. The U.S. Department of Agriculture required production workers to wear white clothes, which the company furnished, but the sanitation workers didn't have to wear special clothing because we didn't work around the meat. We stood in water and used caustic soap to scrub plastic containers for reuse. The work was cold and wet, and we didn't even have boots. The soap would eat holes in our clothes and skin. If the soap splashed on us and we didn't clean it off, it would keep eating us. I had holes in my feet from it. When we washed the production equipment, remains from the meat processes would splash all over us. We were gross. To protect our clothing, we wrapped and taped fifty-five-gallon garbage bags around our arms and legs. Then we'd fix a bag to go over our heads and add two more holes for our arms.

One time shortly after the plant opened, a stockholders' meeting was held there, complete with a tour. We looked out the back door and saw Cadillacs coming down the driveway. The production people were posed like a picture in their spotless white clothing, and there we were, grungy and disgusting in our spattered plastic bags. It was quitting time for the sanitation crew, but the company didn't want us to pass the touring bigwigs on our way out of the plant. They didn't want us to be seen, so they paid us overtime to stay and our foreman hid us in the Dumpsters and the ovens—which had been turned off—until the tour was over.

I did graduate to a white coat, but it wasn't always picture perfect. Our jobs were bloody; we unboxed frozen meat, and sometimes we got splashed with blood. One time I needed to renew the license plates for my car because mine had expired. A friend offered to take me downtown to the license bureau after work, and he was in an awful hurry that day. We rushed out of the plant still wearing our white coats. My friend let me off at the license bureau and went to park the car while I got in line. When he came in, he said, "Doctor Barnett, you're needed in surgery." Everyone let me go to the head of the line, and the woman doing the paperwork was working at the speed of lightning. It was my bloody white coat that did it.

The people who knew me back in Glen Ferris would have been surprised to see me at work. They might remember that other Joe. An alcoholic mom and a dad whose business attire needed help had produced two clothes horses in my sister and me. When I was a kid, Mom always commented on what I wore. It was the same for Jane, and later for our children. Mom wasn't much of a shopper, but she understood the importance of making a good impression, and both Jane and I grew up wanting to look nice. For me, clothes have always been another way to hide. I didn't know until years later that "Always look good" is one of the messages communicated to children of alcoholics. What we show on the outside is what counts, even if we are falling apart within.

I dressed well growing up, but I was behind the curve when it came to basic male routines. One time after Dad was gone, I was at my friend Rodney's house when he was shaving. He was using a blade. I'd always used Dad's electric shavers; he kept two or three. I didn't know how to shave with a blade. Rodney said, "Your dad didn't even teach you how to do that?"

On Dressing

The only thing I got in the grooming department came from Mom, and it was all about fingernails. She was obsessed with fingernails and cuticles. Mom bought special brushes for Jane and me from the Fuller Brush man, who used to come around in a truck and sell door-to-door. We had to clean our nails with those brushes and push our cuticles down every day. We went through so much with Mom, but at least our cuticles looked good.

Mom might have been a nut for fingernails, but she cleaned our faces in the crudest way. Even sober, she wasn't a gentle person. When we were kids, she used to lick a handkerchief and rake it over our faces. It was like being cleaned by a cat—a wildcat. I remember her whipping my head in every direction. When I think of it, I can still smell the inside of her mouth on that handkerchief and her lipstick, inches from my nose.

As a boy I didn't feel good about much, and looking sharp made some of those bad feelings go away. Though some people might, I didn't think of dressing well as a shallow pursuit because of the way Mom had emphasized it to my sister and me. I studied good dressers, people I thought stood out, and all of a sudden I just got it. The first person I noticed was Grandpop. He was impeccable, and I loved looking at him. Grandpop was so thin that clothes hung well on him. He always dressed well: suit pants with a good crease, a vest, his watch in his watch pocket, and nice tie shoes with thin soles. His shoes were always shined.

He had gotten the watch in 1946 after twenty-five years of service to EMCO. It was engraved on the back. He was very careful with that watch, which might be the reason I have it today.

I liked to see the clothes lined up in Grandpop's closet. Most of his shirts were white or tan. He had some pinstripes, too, but nothing too bright. Grandmama ironed his shirts. I don't think she ever sent them to the cleaners. Once she ironed a couple of mine, and they looked so good that my teachers commented on them.

Dad liked to get dressed up when he went someplace, but he couldn't hold a candle to Grandpop. He just wasn't built that way. He always had to watch his weight, doctor's orders, but he was never slender. I don't think there was a suit made that would have made Dad look well dressed. Mom bought his clothes sometimes. She would even order them from mail-order houses. When I was little she'd buy pants for Dad and say to me, "Don't tell him how much these cost."

They were four pairs for twenty-four dollars. I didn't know it was cheap; I thought she was saying she'd spent too much.

Mom did our family's laundry, and I had no complaints until one day when I noticed Rodney's T-shirt. It was smooth. The neck lay flat against his skin, and there were no wrinkles in the body of the shirt. Mine, in contrast, looked like someone had wadded it up until I put it on. That was when I realized that other moms didn't put the clean underwear, T-shirts, and socks in the drawer in one tangled bunch. In our house there was no separating, no folding, no rolling; the clothes went straight from the dryer to the drawer, and not necessarily on the same day. I couldn't change Mom, so I started doing my own laundry.

I ironed my own clothes all through high school. Mom used to tell me I was going to cut myself on the crease of my pants. I would iron them forever. When I went to my friend Steve's graduation wearing a double-breasted pinstriped suit, he told me I looked like a senator. Mom and Dad had a charge account at local department store I liked. I didn't buy a lot of clothes, but when I did get things, I charged them there. Mom and Dad didn't say anything; maybe it was the fact that I could shop by myself and wouldn't inconvenience them. Or it might have been my gestures to turn Dad into a better dresser.

My friends and I used to compare dads, how they looked when they went to work. We'd see them walk past the school bus stop. Steve called Dad by his first and middle initials, C. M., and I called his dad Ray. So, Dad would be walking down the street dressed for work, and Steve would say, "How does C. M. look today?" Not so hot.

I was always trying to help Dad look better. What else was I going to give him? So much in life is about appearances, and I was embarrassed by the way Dad dressed. He was clean and well groomed, and his clothes were clean; but things weren't matched well, or his tie wouldn't be straight, or he wouldn't have a nice knot. I took him to my favorite store one time to buy shoes and dress pants. The pants were off the rack, and they were tight all the way down. Dad usually wore pleated pants, which were very full. Besides being overweight, he was a bit bowlegged, and that's not a good frame for pants.

I got so I'd lay stuff out for Dad, try to match things up. I tried to get him to buy good belts, ties, and shoes. I started tying his ties for him and shining his shoes. I think he liked it. He had tried to do those things himself, but he didn't have the eye. Sometimes I let him use my shoes and ties. We wore the same size shoes. It's an inherited thing; both of my sons wear the same size I do.

Once in high school a boy named Tommy showed me the first pair of Bass Weejuns I'd ever seen. They laced up and had a pebble-grain surface. Those shoes were like new, and he was going to sell them for eleven dollars. He thought I might be interested. I took them home to show Dad and asked if he'd buy them for himself. It took a couple days to talk him into it, but he did it. He wore those shoes to work, and the guys commented on them. He ate it up.

In college, my passion for clothes got me hired in a men's store. My grades were going to hell, but I was thrilled to be earning money at something I understood. It came about when I rented the apartment upstairs and made a deal with the store owners to pay my rent by working for them. The location couldn't be beat; all I had to do was go up or down the stairs from home to work and back.

I wanted to be an example of how to dress, but on that job I became a fanatic. There was never a smudge on my shoes, and my tie was always perfect. I'd go across the street during lunch and get my pants pressed at One Hour Martinizing. I was working in dry-cleaned clothes, and I would go in the middle of the day and get them re-pressed.

Even though I had a feel for fashion, I didn't always know the correct terms, so the store owners would tell me the name of a certain look and where it had originated. In the meantime, they complimented me on the way I dressed. In particular, they said my color coordinating was unbelievable—which was ironic because of my color-blindness.

I'd just found out at age eighteen, when I took my physical for the Air Force, that I couldn't see certain colors. That's a liability in the Armed Services, and it kept me out. It's also a liability in a men's store. I kept it to myself, but if a customer asked for something by color, I couldn't find it. One time I couldn't find the pajamas in the store—any of them. That had nothing to do with color, but it helped me because after the owner showed me the cabinet where the pajamas were kept, he gave me a tour of the whole store. On the tour I asked him questions phrased around colors, and he showed me where the different colors were.

I didn't do alterations, but I did mark men's pants for hemming. Some of my customers came back and told me how much they liked those particular pants. I measured for suits, too. I couldn't do any sewing and wouldn't have wanted to, but I could mark alterations and I could size someone up. I was sure I was right and that I knew what would look good on each person. If the customer didn't know what he wanted, he would walk out with what I'd picked.

My retail career ended with my return to Glen Ferris two years later, when I quit the university. It made no sense to continue. I would have stayed in school for Dad, but he was gone. I would go on to a completely different life, one far removed from the world of gentlemen's wardrobes. In my subsequent jobs I barely noticed the years of fashion passing me by. My work clothes for the meat plant were humble, but functional. My school uniforms were standard styles and colors. Instead of minding, I felt lucky that most of my work clothes had been provided free since 1970. I couldn't predict that my pickiness about clothes would come back to haunt me later.

18
Vacation

Cincinnati and Points Northwest, 1998

My second winter at the kindergarten school was long. I'd settled into my job and still liked it, but between my sweat-soaked nights dreaming of the overcoat ghost and my constant exhaustion, I was ready for a break. The coming summer would be a big one for me, but not because of anything happening at work. I was planning an actual vacation—a trip. It had been years since I'd gone away, and I couldn't wait for June to arrive.

I had been writing to a woman, and now I was going to see her. It was 1998, and I'd been divorced since 1980. I'd been single *eighteen years*. I'd had a couple girlfriends during that time, but the relationships hadn't worked out, which was why I was initially reluctant to start another one.

My son Mike had met Peggy on the Internet and thought we might be a good match. That was before I had a computer or knew how to use one, so she and I began exchanging letters through snail mail. Mine were full of stories about my life and family. No one would have called them love letters. Even though I could see the possibility of romance ahead, I preferred to keep my correspondence with Peggy platonic—especially since I hadn't even met the woman.

She sent me a photo of herself and asked for a picture of me. The only one I had was a snapshot taken in the 1980s when my kids were young and I was still in my thirties. When she noticed that the photo wasn't recent, she asked me why I'd sent an old picture. I told her I still looked about the same—same weight, same build—with the possible exception of a few wrinkles.

It was Mike who suggested I should visit Peggy.

"What if it doesn't work out?" I said.

"Either way, you'll get to see a pretty part of the country."

Peggy lived in the Northwest, in a state I hadn't visited, so I mentioned the idea to her in one of my letters. I was surprised at her answer, "I don't think it's a good idea." We had hit it off—that I knew—so I brought up the subject in another letter. "It might be fun," I wrote, and she turned me down again. I thought she was being skittish, but why?

Eventually she did invite me, and I was excited. After all the back and forth, I suddenly had a trip coming up. I even talked it up at work—work, where uniforms were my entire wardrobe. I realized I had nothing to take with me, not even a pair of swimming trunks.

I had lost my feel for what was in style and needed help. By then Hannah and I had become friends. I had openly admired her taste in clothing, and maybe she reminded me of my old self: the one who would have had a travel wardrobe. I asked Hannah if she would consider going with me to a store to help me pick out some items for my trip. I guess she couldn't wait, because she went shopping alone on her day off and practically raided the men's department of Kohl's. She chose shorts, slacks, belts, shirts, swimwear, and even a pair of tennis shoes for me and put it all on layaway so that I could pick up what I wanted to keep. Hannah had coordinated all of the pieces perfectly. I bought everything. Between the new clothes and my flight, my vacation was turning out to be an investment.

People at school cheered me on as I counted down the days. "Take lots of pictures," some had said. "We can't wait to see them when you get back." It was nice to be on the brink of something new.

June came, and I was on my way. I was looking forward to the change of scenery, and not just the flowers and the trees. I was excited about being with someone new. I felt like I already knew a lot about Peggy; obviously we liked each other, so seeing her in person should be a definite improvement over writing letters. However it worked out, I had to admit that the fact that Peggy lived thousands of miles away was a comfort, not an obstacle. I still felt the sting of my previous relationships, especially my marriage, and I wanted to avoid the pitfalls of the past. In particular, I needed to pace the relationship and not get caught up in the woman's idea of how it should go. Distance and control were the weapons I had to protect myself.

The second big thing that summer happened on the plane to Peggy's. I found a book in the seat pouch in front of me that someone had left behind. I wasn't a big reader, but with a flight of several hours ahead of me, I decided to give it a try. I don't remember the title or the author, but the subject was a woman who told of dying and going to heaven. I'd had so many negative experiences that I thought I'd already been to hell a few times on earth. I wanted to believe in heaven.

The book held my attention, and I read it all. The author's beautiful description of heaven seemed real, and I believed it. What a coincidence: of all the seats on that plane, I'd sat in the one with the book in the pocket. By proving the existence of heaven to me, that book gave me hope.

Growing up next door to the Glen Ferris Methodist Church made it hard to ignore the goings-on; half the town passed by our house every Sunday. Even with the craziness of Mom's drinking and all my parents' sniping, we were involved in church activities. Mom played the piano for a while. My sister was in the programs the Sunday school put on. She and I went to vacation Bible school in the summer and more than a few church picnics. Dad was active for a time, too, serving as an usher and even teaching Sunday school.

Sometimes we stayed home, and in summer when the windows were open, the clear sound of every hymn and snatches of sermon would float out over the churchyard and alley like a hand reaching toward our house, so it felt like we were there — or should have been.

Grandmama was the most religious person in our family. She wanted us to take the Lord as our Savior, so she must have been thrilled when I decided to become a preacher at age eleven. I don't mean that I decided to be a minister when I grew up; I mean that I learned to preach as a boy.

By far, the most exciting thing to happen at our church was a revival when I was eleven years old. It lasted for several nights and grabbed me right up. People filled the pews; it seemed like the whole town was there. Even Jane's friend, Billie, who was Catholic, bobby-pinned a Kleenex to her head and went.

My revival attendance didn't begin and end in Glen Ferris. The evangelist, who was from New York, also held meetings in neighboring towns. The point of a revival is to bring about a reawakening of faith, a commitment to it, and I signed on in one of those other towns. Young boys played a crucial part in spreading the Word for this man, and a good friend of mine named Scott had already been recruited. He told me all about the sermons I would learn and deliver; the youth camp on a lake whose mission was to turn young boys into ministers. The camp was free, and if the owner liked a boy, he might be invited. Then Scott told me the owner did magic tricks. That's what drew me in. Dad had brought me a trick once from Cleveland, and I'd been hooked on magic ever since. I had continued to hone my skills with a Sneaky Pete's Magic Show in a box.

I had to write a letter explaining why I wanted to attend the camp. Mom helped me with it, or at least she read it when I was done. I don't remember what my letter said, just what I thought: that it would be cool to go all the way to New York for a camp. The whole experience was about religion, but I looked forward to the magic tricks that Scott indicated would be worked into the program.

In response to my letter, I was welcomed to camp for the coming season. A session lasted a minimum of two weeks, and there was a chance a boy would be asked to stay longer.

Scott and I went to New York together. It was my first time on a plane, and the trip excited me as much as the idea of camp did. We stayed overnight with some of his relatives on the way to the airport. Once we landed in New York, we were driven down a country road to get to the camp, a big barracks-type building partly under construction. It was in a wooded area right on a huge lake. The walls weren't all up yet, and it was cold there.

As part of our education we'd memorize ten-minute sermons written by the owner of the camp. Each boy was assigned to a gospel team. The teams would go out into the woods with a counselor and practice their sermons. The counselor would coach us. I was one of the last ones to speak, so I listened and learned what he was looking for. Some boys accented the wrong part, and he would correct them. We all did the same sermon, so by the time they got to me I knew what the counselor wanted.

Our days were planned pretty tightly between mealtimes and gospel time, but we also had free time. We could go on our own to the various cathedrals in the woods to memorize; the open structures were all over the place. Sometimes instead, we ran the road leading to the camp and timed each other. It was four tenths of a mile.

Some of the gospel teams went outside the camp to preach. Every weekend the camp owner/evangelist would be gone for a few days with a team, sometimes out of state. Once they were even on the radio. I wanted to be picked for that one, but I wasn't good enough. I never went on an overnight trip, but I did get to go to some of the area churches. The boys took turns going out and speaking. We knew a bunch of sermons. I probably knew a dozen by the end of camp. It was all right, but we didn't get to practice magic.

We could buy tricks from the camp canteen. Depending on our level of expertise, we were allowed to buy magic tricks off different shelves: the higher the shelf, the more advanced the trick. I didn't have money for magic tricks, but the owner gave me one for my twelfth birthday, which came in July while I was there. The trick was called the Squared Circle. I was called up front at supper one night so he could present it to me.

We campers could go swimming in the big lake, but it was cold. I only went in when I thought I had to, to fit in. Every day after lunch they would bring tables outside. After we swam, we'd walk up from the lake, and those tables would be set up across the driveway for selling snacks. My favorite treat was an ice cream sandwich, and I got one every day. The first time I went up, I asked for an ice cream "thandwich." The guy asked me again what I wanted, and I told him. He kept asking—three or four times in a row. I was getting mad. Then he enunciated "sandwich" and I got it. He wanted me to say it differently.

Every day I'd line up at the canteen. I dreaded the confrontation I knew would happen; I didn't learn the lesson in one day. The guy wouldn't give me the ice cream unless I said it right. I'd hold up the line trying to say "sandwich," and I was embarrassed, but I loved the ice cream so much that I kept going back and putting up with it. Over the time I spent at camp, my pronunciation was corrected. I'd learned to say my *s* sounds.

Sometime after I was home from camp, I found a note to Mom and Dad from my sixth-grade teacher advising them to get me into speech therapy. It had been sent at the end of the school year, but neither Mom nor Dad had said a thing to me. In fact, no one had ever said I had a speech problem, so I hadn't even known it. With my new-found talent for delivering sermons, I did some preaching here and there and started entering my magic in local talent shows. My improved speech and ability to get up in front of people were huge benefits of my experience at camp.

Some boys returned to the camp, but I never did, and by the time I got to high school my preaching fervor had faded. I was a normal boy again—or as normal as I could be. Twenty years later I would be studying Catholicism and attending church as a young father, until life took me in a different direction. After that, it would be another twenty years before I felt the impact of religion on my life, and that happened the day I read the book about heaven on the airplane.

The plane touched down, and Peggy met me at the airport. She had told me what color dress she'd have on and where she would be standing. I scanned the crowd and saw her. The photo she had sent me was clearly out of date, and yet she had made a point of quizzing me about mine. I knew right away that her picture had shown a much younger and slimmer version of Peggy.

We had discussed our relationship for weeks beforehand. Both of us were expecting a romantic week. However, we weren't staying in Peggy's city. She had arranged for us to drive down the coast to where a friend had offered us a place to stay. On the way I discovered why we were leaving the city and why Peggy had been reluctant to invite me there in the first place: She told me that she was married and had children. I'd saved my money and used my vacation time to see her, never suspecting that she merely wanted a temporary getaway from her own family; but that's what she said I was: a getaway.

What the heck had happened? I'd been used before, but how could I have been that blind again? Peggy was a nice person; I wouldn't have written to her all that time if I hadn't liked her, but this was wrong, and we had words about it. I tried to make the best of a terrible situation. What else was I going to do? Everyone who counted knew how long I'd planned to be gone. Why turn around and go home? I wanted a getaway, too. But it had to work for me.

Peggy and I spent several days together, strictly as friends. Just like my other relationships, that one was flawed, but at least I could board a plane at the end of it. Peggy and I exchanged a few letters after I got home, but I let her know that I wasn't going to pursue a married woman. After that, it was over. I wasn't sorry, but I was sad. The feeling of being on the brink of something no longer existed for me. I wondered if I would ever have the kind of relationship I wanted.

19
Mom Again

Cincinnati, 1998

A third notable event took place in the summer of 1998: after taking my first vacation in years and being enlightened by the book I found, I reunited with my mother. Maybe *reunited* is too strong a word, but shortly after I returned from visiting Peggy, I saw Mom for the first time in years. It was July eleventh, my fiftieth birthday.

What does a mother think when her "baby" turns fifty? That has to be a trip, although Mom had never called me her baby the way some mothers do. That would be the sentimental ones, the ones who openly love their children. I couldn't remember Mom using any endearing term with me; "son of a bitch" didn't qualify.

I'd successfully avoided my mother for years, and there was one reason: I hated her. Because of Mom, my childhood had been terrible. Any parental support for me had been a joke. As I grew older, especially after Jane went away to college, I had so much "freedom" that I'd practically raised myself. I had no intention of resurrecting my dysfunctional relationship with my mother, even though I'd heard she had quit drinking. When I thought of Mom, I thought only of heartache.

How many years had it been since I'd even seen her? I had to think about it. Our paths had crossed maybe twice in the last twenty or thirty years. The last time Mom had visited me, she had lived in West Virginia and I was still married.

Mom had moved to Cincinnati and had been trying to get together with me. In addition to calling the house, she'd sent me birthday and Christmas cards. Each card had a check in it for the same amount, thirty-five dollars. I tore them up. One time she sent me a card with a note saying that if I'd have lunch with her, she'd give me a thousand dollars. As broke as I was when I got that card, I didn't even answer it. In my mind, nobody could blame me for avoiding her.

When I was younger, Mom had wanted me out of her life. Now she wanted me back in it. Finally, I wanted the same thing. What had changed my mind? I guess I got a soft spot from somewhere. The book I'd found on the plane to Peggy's was fresh in my mind, and so was Dad. When I turned fifty, I was reminded that he had died at age fifty-one. What was my life span? I needed to make things right, to move past the bad times and heal.

Mom had an apartment in a nice section north of the city. I'd found it all right. The sun was hot and bright as I waited in a hallway for her to answer her front door. I couldn't stop my stomach from churning. What would it be like, coming face to face with my mother after all this time?

I'd finally left West Virginia University in 1968. Once I was home, I had soon realized I couldn't stand being there. Mom was still drinking; that hadn't changed, except to get worse. She always made it to work and managed to look good during the week, but she was drunk the rest of the time, and we didn't make great roommates. By then I was twenty, no longer the timid little boy, but when we were together in the house, I was still physically afraid of her. She had become much more aggressive toward me. Sometimes when I came home she would be in the bathroom, drunk, just like in the old days when she gave herself a facial; only now she ambushed me before I got upstairs. She would come to the top of the steps and jump at me, trying to choke me. If I reached the second landing of our staircase and saw Mom at the top, I knew what was coming. Who knows what provoked it? It might be the first time I'd seen her all day, and she'd jump down the stairs at me.

I'd started catching her when I was in my teens, because I could. I could hold her off, but that didn't mean I wanted to be attacked. If she would try to choke me, what else might she do? When these incidents happened, she would always say, "You son of a bitch," and one day I said, "You're right, I am."

Sometimes a friend from those days will ask me why I never talked about Mom's drinking back then, and it surprises me because I thought my friends knew. Wasn't it obvious when Mom wanted to jitterbug with them when they came over?

Mom loved to dance. She had this move she'd do the moment she heard the first notes of a danceable song. She'd put her right arm up with the elbow bent and her thumb and index finger extended the way you would to simulate firing a pistol, only her finger would be pointing upward. Then she'd sort of click her mouth and turn her hand back and forth, like she had the beat. My friends thought she was fun. Hank would even dance with her. It made me sick.

Mom Again

When I look back on my childhood, I see a big void where Mom and Dad should have been. As one example, I played sports from fourth grade through high school. Baseball and basketball were my favorites. I played on Little League and Pony League baseball teams. In grade school I was first string in basketball. Mom and Dad never took me to practice or came to any of my games. Not one. I'd have to ride with some other kid's parents. When I got older I hitchhiked. Other boys did it, too, and we'd compare stories about being picked up by homosexuals. Fending off inappropriate advances was routine. There were times I'd ask the driver to slow down, and I'd open the car door and roll out onto the ground to get away from him..

Even when Mom was present in my life, I usually wished she was absent. She rarely had her head on straight. There are way too many stories like this.

One muggy summer day Rodney and I wanted to go to the golf club pool. Mom had been drinking. She pulled our second-hand Rambler station wagon up to the sidewalk out back and said that if we washed it she'd take us to the golf club to swim. We washed the car, and she drove us there—drunk—and dropped us off. The point is, I was praying for her not to stay. It was always that way. The prospect of swimming wasn't what drove me to wash our car; I would have *detailed* the Rambler to get Mom out of my life for the next couple of hours.

On the way to the pool we passed the Lions Club Park above Gauley Bridge, and I looked over at the groves of trees along the river where campers had set up their tents and trailers. I thought of Rodney's family. How many times had they invited me to that park? They were the first people who ever took me on a picnic.

They would set up a picnic table and fill it with food. I'd never seen anything like it. I could go to that table and get a cold drink whenever I wanted it. I could get a grilled hot dog, a hamburger, and homemade potato salad. That stuff didn't come from the Kroger deli; his mom made it. Rodney's parents went to so much trouble for their family. They had a boat that could pull a water-skier. I didn't ski there, but they drove me around in the boat and treated me like gold. I always thought how wonderful it must be to have a family like that. I would have given anything.

At home on Saturday nights, they sang. Rodney's father and a co-worker from the EMCO plant would open a fifth of whiskey and sing and play country music for hours. It took me a while to get used to the drinking, but the men didn't try to hide their whiskey like Mom and Dad did. They sipped on it all night, and they didn't get mean and turn on us. It was a happy time.

Rodney had moved to California. After college I didn't want to stick around Glen Ferris with Mom. I had a bit of money and nothing good going on at home, so I flew out to see him, and he got me a job in the store where he worked. As it turned out, Rodney was ready to leave California, and we drove back across the country in his yellow 1965 Corvette, taking turns at the wheel. We were pulling a U-Haul with his clothes and motorcycle in it.

We took the Will Rogers Highway, otherwise known as Route 66, out of California. In Las Vegas we slept under the Corvette by the side of the road. In Arizona we got lost in the desert. I turned twenty-one in Albuquerque. When we stopped for gas in Joplin, Missouri, we found ourselves surrounded by a group of locals who challenged us—and the Corvette—to a race. Someone in their group promised to watch the U-Haul while we were racing. The motorcycle was visible, and Rodney figured they were planning to steal it. He let me know he had a rifle in the car. Luckily, we didn't need it. Instead of racing, we moved on.

After thirty-four hundred miles of driving, we were almost home when the brakes on the Corvette locked up on a bridge two miles from Glen Ferris. The Corvette, with its fiberglass body, didn't fare well when we hit the side of the bridge. The car was declared a total loss after the garage's tow line split the back of the car in two. I don't remember how we got home.

Mom was gone, to our relief. She had moved for the winter months to Fayetteville, where she worked, to avoid driving the fifteen miles of winding road over Gauley Mountain in bad weather. Rodney and I settled in at the house—he had nowhere else to live—but we didn't have it to ourselves very long. When Mom heard I was home, she moved back. She was furious. Rodney left, and I enrolled in a computer programming course in Charleston to calm Mom down. Dad's Social Security paid for the course, and I finished the program with an associate's degree.

In the winter of 1970 I took the Civil Service test, hoping for a shot at a good job. Mom suggested I try the State House in Charleston, where she'd worked in the past. While I was waiting for my test results, I ran into Perry, a childhood friend who lived in the Cincinnati area. I had no car, so when he said, "Come out and stay with me for a while," I rode back with him, and that's how I got to Cincinnati.

I hadn't intended to stay in Ohio, but after I arrived I saw the possibilities for a future there. Why go home to Mom? That visit with Perry became my official departure from Glen Ferris and our house. Some years later Mom told me I'd passed my Civil Service test and had received a job offer, but she'd intentionally withheld the information from me. I was surprised, but when I thought more about it, I figured she just hadn't wanted me living at home. I remember thinking that she could go to hell, and probably would.

Now, as Mom's apartment door swung open, I fixed my eyes on the spot where I expected to see her face, but I had to look down instead. She was in a wheelchair. She hadn't been expecting me—not in a hundred years—so her expression of surprise was worth the trip. It made me wonder why I had waited so long. My son Jay, who by then was twenty-one, had been after me to contact both Mom and Jane. I hadn't seen my sister in a long time, either, and he wanted our family back together.

I bent down and hugged Mom, and then we sat and talked. I told her about my job at the kindergarten school. One of her feet was swollen to twice its size; that's what I noticed. She said she'd been on a cruise with Jane and had fallen getting off a bus in Puerto Rico. The ship's doctor had said her foot wasn't broken, but that ankle looked nasty. I felt bad for her; it must have hurt, but Mom didn't complain. She was nice that day.

I didn't feel the world had changed after that first visit, but I felt a lot of relief; if anything happened to me, I'd hugged my mom and told her I loved her. I'd broken the barrier.

20
All I Ever Wanted

I was still having occasional dreams about the ghost in the overcoat. Those dreams, combined with my disappointing vacation, underscored one fact: I was fifty years old, living by myself in a basement apartment. Both Mike and Jay had moved out. I valued my alone time, but there in the middle of the night, waking up from that dream again and again, scared silly, it was loneliness that I felt. And loneliness wasn't what I had envisioned for myself.

I'd thought I had it all when I met my wife. It was 1970, and I was new in Cincinnati. I had found a job working as a ticket writer and dispatcher at a concrete company for a hundred dollars a week. I was renting a room and had just bought a van for four hundred dollars. At last I could get around and thus begin my social life in Cincinnati.

Mary and I met at a church-sponsored singles event. She was attractive and fun. She had a nice figure; big, brown eyes; pretty skin; and hair that shone in the light. When she smiled at me, well, I felt like a millionaire.

At five feet eleven and one-sixty, I'd been told I was good-looking. I had my mother's coloring, dark blond hair and hazel eyes. With some effort my skin tanned in the summer, and I still had hair on my head. That said, you never know what will appeal to someone. Mary liked my ankles. Her previous boyfriend had had thick ankles, a turn-off for her.

Our first date was a foursome with her sister and brother-in-law. We went to the stock car races. I'd never been. I wore nice dress pants and an alpaca V-neck sweater in light cream. We sat near the front. It was a dirt track, and the first time those cars went around, my sweater was "al-blacka": filthy. We moved to different seats, but it was too late for the sweater.

That first date led to others. When Mary showed me a picture of a ring she liked, I didn't say much; it seemed too early for that conversation. We dated for two years, topping it off with a wedding. I hadn't proposed, but I was ready to get married. As with many other events in my life, that one seemed to slide into place. By then I was working at the meat plant, feeling more settled than I had in a long time.

Mr. Joe

The ceremony was quick and small: the two of us and a justice of the peace. I had an envelope of money in my coat pocket to give him after the ceremony. I'd guessed at the amount. "How much do I owe you?" I asked when he was done, and it was more than I'd set aside. I had to go into my billfold for more—slightly embarrassing. It reminded me of the story Mom and Dad liked to tell about their wedding in 1941. Dad gave the preacher an envelope with ten dollars in it, saying, "I don't know if this amount is right." "Just pay what you think she's worth," was the preacher's reply, and Dad took the envelope back and removed five of the ten dollars. My parents always laughed at that story. Maybe it was funnier in the 1940s.

For our honeymoon, Mary and I wanted surf, sun, and sand. I made hotel reservations for two weeks in Myrtle Beach, and we drove there, nearly seven hundred miles. Just as we pulled into the hotel parking lot, it began to rain. "Huh," the clerk said. "We haven't had a drop of rain for months."

It rained every day for the first week. We had plenty of together time, so we went out one day and bought a deck of cards. Watching the weather on television became the highlight of each morning; if we saw it was going to rain again, we knew we were going to play a lot of rummy. I didn't drink it, but after five days of gray skies and rain, I found myself wanting to put the "gin" in rummy.

Finally we saw the sun one day. Before it could prove to be a mirage, Mary and I quickly put on our bathing suits, grabbed our towels, and ran out to the beach. We lay down on the sand and looked up just in time to see a big, black cloud pass in front of the sun. That was it for the good weather. I'd already paid for the hotel, but I convinced the manager to give us a refund for the second week. We went up into Tennessee and stayed in a hotel with a pool, and it was sunny every day.

Mary and I bought a house in Cincinnati and had our two babies during the first five years we were married. Recalling those years as a young husband and father, I suppose the same can be said for any life: Some of it was good; some was bad. Our sons were the pinnacle to me.

Mike was born in 1974. He was beautiful, perfect. I may be saying that with so much pride because he resembled me, right down to the cowlick in his blond hair. When he was a few months old, we took him to West Virginia to show him off. Yes, the boy who hated to go home could not wait to walk up to Mom and Grandmama and all the neighbors with his wife and baby. I thought I would burst with happiness. We were a family: Dad, Mom, and child—young and happy, with the whole world ahead of us. It was what I had always wanted.

Jay, our second son, was born in 1977. I was so proud to have a new son. I called everybody with the news; and then, because I'd been up a long time before he was born, I went home to sleep. The hospital called and woke me up. They thought our brand-new baby was going to die. He had come down the birth canal the wrong way and had swallowed my wife's body fluids. "We don't know if he's going to survive," the doctors said. They didn't sugar-coat it. I called the family back. "Something's gone wrong. If you need to get hold of me, I have to go back to the hospital," I said.

Jay was in an incubator the first few days of his life. It was touch and go, and I touched my baby through gloves. When he was out of danger, Mary and I brought him home and life resumed, with a bit more wear and tear on us. I hope I didn't complain, because God had been good to me.

I loved being married and being a dad. Back then, when I had a young family, Mary would cook a late meal for me. She'd have it ready after my shift at the meat plant and would sit with me while I ate. This could be at eleven-thirty or midnight. Mike liked to stay up until I came home. He was too young for that, but I wouldn't trade all those times for the world. Usually he fell asleep in his clothes, sprawled out across his beanbag chair, while I was eating. Jay was still a baby. He'd be asleep when I got in, but I'd look at him in his bed or playpen. I needed to see my children.

On my nights off I tried to adjust my sleep schedule in order to spend time with Mary and the boys the next day, but it was hard. I was used to being up late and not having to be at work until afternoon, so I couldn't fall asleep when I wanted to. When the kids were small, it was important to be present; the void in my own childhood had told me that. With them I was there, but I was dragging.

I was working a lot of overtime and getting in late. Mary had a job during the day, so I had to get up early and watch the boys so she could go to work. Sometimes I tried to put Mike and Jay down for a nap, just to get some rest. One day, I was the one who fell asleep. We had a white crushed-velvet couch we'd bought before the boys were born. I lay down on it that day while they were playing nearby and woke up in a panic because they were gone. They were small—Jay couldn't even walk yet—so where could they be?

I ran through the downstairs, yelling their names. Then, circling back, I happened to see that the fireplace doors were open. We had a wood-burning fireplace we used on occasion. It had a glass enclosure with folding doors. My kids were playing in the fireplace! They were safe, and the couch was still white, but both boys were covered with black soot. I scooped them up, one in each arm, and held them to me before heading straight to the bathtub.

Being a father kept me running. When Mike was still in diapers, he liked to play with my car keys. He was getting around pretty well, pulling himself up and grabbing things off the tables, and we were in the process of childproofing our house—a continual process, I might add. Whenever Mike saw my keys and could reach them, they disappeared and I'd have to find them. I knew to look low—down at his level—and I would get on my hands and knees and begin searching. One of his favorite hiding places was the toilet. Once I even found the keys in his diaper when I changed it, so I knew that if they weren't in the toilet, they might be there. I'll just say that those keys were washed many times.

I had the kids every day until the babysitter got off school. She filled the child-care gap of two or three hours when both Mary and I had to be at work. As soon as the babysitter arrived, I had to leave. Some days the timing was so close that we'd pass in the doorway, or else I'd be out on the front porch watching for her, afraid I'd be late.

Schedules at our house were a stretch and a strain. It was just bang, bang, bang—not a leisurely life at all. After staying up late with me, Mary would rush out in the mornings to catch a bus downtown, and I'd scramble to keep up with the boys after a few hours' sleep. We started putting our alarm clock on the other side of the bedroom to force ourselves to get up and turn it off, but sometimes we still slept through the alarm.

The last few years of our marriage were less idyllic than the first five. Sometimes it seemed that my ideal family life was slipping through my fingers. My sons were amazing, but things between Mary and me were increasingly stressful. It wasn't just our busy schedules and the fact that we had two young children. Our life patterns and family histories were working against us.

My parents' fights had changed the way I looked at my life. I refused to yell or argue in my relationships. I couldn't; Mom and Dad had turned me off to that. Of course, the addition of alcohol to the mix was deadly.

I saw Dad hit Mom once. They were sitting on the couch. She was drunk, and she was going on and on about something. When she got that way, it wasn't pretty; it wasn't going to turn out well. Mom could drive us right up the wall because she didn't know when to quit. It didn't matter what anyone said or didn't say in response; she kept repeating herself. That time she wouldn't let up on Dad. Finally he hit her right on the chin. She said, "You hit good."

In my marriage I would do anything to avoid an argument. When the kids were young, I told them I was raised with screaming and arguing, and I never wanted my home to be like that. I especially didn't want to argue around them. But it happened.

My wife had come from a family with substance abuse issues, as I had. I'm sure I didn't get the full drift of that, seeing her parents as seldom as we did. I simply didn't have the means to put it together. Even with my background, I'd never thought it through—that the awful reach of the family disease could turn Mary into a different person, too.

I don't know when things changed in my marriage, or even when I noticed it. Certainly we began to see things differently. When that happens, ugly patterns can form. For instance, I started to dread my days off. Mary would want us all to go shopping. I was usually exhausted and would have loved to stay home, with or without the kids, but Mary wouldn't go shopping alone—and she would not take no for an answer. Her style was to cajole me into it, which was like a slow beating.

I was at a disadvantage during these differences of opinion, because I'd reach the snapping point and find that I was incapable of snapping—except to myself. When push came to shove, I wouldn't even push. Instead, I was pulled by my old refuge, hiding, but hiding of a different kind. I was in plain sight, but I held all my negative feelings inside and gave my wife what she wanted. I always wanted Mary to be happy—first out of love and later to avoid an argument.

The strain of our differences was made worse as my wife began to exhibit some of the same behavior as our parents. Sometimes she was chillingly like Mom: insistent, repetitive, and—to me—illogical. The pattern of my childhood, at once familiar and repulsive, had invaded my grown-up world.

I was increasingly uneasy at home, with shades of my boyhood fear amplifying the loss and sadness I felt as my relationship came apart. You might think that two people in the same situation would perceive it the same way, but you'd be so far off the mark. When I was living through the last months of our marriage, I reached the point when I could barely hold on any longer, but I seemed to be the only one. Life went on, and I was in agony. I knew I had to get out, but I couldn't quite take that next big step. Something had to give, yet how could I make a decision I knew would hurt everyone? Every time I thought about it, I got sick with guilt.

In trying to make Mary happy and keep my family together, I had put my own happiness at stake. My sanity wasn't far behind! And, yet, I couldn't stand the thought of leaving my wife and children—especially the boys. It went against everything I'd ever wanted.

21
The Long Way Home

Home is supposed to be our safe place, but many times over the years I've hated to go home, to the point I've deliberately put it off. The location of "home" has changed, and the people waiting for me have changed, but my response is still the same: that of the little boy who always had to wonder what was waiting for him; the one who loved to hide. It had started with my parents. By the time I was hiding in my marriage, I was so tired—tired and sick and guilty and still confused about what to do. I was a thirty-year-old man with a huge problem, and I was avoiding my wife.

Sometime between 1978 and 1980, I began taking the long way home. When I got off work—this was after third shift at the meat plant, early in the morning—I'd take a drive on the way home. It wasn't because of anything that had happened at the plant; I just didn't look forward to going home. I'd begun to dread talking to Mary. She would get on a topic that had "fight" written all over it and wouldn't leave it alone.

Mary thought my family didn't like her, and lately she always seemed to find a way to bring that up. Once the subject was on the table, all I could think was: *Here we go again.* I'd heard it over and over, and frankly, I was starting to understand why my relatives might not like her.

I was pretty sure she was stopping by a bar near her bus stop after work. Sometimes in the evenings she had a buzz on, and it wasn't as though we had a storehouse of alcohol. Was Mary taking the long way home, too?

Drinking didn't agree with her; when my wife drank, one thing was sure to follow: she would get on the phone. I wasn't always home when it happened, but I heard about it. Her tirades about my family escalated until they were no longer directed only at me; they spread to my relatives through the trusty wires of the Bell Telephone system. Mary would call my mom or grandmother at any time of the evening, sometimes repeatedly. In my lighter moments I have wondered what sort of conversation took place between my wife and my mother, who were so much alike.

I had to wonder: Did Mary want to be a mom the way I wanted to be a dad? She left a good deal of the child care to me. I had a vasectomy when Mike and Jay were still quite small, and afterward I was in pain. I had to be in bed, doctor's orders, so I was surprised when Mary came upstairs and put one child on either side of me in the bed so that I could watch them.

When I wasn't home, I worried. Mike used to get out of the house. He was just a toddler, but he got around. One time he climbed a ladder to a neighbor's roof. Someone saw him walking around and went up there and got him. I was at work and don't know how it happened.

Another time Mike walked down the street to the gas station wearing only a diaper. The station was located at an expressway exit, and there was so much traffic. How did he even make it? Someone from the station brought him home. There was our payoff for teaching a little child his address and phone number. Again, I wasn't home, but I got my gas there, so I heard about it the next time I stopped.

I'd known for a long time that my marriage wasn't working, and clearly, our life wasn't good for the kids. It was killing me. I was worn down from being sweet when I didn't feel sweet. I was down to 140 pounds from my usual 165, and my hair was falling out so fast that my barber was giving me treatments for free. I felt like the main character of a movie I'd seen as a child, *The Incredible Shrinking Man.* I was disappearing, day by day. Even then I did everything possible to work things out.

It didn't help our situation when Jane and her seven-year-old son moved in with us for two months after they relocated to Cincinnati. My sister's furniture filled our basement, and she and Greg shared our spare bedroom until they could rent an apartment.

All of the adults had different work schedules, and Greg was in school. Jane had enrolled him in a Catholic elementary school near our house, and that was on my advice because we didn't live in the best neighborhood for public schools. He had to wear a uniform, and she had little money to invest in clothing, so she washed his pants and shirt in the sink every evening. One night Mary had a fit when we came home to find his school clothes hanging out to dry on the front porch for all to see. Another time Mary accused my sister of turning our bathtub black with dirt. And I know that my wife snooped in Jane's room when she had a chance.

Our lives grew more chaotic all the time. Mary had expectations that were not met—I think she had hoped for babysitting from Jane—and we gave up what privacy we'd had. I ended up taking my family to Myrtle Beach just to get us out of the house. When we came home, Jane had moved, but my wife didn't settle down. She was reminding me more of Mom every week, and I couldn't think of anything worse.

Mary was Roman Catholic. Even though I wasn't, I initiated an interview with a priest at a local university. He said, "Mr. Barnett, there's no way I should say this and no way I'll admit to saying it, but I think you should get divorced right away." A *priest* had advised me to get a divorce.

Even when I went to see a lawyer, I asked if I was rushing into a divorce. "Is this my fault?" I asked. "Is this enough to leave her for?" He looked at me like I was an idiot. The idea of breaking up my family still destroyed me, but I went ahead with it.

When I left our house, I left like Steve Martin in *The Jerk*. I had a nine-inch TV under one arm and a wicker chair with one of those big fan tops in the other. That's what I left my marriage with, because I didn't want to take furniture from the house where my children still lived. I subleased a one-bedroom apartment for three months. I had no furniture but that wicker chair and a sheet. I made a "bed" on the bedroom floor when the kids came over. Somebody gave me a card table out of their garage; that was my dinette, but I had no chairs to go with it.

Splitting up my family was the end of my dreams. I didn't get a huge sense of relief, just guilt and more guilt; guilt piled upon guilt. I never forgot that I'd initiated the divorce. It haunted me every day. What was new? My whole past was a ghost chasing me through the dark.

I had to admit that I didn't know how to have a happy family. Maybe I never would. But driving to my new apartment, humble as it was, was a straight shot; I no longer needed to take the long way home. In the wee hours of the morning, in the quiet of my car, I found myself beginning to dream of better days ahead.

22
Transitions

It was the spring of 2000. The kindergarten school was as creepy as ever, and that wasn't just my opinion. Dave told me the women who worked in the offices didn't like coming in on weekends, even during the day. They got a funny feeling there. So did I, and the incidents continued; but at least each one wasn't big, and every one didn't happen to me. My teacher friend, Karen, told me about an experience she had when she was working late one night.

"I noticed a boom box sitting at the end of the hallway. No one was around," Karen said, "and it was completely quiet. I was in my classroom, working, and suddenly that radio turned on full blast, playing the national anthem. It was like the start of a ball game. I got up to see who was out there. It had to be either you or Dave. I was going to say something about the radio, but no one was there." I knew that boom box was mine.

"There's an eerie feeling in this building at night," she said. "I've felt it so many times, and that radio coming on was just another example. In the daytime, with students in the room, I'm busy and don't think about it; but things happen at night that I can't avoid noticing, for instance, the printers and televisions turning on and off by themselves. It isn't terrifying, but it's unsettling. I never get used to it, but in the case of the radio, I just turned the volume down and went back to work."

A psychic told me once that ghosts can duplicate sounds and smells. They can manipulate objects. She said they can even stack chairs. If you buy that, you know that a ghost can definitely turn on a radio or move a vacuum cleaner.

I was glad to have a job. I liked my principal, even though she was demanding, and I loved the little kids. The kindergarten school was where I had become Mr. Joe. But, for all the good things about my job, it was killing me. Between the teachers working late and the ghosts, I still couldn't get my work done the way I knew it should have been done. I was frustrated, but at least by then I knew it wasn't just me failing to make the grade. Hannah liked me—she even kidded with me sometimes—and I think she respected me, too. She knew I did good work.

The bottom line was still that the job was beating me up. I was hanging on in spite of that when a miracle happened. I had a new baby granddaughter! My son Jay was the proud father. I was thrilled when Adrianna was born, but my work schedule left me no time to see her in the evenings. That was the last straw. Besides being spooked and worn out, I missed having that time with Adrianna. In May, when I got a chance to work at the high school, I jumped at it. I couldn't resist the opportunity to go on third shift instead of second, in a newer school that was *not* rumored to be haunted.

There was another reason I wanted to be on third shift. I worried about what the students would think. I'd liked being around the young kids at the kindergarten school; they were friendly and didn't look down on me the way high school kids might. Little kids were cool, in my opinion, but teenagers would have lost their innocence and might make fun of me for being the custodian. I didn't want to deal with them. On third shift, I wouldn't have to see the students.

As it turned out, I loved working at the high school. I started late and worked all night. This meant I had my evenings free before reporting to work, and once I got there I was alone. No teachers remained in the building, so I could do my job the way I had tried to do it at the kindergarten school. I was happy there; every condition was just right. And then Carl, my old acquaintance from the meat plant, called me.

Carl had left the plant after a close call with the USDA inspector. I could empathize. When I became a foreman, the inspector was rough on me because he didn't like my boss. He even warned me that things could get difficult for me, but that extra ten thousand dollars I was making had overruled everything he said.

The situation between the inspector and my boss became so volatile that the quality control people were afraid of the inspector. Their usual procedure was to place tags where they found violations, and they began tagging everything. One time, when I saw how many tags they'd put on the equipment, I started getting acute chest pains. The other foreman saw me grab my chest, and in minutes I was on the way to the hospital. They shaved my chest and hooked me up to a monitor. The upshot was that my pains had mimicked a heart attack and had lasted just as long, but weren't the real thing.

Meat production took place in a huge room, and sometimes the air conditioning units would break down. When it warmed up in there, water would drip from every square inch of the ceiling, just like it was raining. We couldn't run production with any water on the ceiling, the pipes—anywhere—so we had to wipe it all down every day using sponges on twenty-foot poles. One time it happened fifteen minutes before the inspector was due to make his rounds. People were yelling at us to get the ceiling dry, and that was when Carl quit and became a custodian.

Carl had called me from time to time, usually to tell me how much better his new job was than his old one. Now we were both working in the same school district. His latest call was to tell me that a custodian was leaving one of the elementary schools because the job was too hard for him. Carl knew that no one would bid on the job, and he asked me to take it. He *begged* me to take it. It was another third-shift job, which I liked, but I didn't want to move. The only enticement was to get to work with Bob, another good friend from my days at the meat plant. He and I would be working the same shift, but in different areas of the school. When I said yes, I didn't do it for Carl. Bob was the reason.

My new job was cleaning classrooms in a building that housed first and second grades—little kids again. I was working like a field hand every night. Sweat dripped off me. The floors in that school were all tile, and I had to get down on my knees to scrub them. It was a pain; my knees couldn't take it. Besides that, the blackboards in Bob's school were covered with writing every night. I'd ask him, "Is there any spot they didn't get?" The kids were learning to read and write, so I had to erase and wash those blackboards and clean the chalk trays every night.

In first grade, the students also got pencils for the first time, along with those little hand sharpeners. They sharpened their pencils all day, and sometimes the leads would break and get stepped on. Sometimes the students deliberately rolled them under their feet. Or, if I didn't pay attention, a wheel of my cleaning cart could roll over one of those little pencil leads and leave a black trail for forty feet that I would have to remove.

Besides the brutal work conditions, there were once again rumors of ghosts. I'd had enough ghosts, and fortunately I didn't see any there. But little did I know that other changes were in store.

Mr. Joe

The next year Dave was promoted to head custodian at the kindergarten school. The administration wanted him visible and available during the day, which meant that his old job, cleaning the administrative offices on third shift, opened up. I was surprised; I didn't think Dave would ever give it up.

I didn't expect the job to attract many applicants, for two reasons. The first one was the bosses. Whoever took that job would be working for the district big shots, and that made it a hot spot. I knew from Dave that the custodian in that job had to do everything just right, had to know what he or she—we had a few female custodians in our district—was doing. If a custodian tried to get away with anything, it would be discovered right away. Anyone caught sneaking smokes would be fired. And it wouldn't be wise to knock the work out and then take a long break the way some custodians liked to do. Because of the built-in conditions, nobody wanted to work for the bigwigs. Well, that's not exactly true; I did.

The second reason Dave's job would not be popular was the stairs. Other schools in the district either had elevators or were built on a single level, but the kindergarten school with its multiple levels was too old to have an elevator. This meant all kinds of inconvenience for the custodians. In a nutshell, even if there hadn't been any ghosts, that building was against us.

A job that might take only a few minutes in another building couldn't even be timed in the kindergarten school. When I did the floors, I had to pull the buffer and the carpet scrubbing machine up and down those stairs. And then sometimes the administrators would change offices or get a new desk. Dave and I would have to move the old desk to some other office or out to the Dumpster. We took those big, heavy, expensive desks up the stairs and down the stairs. One day they were getting rid of a piano. Try to carry that.

Of course, I knew when I considered going for Dave's job that the kindergarten school had stairs. I knew it had ghosts, too, but I signed up for it again because it beat the job I had at Bob's school. The offices were carpeted, so my knees would get a break. I also would not miss cleaning blackboards.

Dave's job was posted in every building, with so many days for applicants to sign up. I waited to see if someone above me was interested; if not, I had a chance. That was the job I wanted most in the district. If I got it, there would be no classrooms to clean—therefore no glitter, no vomit, no finger paint to clean up, no blackboards, and no one in the building but me. When I learned that no one else was going for it, I applied for the job in a heartbeat, and I got it.

23
A New Start

I was back in the place I'd started—the kindergarten school. I loved my shift and the fact that I wasn't cleaning up after children. I rarely saw Hannah now, but losing my job was still a fear. It must have been stronger than my fear of ghosts, because there I was, back to working nights in the building where I'd seen my worst ghost—the building with an old graveyard for a neighbor.

This time around I was cleaning offices, and one of them belonged to the superintendent of schools. He was very particular, especially about his desk. I'd learned that if he left half a cup of cold coffee on it, he didn't want it thrown away. Because his desk held so many items that were important, it was not to be disturbed, and I didn't touch it.

The superintendent left his chair in the same position every day when he went home. When I came in at night to clean, his office always looked the same—until the night I noticed the chair was at a different angle. Instead of being straight, the way he always left it, it faced an empty spot on the desk, as if the occupant of the chair was sitting back with his feet up on the desk—but of course at that hour there was no occupant.

I also noticed a lingering smell of cigar smoke. The superintendent didn't smoke, so my first thought was that if the office personnel smelled it the next day, I could be blamed. It was irrational: I smoked, but not cigars—and I wouldn't have sat in the superintendent's chair with my feet up for anything. I cared about my job too much. I decided to work a while over my usual quitting time that morning, so that when someone else came in I'd know if they smelled the smoke in the office.

I was paranoid about smoking because I'd been caught once. It wasn't unusual for me to take a cigarette break when I took the trash out. After all, it was nighttime and I worked alone. It was rare to see anyone walking around outside, but one night a man in a suit walked by me when I was holding a cigarette. I wasn't alarmed at first; I thought he was a businessman from town. He turned out to be the principal of one of the other schools. "If I catch you smoking again," he said, "I'll take it upstairs," meaning that he would tell the superintendent.

When you smoke, you have no idea what you smell like; at least, I didn't. I'd quit just before going to see Peggy, and when my granddaughter was born, I started again—stupid. We had a product at school called Smoke and Odor Remover that came in an aerosol can. I used to spray it in the air and let it fall on me, thinking no one would know I was smoking again. I was only fooling myself, but fortunately no one said a word about the cigar smell in the office. I was safe. But who *had* been smoking the previous evening?

The big shots came in after hours a lot, so if they were going to be working, they checked in with me. I knew the superintendent wasn't working the night of the cigar smell. I'd been the only one in that building. The way the entrances are positioned, you can't sneak in there, and why would he?

From time to time Dave and I had suspected kids were breaking in and using our spaces to sit around, smoke, and even skateboard in the halls at night. We'd see the lines in the wax the next morning. I didn't think kids had moved the superintendent's chair and smoked in his office, though. There was no way anyone else was inside my area that night. I kept the halls in my section so nice that if anyone had disturbed my wax, I would have known it.

The possibility of a ghost didn't cross my mind that night, maybe because I'd been away for two years. I was thinking about people.

The kindergarten school had a large reception area in front of the offices. One night I was cleaning it when I saw movement in my peripheral vision. I looked over to my left, past the receptionist's desk. The door to one of the offices was open, and the light was on. A woman was walking across the room.

She was almost past the doorway, so I didn't see her face clearly, but I could tell what she had on. She was wearing a dark skirt that came to the middle of her calves and a white, long-sleeved blouse with ruffles on the collar and sleeves. I saw a cameo pin right where her blouse buttoned at the top. She had on what I'd call "teacher shoes," old-style and orthopedic looking. The little bit of her hair I saw was in a bun.

I called out, "I didn't mean to disturb you. I didn't know anyone was here." When I didn't get an answer, I walked into the office. No one was there.

Weeks later, when I was cleaning the same reception area, I thought again of the woman I'd seen. I wasn't afraid, exactly, but it didn't help my state of mind to reminisce about her. Can thoughts alone cause something to happen? I saw her again that night, in the same place. She reminded me of my high school history teacher. She looked busy, the way she was walking with a purpose. She had on the same outfit as before. Her blouse was crisp, her skirt was neat, and her hair was in a bun. I thought she would have looked sharp in her time—and right then I knew that the present wasn't her time.

She was in black and white, and the thing was, she was doing the exact same thing she'd done before. She was passing by the doorway, heading in the same direction as before, her face already out of view. It was like I had replayed a movie.

I didn't even go to check that time; I knew. The first time, I'd thought it was a person. I'd just caught her for a step or so, but it seemed to me she was real. I didn't even think of the other. This time I just kept working. There was nothing else I could do; I'd have to clean that office eventually.

I showed a photo of the kindergarten school to a psychic once—the same psychic who told me ghosts can manipulate the physical world. When she looked at the picture, she told me that ghosts were all through our building. She pointed to an area of the photo that was very familiar to me—the offices—and proceeded to describe a ghost she saw there. It was the woman I'd seen twice walking past the office door.

It seemed to me that some people—for example, my teacher friend Karen—attracted ghosts. At least they were *unusually susceptible* to the unseen. It was looking more and more like I was one of those susceptible people.

24
Hunches

Back when I worked at the meat plant, the night shift workers would go into the locker room after they'd punched out and gamble. Playing cards or dice for money was their incentive to stay on instead of going home. Typically, half a dozen guys would squat or sit in the aisle between the lockers.

Cleaning the locker room was one of my jobs. I was the only one who was supposed to be in there, but these guys would smoke and gamble and take their sweet time. I had to wait until they were done with their game. I could have run them out, but everyone would have hated me. That isn't pleasant. Also, I was such a perfectionist that I didn't want to clean the area until they were all gone. I'd clean what I could and then watch the gamblers until they vacated that last aisle.

The men sat roughly in a circle, with space between them. As I watched them one night, I started seeing something amazing. It was a yellowish light about the size of a marble. It was like a blinking bulb. As I watched, that light went around the circle of men a couple times and then stopped on a particular man. Obviously no one else could see it; this was something weird and known only to me. When the poker hand was done, the person the light had stopped on was the winner. The same thing happened two or three more times.

I went out into the plant and got a piece of paper and a pencil. When I came back, I watched that light go around the group six times. Every time it went around, I wrote the name of the person it stopped on—not six different people, but the ones I thought would win each hand. Another guy named Jim had been watching the gamblers with me. I said to him, "Watch this list. These are the next six winners in a row." Then I left to do my job. I had to clean the cafeteria, too.

When I came back, the gambling was still going on and my friend came over to me. "How in the hell did you do that?" he asked me. I told him. Did he believe me? I say he had to. I'd predicted every winner correctly.

I liked to play the horses, and especially to read about them. Sometimes when I looked in the paper at the listing of horses running that day, I saw the same light I'd seen in the meat plant. It didn't always happen, but when it did, I didn't question it. I would open the sports section and look slowly down the list of entries. After I got to the bottom, I'd start at the top again, and sometimes the light would appear on a certain number. I had no control over it. Sometimes I'd try to make it appear, and it wouldn't. But when it did, it was always right on.

At first I just checked the race results the next day. After all, I couldn't always run to the track; I didn't have the money, and my work shift didn't always allow it. I couldn't take off work for a light I'd seen. But one day three horses were lit up.

It was the day before payday. I was still married then. We rarely had extra money, but that day we had gas in the car and I had six dollars in cash. The light had identified three horses in the last race. I wasn't drinking then, but I made an exception: I drank a tall can of beer to give me some nerve, and I took my six dollars to the track. I told Mary, "I've got to go do this."

I just made it in time to bet that last race, which was a trifecta: I had to choose the first three horses I thought would finish. That part was easy. There are two ways to bet a trifecta. You can bet straight, which is to specify the order in which the three horses will finish the race, or you can bet a box. With a box, the horses can finish in any order as long as they're the first three. I bet the box and handed over my six dollars. After I'd placed my bet, there was a late jockey change on every one of my horses, which is rare. I left; I didn't want to get stuck in traffic.

The race was on the radio when I was driving home. All of my horses came in. Then the radio station went to a commercial, so I knew I'd won, but I didn't know what it paid. All of my horses had odds of twenty-one to one, or better.

When the radio announcer came back on the air, he said, "Hold onto your hats. This is a big one." No one had called it straight — guessed the winning horses in order — meaning that no tickets had been sold with the winning combination. Therefore, that pool of money had rolled over to the boxes. I'd won more than five thousand dollars!

I'd thought of betting it straight. If I had, I'd have held the only straight ticket there, and my winnings would have been more like twenty or thirty thousand dollars — but I'd played it safe. I had my winning ticket with me that night at work. I wanted to show it to the guys. A race that big was the talk of the plant, and that ticket was my proof that I could pick horses.

I feel like I've always had to prove myself. Things have happened to me that are out of the ordinary. First there was Grandpop, appearing in every mirror after he died. Later I had that conversation with Dad after he'd passed away. Next came the golden light. Then I saw ghosts as a custodian. I have something. Maybe it's ESP, extrasensory perception; a sixth sense. I'm sensitive, receptive, or *something*, to things I often keep to myself; things others would doubt.

When Jane was in college, she got a Ouija board. It was a Parker Brothers game by which players could receive supposed spirit messages via movement of a planchette, or pointer, over a board printed with letters and numbers. Though it was developed as a parlor game, the Ouija board was believed by some to draw evil spirits into a home.

When Jane and I worked the Ouija board together, the planchette flew to spell out its messages. People accused us of faking it, but we were innocent. One time we demonstrated the board for Mom and Grandmama, who watched silently as we asked it, "Who are you?" Immediately the planchette began to move. It spelled out, "I am known by many names." It then proceeded to spell "I want 90" over and over again. The toy billed as "the mystifying oracle" had us mystified. We kept asking, "What's ninety?"

"I'm ninety." It was Grandmama speaking. We all turned to look at her. "I'm ninety years old," she said, and that's when we got rid of the Ouija board. I'm happy to say that Grandmama lived to be 102.

Sometimes now when I'm watching TV, I see shadows go by in my peripheral vision and I wonder what they are. Dark shapes will flit across the arm of the couch or swoop over the end table. I wonder how many times I blew such experiences off when I was young. My tendency was always to play it down and tell no one. Like the little boy in *The Sixth Sense*, I had premonitions. Consider this dream that played out in real life when I was only in my teens.

It was the 1960s, and I had just started driving. The car we had was a green Ford Falcon. One night I dreamed I was driving that car toward Glen Ferris. It was summer—evening, but not quite dark. I was on Route 60, which had two lanes, and I'd passed the Silver Bridge going east. I had almost reached the railroad tracks where they cross Route 60 at an S curve. That curve created a blind spot for drivers.

I always noticed the houses that were to the right of the road, down over a hill just before the curve. In my dream, I glanced over toward the houses and then drove across the tracks. As soon as I could see traffic coming from the other direction, I saw a black '57 Chevy convertible roaring toward me in my lane. The people in it had their hands up like they might on a rollercoaster. I can still see them now.

The convertible top was down. People were sitting in the front and back seats. They were all laughing; the radio was blasting, and they weren't paying attention to the road. People tended to speed up going west from Glen Ferris because of the wall below the bowling alley: it would produce an echo, so everyone always floored it past that wall.

I dreamed I swerved to the right and shot off the right side of the road just past those houses, where the terrain drops off sharply above the island. At the end of the dream, the car and I were airborne, headed for the tops of the trees. I had the dream two or three times that night; it would wake me up, and then I would fall asleep and have it again.

The next night I was in the Falcon, going the same route at the same time of day as in the dream. Suddenly I remembered my dream and turned right. I left the road, aiming for the driveway of one of the homes I always looked at driving by. As soon as I drove onto the gravel, that black Chevy came along. The top was down, and the same people I'd dreamed about were in it. They were in my lane, taking the "S" out of that big curve. I missed them by two or three seconds. When I turned off the road, it saved my life.

25
Oops!

I didn't always know things or see them coming; not by a long shot. Sometimes I made mistakes.

When I took over Dave's job, I began using his supply carts. He had one on each floor to avoid carrying them up and down those infernal stairs. When one of the administrators saw me struggling with a heavy object on the stairs, he'd always say, "We have that escalator on backorder." *Hardy-har-har.*

I knew what a good a job Dave had done, and I wanted to make a great impression, too. Dave's cart had a spray can of furniture polish on it, so one night I polished everyone's desk. The next time I came in, he told me that had been a mistake. "The desks look like real wood," he said, "but they aren't." The furniture polish hadn't soaked in, and the employees were upset because their papers stuck to their desks. I had learned my lesson before Dave's advice—"Don't ever use that stuff again"—ever left his lips.

He'd made a similar error once. I guess he told me to make me feel better about the polish. While cleaning a hallway that had ceramic tile halfway up the walls, Dave and another guy decided to put oil on the tile to make it shine. Unfortunately, that was before they'd buffed the floor. During buffing, the dust from the floor flew onto the walls and stuck. He said those walls looked like Chia Pets.

We had a storage area for paper on each floor. When a paper order was delivered, the day-shift custodian carried all the boxes from the truck to our gym, and then they had to be carried to the various storage areas. Dave mentioned to me that he was going to have to carry thirty boxes of paper upstairs, and I wanted to help him out, so I did it during my shift at night. The next day I found out I'd taken the wrong paper. Dave said, "The first thing I heard when I got to work was, 'Who got into our paper?'" My intentions had been good, and I'd worked my butt off, but I'd made another mistake.

In the 1970s, the Cincinnati Reds baseball team became known as the Big Red Machine, a pennant-winning dream team led by Pete Rose, Johnny Bench, Joe Morgan, and Tony Perez. I'd been living in Cincinnati for several years by then, so the Reds were my hometown team, and I collected Big Red Machine memorabilia. My most prized possession was a baseball signed by nine of the players.

Several years after their baseball careers ended, some of the players from the Big Red Machine gathered for a softball game at Riverfront Stadium in Cincinnati. It was one of the rare times they appeared together. That day, the first twenty thousand game attendees were to receive a special Pete Rose bobblehead. That bobblehead was a big deal to me as a collector, and I went through some trouble to get tickets and then to make sure I was one of the first twenty thousand fans through the gate.

The director of human resources for our school district was a big collector of sports memorabilia, too. People often brought him valuable souvenirs as gifts, and some of the items in his collection were displayed in his office on the administrative side of the kindergarten school, an office I was assigned to clean.

I knew the HR director slightly and looked forward to telling him about my bobblehead. When I went in to clean his office, he wasn't there—it was ten-thirty at night—but what I did see was an identical bobblehead on the corner of his desk.

I was sweeping that night, and any time I vacuumed I held the cord up in one hand so it wouldn't catch on anything in the narrow spaces between the furniture. My eyes were on the floor, so I missed it when the cord caught the precious bobblehead, knocked it to the floor, and broke Pete Rose's head off.

There was no way to obtain another bobblehead; the one softball game was the only time they'd been given out. I wondered if this man had worked as hard as I had to get his tickets. Had he even gone to the game? It didn't matter. I had no choice but to substitute my bobblehead for his. If I'd ever wished to take a moment back, to do it over, I wished it that night. I took his broken bobblehead home with me and left a note explaining what I'd done. I said I would bring mine in the next day to replace the one I'd broken, and that's what I did. He never mentioned the note or the substitution to me, but I still think of that night when I look at the rare baseball souvenir that's glued together in my den.

Sometimes I got surprised on the job. One time I was going into the board of education meeting room to clean, when all of a sudden I heard, "Stop! Stop, right now!" It was like someone yelling at a thief.

I kept walking; I didn't think the person was talking to me, and when I looked around, I didn't see anyone else.

Next somebody screamed, "Get down. I said to get down now!" That time I hit the carpet—flopped down right on my belly. I heard three shots go off. I could see the flash from a gun. Was I shot? I got up on my hands and knees, turned around, and looked toward the principal's office. Hannah and two secretaries were peeping around the corner to see what had happened. All I could see were their heads, stacked above one another in the door frame like a human totem pole. I went downstairs and found out that the police had been holding a community awareness demonstration in the basement, and with our acoustics it had echoed so much that it had seemed real. Some of the police and parents were still there, and I said to the cops, "You really scared me."

"We're professionals," one officer said. "We were trying to make it seem like a real scenario." They had been using blanks.

After everyone left, I had to clean the room where the presentation had been held. I looked over in the corner and saw a dead body with a knife sticking out of its back. It was a dummy with hair and clothing like a real person. The police had left it because they were going to use it again. If I'd come upon that without knowledge of the meeting, I probably would have run outside.

The big shots' offices were located on the top floor of the administrative side of the kindergarten building. A reception area near the entrance led to their secretaries' desks, and behind the secretaries was the office of the assistant superintendent, a man named Tom.

One morning toward the end of my shift, I walked into Tom's office to clean and saw two of his framed pictures smashed on the floor. They were family photos he had displayed on a wall shelf. The frames were totally messed up, and the glass was broken.

No one else was in the office complex at that hour, so I took the pictures off the floor and left them on Tom's secretary's desk with a note: "I don't know what happened to these, but if I can do anything to help, I will—Joe."

Dave was in charge of the building then, and when he got wind of the broken pictures, he was upset. He came to me and asked what had happened. I told him I hadn't done it, but when I looked into his eyes, I thought he didn't believe me. After all, what other explanation could there be for something that had occurred in my work area in the middle of the night? I could have suggested a ghost, but I didn't think a ghost had broken the pictures. More important, I didn't want to open that subject with Dave. Even if he believed in ghosts, he didn't let on.

All I knew was that I'd had nothing to do with those pictures falling. I understood that Dave felt responsible for me. I was his protégée, and he hated for me to look bad. Dave never wanted me to be at fault for anything that went wrong or prompted a complaint. I got that, but I had nothing else to say in my defense.

"It was probably from the jack-hammering outside," a voice said. "Ever since they started demolishing the entranceway, the whole building has been shaking."

It was one of the secretaries. She had come in and overheard our conversation. The office complex was right above the site of the jack-hammering, and that lovely woman had just saved me from my friend's doubting eyes.

Not everyone felt so sympathetic toward the secretaries, and I soon learned why: they were pickier than Hannah!

The superintendent's secretary was the person who received visitors. She worked behind a counter. The front of it, the side facing the public, was solid, but her side held shelves stacked with paper. One morning Dave came up to me at the end of my shift and said, "Come and walk with me. I have to show you something."

He and I walked to the superintendent's reception area, and Dave took me around to the other side of the counter. He showed me two dead flies lying between the stacks of paper. The secretary had complained.

I was tired of being picked apart after doing my best. I said, "Did you take their body temperatures? Maybe they were still flying around when I was cleaning and they died after I left for the night." It was a sarcastic answer that he didn't deserve, but I'd had it. I knew how picky people could be; my friend Bob had been busted once for a single strand of a spider web. How long had *that* been there?

We had surprise inspections once or twice a year and the result counted toward our evaluation. The person who did it was a manager. One morning he walked in to the office side while I was still cleaning. We started talking. I noticed that he was looking around as we talked, but it took me a minute to realize he was doing an inspection. Once I knew he was checking on me, I asked if I could walk around with him to find out if I was doing anything wrong.

Oops!

He inspected the rooms on that floor and two other floors I'd already cleaned. He'd been told to find something in every room. This was the mentality that "no one is perfect." The only things this manager found were two dead flies in a light fixture. Flies again; I was getting sick of them. I was all set to be indignant, until he spoke.

"Joe," he said, "I don't see how you do this. If I want to find any dust in here, I'm going to have to bring it from home."

I told him I did it by getting to work early, staying late, and working through my break. The truth was that I barely finished my work, even when I did all of those things—and I received no overtime pay.

26
Custody

Particularly after my divorce, pay figured into my life many times as inadequate, interrupted, divided, or worse, nonexistent. That proved especially true once I knew I wasn't just one guy trying to survive. Things changed when I had my two children living with me.

Toward the end of my marriage, when Mary was working days and I was on second shift, we had turned to a neighbor for help with the boys. They were still at home, too young to go to school. Ann was a single mom, a bit older than we were. I knew her better than Mary did, but she liked us both—until we separated.

After I left, Ann hated me. She couldn't understand how I could ruin such a beautiful family by moving out. It's funny how other people perceive our most intimate relationships, the ones we know best. Ann thought the world of us. She had no idea what was really going on in our house; that, for me, living there was like being back in Glen Ferris.

One day I went to Ann's house and explained what my marriage had really been like. By doing that, I got her on my side. She even agreed to check on the kids. I was worried, now that I lived miles from my children. Ann would go down the street sometimes and look for the boys in the yard, or even stop by the house for a visit. Once when she dropped by, Mike and Jay were alone in the house. She told me then that I had to try for custody. The idea of full custody was overwhelming to me, but the thought of ever losing my boys was unacceptable. I didn't know what was ahead, but I knew I wanted to be with them.

I'd been seeing my kids on weekends. That was tough on all of us. *Visiting* my own sons? It was strange. The first time I picked up Mike and Jay, I took them to a park near their mom's house. When I brought them back, I wanted to give each boy a hug and tell him good-bye before I left. I hugged Jay, but I didn't see Mike. I knew he was upset that I was leaving, and he had my habit of going off alone. When I got in the car to pull out, I discovered him on the floor behind the driver's seat, hiding under a blanket. He wanted to go with me, and I had to tell him he couldn't.

Mr. Joe

In the early days after my separation, I didn't have many toys for my kids to play with. When they came over, it was hard because their toys had remained where they lived most of the time. One afternoon I went to the race track. I didn't always have money to bet, so sometimes I just sat and watched the races, reading the form to take my mind off my problems. That day I did bet. I remember wishing that I could win enough to buy each boy a Big Wheel to ride. That was all I asked for. I won within a dollar of what I needed for the toys, so I stopped on the way home and bought two Big Wheels. Every time I picked up the boys after that, they'd bring their Big Wheels to my place.

When I first left my family, I worried about whether the boys were all right. I threw up all the time. Now it was money. It was always something. Sometimes it was hard to even smile. I had to train myself to forget the bad things. It took me a whole year to teach myself not to concentrate on problems I couldn't solve. Once I learned that, I could cope better. The kids didn't know this, of course. I especially didn't want them to know how much I had to struggle to buy them something new.

I was awarded temporary custody of my sons, but I still had to go to court to make it permanent. When the court date was scheduled, I was living in my one-bedroom apartment, the one with the distinct lack of furniture. I couldn't be awarded custody if I planned to have all of us in a three-room apartment. Someone had said I needed "a suitable place." I wasn't rich then, but I wasn't broke. I just didn't have anything from the marriage, and my credit was shot.

Back then, no one had to rent to an adult with children. Some apartment complexes were called adult communities, and they didn't allow kids. Those were nicely kept. The ones that allowed kids were run to hell. I had kids, and I had no credit. I couldn't get into any of the nicer places. I rented a townhouse a week before my court date, and I'd never even been inside it. I'd only looked in the window.

Before I went downtown with the kids to be interviewed, I got both boys new outfits—nice shirts, shorts, shoes, and socks—and got their hair cut. They looked gorgeous. As we were walking up the steps to the courthouse, Jay tripped and fell. His nose was bloodied, and soon blood was all over his face and his new clothes. He looked like he'd been beaten up. This was a custody hearing! What were they going to think, that I'd been abusing him? Would it look like I couldn't take care of my kids?

When we went in, the boys and I were separated. I was interviewed first, and they went in later. Luckily, the subject of my son's appearance didn't come up in my interview. I didn't ask the boys about theirs. Jay was only three years old and Mike, five.

Ann had given a deposition about finding the kids alone. It would have come into play in court, had my wife fought me for custody, and she knew it—so we didn't get into a court battle. Mary set a couple conditions, including an agreement from me to raise our sons as Catholics, and then she backed off and let me have full custody. After the hearings I took the boys back to my place. "You don't have to leave any more," I told them. "You're going to live with me." I knew they were better off, but I worried about my ability to handle the responsibility. I hadn't hesitated to seek custody after my talk with Ann, but when it became a reality, it was scary. I knew I was on my own.

Mary might not prove to be any help at all. I already knew I couldn't count on her to show up for her visitations. She had rights, but sometimes the kids would be dressed and waiting by the window, and she didn't come. Mom was still in West Virginia when Mary and I divorced. She'd at least said she'd help me pay for the custody procedure, but after I went ahead, she wouldn't give me a dime. My lawyer threatened to sue me if I ever missed a payment, so I was paying off fees for several years—alone. Money, or the lack of money, was always on my mind, but I did my best to keep my worries from my children.

The boys were super. Both had good personalities. It was hard making ends meet, but the three of us got along well and did lots of things together. We played in a local park, or I'd take them to a water park, or we'd get a bucket of Colonel Sanders chicken and head for the lake. They were best friends, too. They helped each other. Love was the key for all of us.

Jay and Mike were well behaved. I could take them anywhere, to any restaurant, and they never got out of line. That made it easier for me. I was blessed that they were polite and friendly, and I didn't have to ram good behavior down their throats. If they'd been a lot of trouble, I never could have made it.

They attended parochial schools, per my agreement with their mother, and it cost. I took classes in the Catholic religion because not being Catholic went against me financially. I didn't intend to convert, but I had to show that I was trying in order to get any financial breaks from the parish. As I began to understand Catholicism, I responded to it. I hadn't expected that. I took the boys to mass and found that I enjoyed being there. It wasn't just that the services were casual and we could get by with our everyday wardrobes. I always experienced a feeling of peace in the church. Any problems I had would vanish for that one hour.

My boys played sports—soccer, T-ball, basketball, football—and they were good. They played all the time. Mike was a great soccer goalie, one of the best in the district. When he started playing, I didn't know a soccer ball from a tennis ball, but I learned the rules. Another dad offered to work with me, and we became good friends. I ended up coaching.

The soccer uniforms came to me, as coach. Jay was too young for the team, but he was a good player. I'd take him to the games dressed in a uniform under another shirt. If we didn't have enough team members, I'd put him in the game. It was against the rules, but it wasn't like he was an older kid taking advantage of the others. He saved the game sometimes, just by being there. If another kid showed up late, Jay dropped out.

I loved to watch the kids play sports. When I wasn't coaching, I would work the concessions stand. In football season, I ran the chains to mark first downs. I really looked forward to the games. It was normalcy, and that was what I was trying to achieve for myself and my kids. I wanted the same thing from a woman, but it never happened, not really.

Once I had custody, babysitting was one of my biggest challenges. Several times I just about lost my job at the meat plant. If either child got sick at school, he was sent home. I had to leave my job and pick up the sick child, then stay with him. I got no sympathy from my employer. In my new role as a single dad, all of that was news to me.

Sometimes I was forced to work overtime. The day-care center charged a dollar a minute if they had to stay open past their usual closing time: sixty dollars an hour until I arrived. I didn't have that kind of money. I could make it, but I had to work more hours to keep up. There was never a problem with working overtime if I wanted it, except that I had the babysitting issue.

Custody

For me, living alone with two young kids and trying to hold onto my job was just too hard. The boys and I moved in with a woman I'd been dating. Alice and I worked together at the meat plant. She was divorced with three children. Her daughter had been watching the boys some, but I needed serious child care. Alice needed financial help, so it seemed like a good trade. It seemed good for the boys, too. Mike and Jay and I had been living in an old neighborhood on a busy street that was full of traffic. Alice's house was on a cul-de-sac in a neighborhood full of kids. Living there, my boys had friends to play with and they were safe when they went outside.

Alice had a house, an ex-husband who paid child support, and parents a short distance away. She was a basket case sometimes, worrying, but she was never in any danger. I would listen to her and think, *I have nothing, and no one cares.* Alice had a safety net, but I had no safe place. I'd thought her home was going to be that for the kids and me; she had actual furniture and some kind of structure in place. I was always looking for a functional life for myself and my children.

We lived with Alice less than a year. I'd moved in with her thinking we'd split the bills and I could do more for the kids. That part worked out all right, but in her house, her rules counted. I discovered that Alice's children didn't have to abide by the house rules, but mine did. For instance, she might say on a pretty day that the kids should go outside and get some air and exercise. My boys would go outside, but her daughter would stay in to watch TV. Alice locked my boys out!

When she asked me to move out, she didn't explain why; she just said we'd get along better if we didn't live together. I thought we were breaking up because of the kids; they hadn't gotten along, and I couldn't make my sons care about Alice. As it turned out, we didn't break up entirely, but my boys and I moved on.

It was as if my life reversed. I found another townhouse, and we were back to being three. After we moved in, I spent quality time with Mike and Jay. I taught them how to swim using kickboards at the YMCA. We saw movies like *Superman.* One weekend I took them to Mammoth Cave. Our outings didn't always cost a lot, but we had fun together. My relationship with Alice reverted, too: we were back to dating and working together at the meat plant. My presence in the Catholic Church tapered off, a casualty of geography and time.

I was in the same place as before, except for one thing—one terrible thing. The plant went on strike.

27
On Strike

When our labor contract at the meat plant was about to expire, two things happened that didn't make sense when taken together. The first one was the company's announcement about how profitable it had been that year. The second one was the company's offer to the union: it amounted to a pay cut of more than $2.50 an hour. The offer was horrible, and it left us no choice but to strike.

When you're on strike, you don't work at your job and therefore do not receive your usual paycheck. Instead, you are entitled to strike pay under certain conditions. My strike pay was forty dollars per week—if I walked the picket line.

The rent on my townhouse was over five hundred dollars a month, and I had the usual living expenses. In addition, with Mike and Jay enrolled in a Catholic grade school, regular tuition payments came due. I'm talking hundreds of dollars, and I couldn't pay it. The people at Sacred Heart School were so good to me through that time. If I ever come into a lot of money, they're the ones I want to help. In the meantime, "No picket, no pay" was the slogan of the day, so I walked picket. I walked in the middle of the night, my assigned shift.

The strike began in April, during a soggy Ohio spring. I remember it raining eleven weekends in a row that year. It rained so hard the gutters wouldn't take it, and we weren't allowed to use any kind of enclosure on the picket line. When it rained, we got soaked; if it got cold, we couldn't build a fire. And we couldn't just stand or sit and hold a sign; we had to keep marching back and forth.

The company brought in a security firm to make sure we walked all the time. In fact, they hired the security company to come in before the strike and make sure we didn't sabotage the plant. We felt their presence all the time. Maybe it was because security personnel were stationed around our work area to watch that we didn't remove machine parts, otherwise damage the equipment, or ruin the meat. They even followed us back and forth to the trash.

Once the strike started, the security people filmed us twenty-four hours a day. We had to walk into the woods to pee. After the bars closed at two in the morning, people would go by and yell at us out their car windows. One night somebody threw a quart beer bottle and hit me in the chest. What we heard over and over was, "Get a f---in' job!"

I wanted a job—how could I make it on forty dollars a week?— but they were hard to find. Most potential employers would figure I'd leave as soon as the strike was settled. I tried entrepreneurship on a small scale, making up three-by-five index cards that said I would shampoo carpets. I was going to rent a shampooer at the supermarket and charge sixty dollars per apartment in my complex. I put the cards near the mailboxes in each building, but no one ever called.

I'd had time to do a little planning. I had no savings, but I sold my vacation days and was able to take out a small loan from our credit union before the strike. That's because no one at the credit union knew the strike was coming. Once they knew, the loan opportunities dried up.

I went to a temporary agency and got a job putting stickers on boxes for the cable company. Then I was hired to dismantle and move cubicle dividers in an office. God, those things were heavy! I was making crap for wages, and I had no rights. As a temp, I had to do anything anybody told me to do. None of those jobs lasted very long, of course, but I got excited if one paid fifteen cents more per hour than minimum wage.

I was still dating Alice. Her parents were helping her, so she helped me when she could. We bought a quarter of beef together and split it up.

I drove a Gremlin then. It was fifteen years old, so you know it wasn't much. It was red, and Alice painted it one day with white shoe polish: "Boycott hot dogs" and "Boycott wieners." I didn't like driving it that way, but the polish was hard to get off. I had to drive to a different area of town to walk picket, and people got to know my car. It stood out. I felt pressure to keep driving it because the other picketers liked it.

In case you're wondering how to exist on forty dollars a week and still have a little fun, Alice and I had a club we liked, where we used to go for drinks and dancing. When we were on strike we were stressed out, but too broke to drink. Sometimes you just want to have a couple. So we weeded her parents' whole vegetable garden for a six-pack. Beer was cheap, but we couldn't afford it, so we worked for hours in that garden just to get a few bottles of beer.

On Strike

To get my forty-dollar paycheck, I had to drive from my northern suburb to the union hall in downtown Cincinnati, which was twenty miles each way. It seemed like I always needed gas.

One day I got pulled over. Everyone in town knew about the strike, and there I was in my red Gremlin with the "Boycott hot dogs" signs all over it. The local police weren't in favor of the strike because it cost the town money, so when I got a ticket for one of my brake lights being out, I thought it was strike related. I hadn't noticed the light was out, but that no longer mattered. I had a court date, and naturally, the court was downtown.

I got to court with five dollars in my pocket. My fine for the traffic violation was either five dollars or having my driver's license held. When I handed over my license, the judge was shocked. He said, "I'm trying to give you a break. Don't you have five dollars?"

"Well, I do," I said, "but if I pay this, I won't be able to get my car out of the parking garage." The judge took my license. I got my car out of the garage and drove home.

It got worse. I couldn't pay my bills; it was everything I could do to keep the utilities hooked up. I got so far behind that I let my mail accumulate before I opened it; that way, I didn't have to look at the bills. One day I got a shut-off notice from the power company saying that if I didn't pay the bill immediately, there would be no electricity in my old house, the one where I'd lived with Mary. *What?* Why was *I* getting that notice? I thought I had requested that the bill be put in her name, but when I tried to find the letter that was required, I realized I'd failed to write it. The amount due was over five thousand dollars! Luckily, Mary's mother stepped in to help with that one.

I waited until the last possible minute to pay everything. With the phone, I waited until it was shut off. Then I'd go to the YMCA and call the phone company to make arrangements to pay something to get it turned back on. Finally, they said, "You can't keep doing this." Everyone was after me. I had nothing. Even my sputtering romance with Alice petered out. I suspected she was interested in someone else.

The strike lasted for seventeen weeks. I broke a lot of rules trying to make it through the rough times. I felt guilty, but I did what I had to do. I had to find ways to survive and get food, gas, and the other things we needed. When it came to extras, we didn't have many. Some of the kids Jay and Mike went to school with were well off. I knew I'd put my children in that position when I agreed to send them to parochial schools, and I didn't want them to feel bad about themselves. Whatever it took, I was going to do it.

When it was time for Jay's first communion, I wanted him to look as good as everyone else, but I didn't have the money to buy him a suit. I went to a department store and picked out a three-piece, navy blue pinstriped suit that cost over eighty dollars. I told the clerk I wasn't sure it would fit my son. She let me take it home to try it on him, and I was supposed to return it the next day if it didn't fit. That's what I planned to do: return it—after he wore it to his first communion.

Following the communion ceremony, we had cake. We knew a woman who painted beautiful cakes; the tops looked like paintings on canvas. Jay was eating cake in his new suit. I wanted him to have fun, but I was scared to death he'd spill something on that suit and I'd have to buy it. He didn't get one spot on it, and I took it back to the store. When I handed it over, my relief was physical. Lying to the clerk had given me a sick feeling in my stomach. I didn't intend to hurt anyone by the things I did; I just wanted my children to look good.

Our food situation during the strike was pretty dire. We got food from the free store downtown. They gave it out by weight, not ingredients. Everyone would get a brown bag of mixed products that weighed so many pounds. One time I got mine out to the car and couldn't wait to look at it. Most of it was dog food, and I didn't even have a dog. There was a box of no-brand cereal, and beans. One time there was a container of stale powdered donuts. I felt like I'd hit the jackpot. I got into those donuts and ate a few on the way home.

My kids and I once ate for two weeks on carnival prizes. One of the local schools had a little carnival. The boys had done without for so long, I just wanted them to have a good time. All of us had been stressed out, so I took them to the carnival with less than twenty dollars to my name. Jay wanted to try throwing a beanbag into a hole. He did it, and the prize was a coupon for a Big Mac, so I let him keep going. Mike tossed a ring onto a two-liter bottle of pop and won it. I kept paying for the kids to do these games, and between the Big Mac coupons and the two-liter bottles of pop, we took home enough to last us two weeks.

In the winter my boys got free coats from the school. I was glad for the coats, but hated that my sons had been picked for charity.

During the strike I did things I never thought I'd do. At one point, I took the boys and went to the Welfare office to apply for assistance.

On Strike

The application was twelve pages long. It took me an hour to fill out all of the information while keeping one eye on the kids. Finally I reached the end, and there—on the last page—was the question that should have been on page 1: "Are you currently involved in a labor dispute or on strike?" *Yes* was not the answer they were looking for.

After we'd been off maybe ten weeks, I applied to be a house painter. It was summer, and I'd painted before. When I applied, the boss said I should have my own brushes and equipment, but I didn't. He hired me anyway because I had experience. I told him that when I'd lived in California, I'd painted some big homes on the order of the Clampett mansion from *The Beverly Hillbillies*.

"This house has a widow's walk," he said. "Do you have any problems with heights?

"No, not at all," I lied. Heights were my worst fear. *Worst*. It seemed I had a few "worst" fears, and that one had become evident in Glen Ferris when I was a boy climbing Chimney Rock, the mountain-top formation that overlooked our town. When I reached the top—a big, flat rock surface—I couldn't stand up like the other kids did. I had to lie down on my stomach.

The house I was to paint was three stories high. It had a slanted yard, so to get up to the widow's walk, I had to use a thirty-foot aluminum ladder with a block under one side to balance it on the hill. Nothing was secure. My legs were shaking as I went up the ladder, and when I got to the top I was clutching onto every possible surface while I painted. I finished that job, but work-wise, it was the hardest thing I ever did in my life.

The strike ended in August.

28
Second Lives

My suspicions about Alice proved to be right. She eventually married a man we worked with at the meat plant. The strike, as well as our romance, faded into memory. After that I decided to get rid of the Gremlin, too. I cleaned and polished it, intending to eliminate the "Boycott hot dogs" propaganda that was no longer relevant so that I could sell the car. I must have done a great job, because the Gremlin was stolen. By the time it was recovered six months later, I had moved on to my next car. It wasn't time then for the next lady in my life, but a few years later I was ready to try again. I was interested in another woman who worked at the meat plant.

The dating culture at the plant was fascinating. Both women and men would get fixed up to go out to the clubs after work. Many of these were married people. The women would get all made up at the end of their shift. Guys would keep nice clothes, a razor, and cologne in their lockers. Some of my coworkers had whole sets of clothing, complete with shoes, for going out. When our shift ended, they'd change out of their plant clothing and assume their second lives.

How did they get away with it? We worked at night. That didn't leave a lot of time to socialize. The people we saw most often were the ones we knew on the production line. Everyone's families were home asleep. Folks who wanted a little something extra took what the plant offered. It was a cruel truth that the best-looking women were always being hit on, even if they might not compare well on the street. That was the mentality.

Finding someone to date at the meat plant was also convenient for those of us who weren't cheating on somebody. I was divorced, so sneaking around was unnecessary, but the same logic applied. Work was as good a place as any to meet someone, and I knew just the lady I wanted to meet.

I'd always been attracted to Marilyn, but we worked in different departments. I'd never even spoken to her. When I first noticed her, she was married. Then her husband, a truck driver, was killed in a traffic accident. By that time, I was married. When I was divorced ten years later, she had remarried. We'd never been single at the same time.

Eventually Marilyn and husband number two divorced. She and I still hadn't talked until one night when I was working overtime in her department. They put me on the job right next to her. Finally, I was standing right beside this woman I'd admired for so long. She didn't have any idea I cared about her.

From time to time our employer would give out free tickets at work. They might be for the local theme park, Kings Island, or a water park. We'd have special employees' days at these attractions. I ran into Marilyn on such a day at a surf park. Because we knew each other from working overtime together, I sat down beside her and talked a while. Dating had always been a slippery slope for me, but I took a chance and asked her out that day. She said yes.

One date led to another, and eventually my sons and I moved out of our apartment and into her place. Marilyn had a house and a young daughter who hadn't even started school. By then Mike was in high school and Jay was in junior high. They could get off to school on their own in the mornings. My babysitting problems had ended at last!

About a week after we moved in, Marilyn went on medical leave. The company challenged her time off; they didn't want to pay, so I ended up paying for everything. I was trying to help her, so in addition to paying for the house and food, I gave her spending money every week. Within a day or so, she'd be broke again.

I started taking the long way home after the first month with Marilyn. I'd moved in on a weekend, and just a few days later she was home every day. As soon as I got home from the plant and went to bed, she'd take her little girl out for the day. My arrival seemed to be the trigger for Marilyn to visit her mother or—worse—to go shopping. I was giving her spending money every day, and she had no hesitation about spending it. One day her little girl said, "Mommy is buying me new clothes and hiding them in the trunk of her car so you won't find out."

I started avoiding the house, just like I had with my wife and with my parents before that. I just couldn't go home, so I drove around. Sometimes I got off work at seven-thirty in the morning and didn't get home until eleven o'clock. When I thought of starting for Marilyn's, I'd take another lap around town.

Marilyn must have been feeling the same way. One night before work, I stopped at a McDonald's to get food to bring back to the house for the kids. This was ten o'clock at night. When I got back with the food, my sons were out in the yard. I asked them why they were outside, and they said Marilyn had kicked them out. She'd thought I was at work and had told them not to come back. "Get in the car," I said, and we took off. We had no place to live. Did it ever end?

What was it about my relationships? I thought I knew. Twice I'd moved into someone else's house when we were dating, which had automatically given my partner the upper hand. I didn't need to be the boss, but I wanted an equal partnership. Our relationship might have been better if Marilyn and I had found a new place together, but that wasn't possible on my income. I knew one thing: I never wanted to move in with another woman—into her house—again. If I was going to pay all the bills, I'd just as soon live with my boys and help them.

When we left Marilyn's place, I didn't have much at all, but at least I had a car. My sons and I went to a hotel that night, and then we began the depressing process of looking for a home on a very tight budget. One day I turned down some road, saw a hotel, and figured it could at least be something cheap and clean while we continued to look for an apartment. We went in to check it out. The lobby had Plexiglas in front of the clerk so that no one would shoot him. It was a place to take prostitutes, a place to get X-rated movies and rent a room by the hour. We were desperate, but not that desperate, so we left and found another hotel I could afford. Right after we got there, I left to go somewhere in the car, and the engine blew. It was my fault; I had things on my mind, and I'd let my car run out of oil. It was a nice car, a Nissan Sentra, and I hadn't even kept oil in it.

So, I didn't have a house; I didn't have a car. My boys and I were living in a cheap hotel. You do what you can, but I still feel guilty about times like that, when I fell short. I had to walk to work every day. For food, I'd walk to Sam's Club and buy things we could microwave. We lived in that hotel for a month, but I couldn't pay the $175 a week and put anything aside for a deposit on an apartment. I could never get out of that financial hole. Finally a friend loaned me some money and I got an apartment near the kids' schools.

I was scraping by, gritting my teeth, and trying to give the kids what they needed; but most people at the plant knew nothing of my troubles. My coworkers thought I was a cheapskate. I learned that people at the meat plant were making jokes about me, like "He turns off his car at the top of a hill to save gas." That one wasn't even accurate. I still had to *find* a car.

I thought I had troubles; a friend who sometimes gave me a ride told me his wife was in the hospital, seriously ill. She passed away. He asked me if I wanted to buy her car, a white Dodge Shadow convertible. It was spotless, a beautiful car. He gave me a good deal, and I was able to swing the loan through the credit union at work. I'd been a member for twenty years, so that place saved my life more than once.

I lost that Shadow when a woman went into a diabetic coma and hit me. I was stopped at a traffic light, way back in the line of cars. I had a quart of chocolate milk in my lap, open, drinking it on my way to work. All of a sudden I got the hell knocked out of me. This woman rear-ended me with a big Ford SUV at sixty miles an hour. Her foot stayed floored on the gas, and she pushed me into the car in front of me. Then she hit me again, knocking my car across the street and into a telephone pole. The airbag deployed and then sagged. The steering wheel bent in the accident, and my legs were locked down. I kept feeling something running down my face. My whole head was soaked, and I was scared. I thought I was dying.

When I looked, I didn't have a drop of blood on me. It was the chocolate milk! It had spilled all over me. I seemed to be all right, but the car was totaled. It was so smashed up that I could just about put one hand on the front license plate and touch the back plate with my other hand. My insurance paid off the car, which was good, but I still didn't have a car. They paid off a wrecked car.

I received a settlement because the accident had not been my fault. With that settlement, I bought another Nissan Sentra and was able to pay cash for it. Like Willie Nelson, I was on the road again. As for my relationships, they seemed prone to breaking down, just like my cars. I was becoming far too good at predicting the endings. After the boys and I left Marilyn's house in 1988, I took a break from dating—a long break.

29
Gambling

I hadn't kept up with Mom the way I thought I would, but after our reunion on my fiftieth birthday she'd invited me back to see her, and I'd gone. That time, Jane was with us.

Gambling boats were just coming into the area then. Mom and Jane loved them, but I'd never been until the three of us went to the casino together one Saturday morning. I was still working at the kindergarten school, and I talked all the way to Indiana in the car—about my job, my principal, all kinds of things Mom and Jane didn't even know about me. It was like I'd been unlocked.

Being with my mom and sister was fun that day. I felt welcome—part of the family again. The mood was upbeat. Jane and Mom were glad to see me and interested in hearing all my tales of life and work. I let down my guard, and some of my lost joy returned, but it was temporary. I couldn't forget the past so easily. In particular, the impression Mom had made when I was a boy could not be cancelled out in a day.

I remember thinking that at least I didn't have to ask Mom for money. That was the pits, asking her for help—rock bottom. I'd had to in the past, when I was desperate. If she didn't flat-out refuse, she made it so difficult that I decided from then on just to go without eating instead.

She could have argued—and did—that I was a poor risk. In 1970, after I'd moved to Cincinnati, I borrowed forty dollars from Mom. I wrote her an I.O.U., but I didn't pay her back right away. She kept asking for the money, saying she *had* to have it, so one day I drove all the way to Glen Ferris from Cincinnati to give her the forty dollars. For some `reason, Mom still insisted I hadn't paid her back, so when I had to ask for help after that, it didn't go well. "Jane is a single parent, too," she said once after I had custody of the kids. "She manages."

"Jane has a house and furniture." Mom didn't get that I, the custodial parent, had given up my home and furniture; that I didn't receive child-support payments like my sister did. It was the opposite; Mary wasn't even paying the bills she was supposed to pay.

Mom told me she was going to put my I.O.U. from 1970 with her important papers so that I would see it upon her death and be remind-

ed that I had not repaid her. I knew I had, but no doubt I would see that
I.O.U. again one day. Aren't parents supposed to build you up? I was
a grown man, but I was hurting, and what had Mom ever given me?
It's because of her that I've encouraged my sons to come to me for
help, no matter what. I might not be able to do a lot, but I will always
do what I can to help them. I never want them to feel the way I did.

One time I had five dollars to my name. I put gas in my tank and
drove to Mom's apartment in Cincinnati. I asked her to help me buy
groceries, and she turned me down. She gave me five dollars, and I
used that to get home.

Another time I had to ask Mom for $240. It killed me. My repay-
ment plan that time was to write her six checks, on the spot, for forty
dollars each. I wasn't rolling in it or else I wouldn't have needed the
loan, so I asked Mom to cash one check a week. The first one bounced,
and the fee came out of the second check. After that it snowballed, and
they all bounced, each one a check fee away from being good. I didn't
know it—I thought things were fine—but Mom told me later that she
was embarrassed to go to the bank.

Fortunately, by the time we made our trip to the gambling boat, my
hard times were in the past. I was working for a great school district,
earning regular pay, and our family was mending—or so it seemed on
the surface. If you ask me, we were gambling on *each other*, and had
been all our lives.

By then Mom had been sober for years. In my view, that didn't
make her a lovable person, but certainly she had improved and was
living a regular life. She was responsible and organized. I wondered
how she had done it, because I knew that drinking wasn't her only
problem.

In my early days at the meat plant, a guy I worked with had become a friend. His name was Johnny. Every night, Johnny would
come in to work on third shift and be as nice as could be. Our first
break came after about two hours, and by then his attitude would have
done a one-eighty. On break, he was hateful. He tried to start fights,
but he was the size of a jockey, maybe 130 pounds soaking wet, so the
other men ignored him.

One night I was in the locker room with Johnny, and he opened his
locker and reached up to get a container of red pills off the shelf. He
told me he took them every night and washed them down with a beer,
which was entirely possible in our plant. He could have hidden a beer

in the equipment or walked out the back door and sneaked one without detection. Johnny's pills were downers, and downers make you mean.

When I saw those red pills, I remembered standing up on the toilet lid back home when I was eight or nine years old, opening our bathroom cabinet and seeing the same pills. Mom and Dad had told me they were sleeping pills and that I was never to touch them. I used to get that bottle out, take the top off, and look at the pills. Sometimes I put them in my hand. They fascinated me. They were bright red, and they were big. I liked them. Sometimes I noticed the level had gone down. I never thought about taking them—I was afraid—but it was exciting to look at those red pills.

They were barbiturates with many street names, including Reds. Once I saw what happened to Johnny, I remembered how quickly Mom's mood could change back home; how mean she would get. Reds will also make you stagger like you're drunk. When you take them with alcohol, it's a double whammy. I never took a Red, even after I was grown. I couldn't see the benefit: Why would anybody want to be mean?

When we got back from the casino, Jane asked me if I wanted to see where she lived. We drove by it, but I had no idea where we were. I lived forty-five minutes away and couldn't have found Jane's place again for a million dollars. She asked me if I wanted to go in, and I said no. I wasn't ready for that. Knowing my sister, I expected that her place would be perfect, and it would just depress me.

The outside of Jane's condo unit was neat, with landscaping in the front. My apartment community had been attractive when I'd first moved in, but now it was rundown. I hadn't paid much attention to the neighbors—they came and went while my life centered on my living room couch—but it wasn't a high-class clientele. The cars in the parking lot were older models, the outsides of the buildings hadn't been painted in years, and the pool was looking scruffy. Some weeks nobody mowed the little patches of grass. I was glad to skip the tour of my sister's place, for obvious reasons.

It also became obvious on that outing that Mom—our nemesis for half a lifetime—now had a buddy in Jane. After I thought about it, I felt betrayed. For so many years my sister and I had survived the awful wrath of Mom together, thankful for each other in our Glen Ferris house of horrors. I was glad I'd initiated contact with Mom again—I'd broken a barrier—but I hadn't forgiven her for those years. Maybe I never would, and now it seemed my sister had aligned herself with the dark side of our family. I kept thinking, *birds of a feather*; couldn't help it.

Even after our day of fun, I was not drawn to either of them. They had each other, and I didn't need to make it three. I'd done my bit and could quit worrying about Mom, but I did go to see her again. The next time was on Mother's Day, 1999, the same day as my older son's graduation from college. Mike was graduating summa cum laude, but he didn't attend the ceremony or invite any of our family. By the time he told me about it, he had arranged to have his diploma mailed. "No big deal," was what he said.

I, on the other hand, wanted to shout it to the rooftops. My son was graduating with honors! One night I took the graduation program to work with me. I wanted to show it to the superintendent of schools.

It was late, maybe even midnight, when I approached the door to his office. It was open a crack, so I stuck my head in. "Do you have a minute?"

I could tell by his face that he didn't have a minute, but he stopped what he was doing. "Come on in," he said.

I handed him the program, pointing to my son's name: Michael Joseph Barnett. "I had no idea you were attending college," he said. He thought I was the one who had graduated.

Even though I was let down that I wouldn't be seeing Mike graduate, I knew that he had made his choice. Instead, I would observe Mother's Day with Mom. She had moved into a gated apartment community, and I had to call from the gate to be let in. Mom had a code to key into her phone, only she hadn't perfected the procedure. Sometimes she didn't realize she had a visitor. "Thank you for calling me," she said later.

"I didn't just call you," I said. "I came over. I was going to take you someplace for Mother's Day. I was calling from the gate, but you didn't let me in."

Mom wanted to see more of me, and I thought I wanted to see more of her, but maybe it was too little, too late. Our stabs at family time were good in one sense, but they brought up old memories for me—bad memories. The memories stirred up raw feelings from the past that I had tried to forget. After all, Mom was still the same woman who'd called me a son of a bitch until I left home. She was still the same one who'd tried to choke me when I came upstairs. She was the same mean person who had held onto my I.O.U. since 1970, hoping it would haunt me after she was gone. Wasn't she?

I didn't want to invest a lot in Mom. Nothing could convince me that she was a good person who loved me. Going to the casino had been fine, but I decided that if I wanted to gamble, I would rather sit by myself at the race track. Put another way, I'd rather bet on a horse's nose than spend time with a horse's behind.

30
Ponies

I've been going to the races for almost forty years. I got interested in race horses back in 1973, before my children were even born, because people at the meat plant would talk about them. One guy had a bookie, and he'd bet the horses every day. He and I were hanging around together, and racing was pretty much all he talked about. We never went to the races together, but I watched him bet.

The first time I ever bet on a race, I won. It wasn't much—maybe thirty dollars—but winning always hooks you. I came home with more money than I'd taken with me. Besides, it was fun. Like shooting pool, racing involved numbers and math.

My days of playing pool had all but ended when I became a custodial father. I taught Jay to play Nerf Pool on the dining room table when he was eleven or twelve, but even if I could have done the bar scene, I had lost interest. With pool, you have to keep your skill up or lose it. My eyesight had weakened, too, but I still loved math.

Because of the numbers—the statistics—the *Daily Racing Form* has always been my favorite part of horse racing. The form includes information on the horses' past performance as well as experts' picks for each race. Many times I'll spend a dollar-fifty for a racing form even when I don't plan to spend another dime on the races. That's how I perfected my system. I would handicap the horses without even betting. I studied each form, chose my horses, and then I looked at the newspaper the next day to see how I did.

I've mentioned the golden light that has sometimes identified race winners for me. That was always nice when it happened—easy money—but I like the methodical route, which is rewarding in other ways. It takes so much concentration for me to work on the racing form that it's a good escape. It calms me down and takes my mind off my troubles, the same thing baths seem to do for women. When I've been unhappy or wished I was alone, I've lost myself in racing forms. They take me away every time.

It's possible to study one race all day, and I have. There are so many variables, but the answers that point to the winners are there in the form most of the time. Things can happen—a jockey can get bumped or blocked in, or even fall off the horse—but most of the information you need to pick the best horse is in the racing form, if you know how to get it out. But you can also spend twenty hours studying the form and then find out it's going to rain, and that cancels out everything you've learned.

Just a few months after I started studying horses, I went to Churchill Downs. I'd never been to a big-time track, and I wanted to see a Kentucky Derby. I went alone and watched from the infield, where the parties were. I was able to see part of the race, but not all of it, because of the crowd; but that day I saw Secretariat, the best horse in history. I had a ticket for Secretariat to win, but it paid only a few dollars because he was the favorite. That turned out to be the first race of the Triple Crown he would win. So, the first time I went to the Derby, Churchill Downs had the first Triple Crown winner they'd had in many years. What are the odds of that?

When I was a young married guy in the early1970s, I had a part-time job selling real estate. I was required to spend at least one day a week in the office, mostly taking phone calls. Sunday was the best day to cover the office because people were always looking for houses on Sundays. The most sales opportunities would occur then, and I'd be the only one there. One Sunday I was alone in the office, and I had my racing form with me. I saw a horse I liked that was going to run that afternoon at Beulah Park, up near Columbus—nearly a 100-mile drive. I liked that horse so much that I called another Realtor to relieve me in the office, and I left. I took $200 with me. I knew I'd have to hurry to get there in time to bet on the race.

When I was a block from Beulah Park, I turned one street too soon. As soon as I did it I knew, but I had to keep driving for a couple of miles before I could turn around. When I came back, I parked in someone's yard near the track for a fee. I ran to the track and stood in the betting line. Just when I got up to the ticket counter, the announcer was saying, "And they're off!" I was too late to bet.

My horse—the one I picked, but didn't bet—came in the winner. It paid twenty-one dollars. Based on my expected bet, I would have won $2,100. When I was walking out of the park, I handed a man my program. "I was too late to bet the one horse I wanted," I told him. He didn't believe me.

When the guys talked about racing at the meat plant, I'd tell them my picks and which ones had come in. Just like the guy at Beulah

Park, they didn't believe me. One coworker accused me of waiting until the winner was known and making up the rest, so we got a paper. I went downtown and bought a form on my lunch break. I picked four horses that were running the next day and worked my system on them. He took the list and put it in his locker at work. The next day, all of my horses had won. He knew I'd picked them a day ahead, so from there on out people would ask me about the horses. They knew I had something that worked.

I once gave Pete Rose a tip at Latonia. Latonia—now called Turfway—is a winter track, so every seat is located indoors. I was up on the top floor, and Rose was sitting with a couple of friends in an area of reserved seats. You had to pay to go in it. This was back when the track was really crowded. I was in a section where I could see Rose and his group. He had on a white, short-sleeved fishnet shirt, and he looked like Superman. I couldn't believe how muscular he was. You could see the muscles in his back through his shirt. I went over and told him I had a horse for him named Big Yonk. He just looked at me. He was paying attention, but he didn't say much—maybe "Thanks." The odds on Big Yonk were fifteen to one. The horse came out of nowhere down the home stretch, splitting the two leaders, and it won. I don't even know if Rose bet it; I didn't talk to him again.

People talk to each other all the time at the track. Once at Turfway I was standing near a man I called Mr. Anything because all during the race he kept yelling, "Come on, anything!" He was hitting his leg with his hand like he was whipping a horse. I kept looking for a horse named "Anything," because I didn't remember seeing it. I asked him, "What number is that horse?" He said he'd bet on every horse in the race, so anything that came in was a winner to him. A lot of people do that just to make sure they have a winner. Maybe they'll hit with a long shot.

As much as I loved racing, I wasn't a frequent bettor—especially while I had custody of my boys. It wasn't just that getting to the track was inconvenient; I couldn't justify gambling our money away. Having a winner might have offset my frantic budgeting for a while, but there was always a chance I could lose—and a loss would have devastated me. When you're fooling with your grocery money, taking chances doesn't make sense.

Even now I rarely put big money on a bet, but in 2006 I bet $500 on a horse named Barbaro in the Preakness, the second big race of the

Triple Crown. Barbaro had been undefeated going into the Kentucky Derby and had easily won it. I bought my ticket at a local racetrack, and then went home to watch the race on TV. While the horses were being loaded into the starting gate, I went to the refrigerator for a cold beer. I had bet on Barbaro to place, giving myself some wiggle room in case he came in second—after all, $500 was at stake—but I thought his win was a sure thing. There's a saying: "There's no such thing as a sure thing."

There's another saying: "The only way this horse won't win is if it falls down." When I started back into the living room with my beer, I heard the TV announcers gasping about a horse being injured. I didn't even have to look; a feeling of dread told me it was Barbaro. The horse had suffered catastrophic leg injuries in the first moments of the race. Later, he underwent several surgeries, but did not recover. Barbaro's injuries were the end of his racing career and my $500.

I still love the horses and the form; always will. I have a "day of hibernation" on the day of the Kentucky Derby. It's a selfish thing I've done for years. The people close to me know not to come over or call, because I'll be reading the racing form and watching the Derby coverage on TV. I want to lose myself in the Kentucky Derby for that one day. Hiding? Yes, but at least I'm not afraid of anything but possibly losing some money.

31
Beth

Even with ghosts roaming the kindergarten school at night, I was able to settle in. More than a year went by, and then something else happened, this time in my personal life. I met a woman I liked.

If you define "single" as "unmarried," the way I do, I'd been single more than twenty years. I'd dated a few women since my divorce, but I'd broken up with the last one—Marilyn from the meat plant—in 1988. Yes, I was definitely single; I'd pretty much missed my forties as far as dating went. The time I'd spent with Peggy, the woman I'd gone to visit on the plane, didn't count as romance.

I was going to turn fifty-five in a week, and I'd been feeling the effects of the lonely nights cleaning and days spent sleeping. I didn't exactly have a vibrant social life, and most of the time that was okay, but sometimes I missed having someone in my life. My son Jay kept trying to get me to go out. One day he said he wanted to fix me up with somebody for a date. She was the mother of one of his friends, so I agreed.

I met Beth for coffee on the Fourth of July. She was attractive and friendly. Before I knew it, we'd been talking nearly two hours. I came home and told Jay that I'd met her and liked her.

"Did you ask her out?"

"No." I wouldn't act on anything. I might be attracted to someone or like her, but I didn't follow it up. I'd never had confidence around women and didn't want to be turned down.

Jay was upset with me. "You should call her," he said. "Ask her out on a date."

I got up my nerve, called Beth, and asked her to go with me to the movies. She accepted, but when I asked where to pick her up, she named a grocery store. I'd never had a woman give me a neutral site for a meeting place. Did she not want me to see where she lived? Maybe she thought I was a stalker. I was a bit offended. Did women learn that on Internet dating sites? We didn't know each other well, but still.

We went out a few more times before Beth allowed me to see where she lived. One night when I took her home, she removed a piece of paper that had been placed between her storm door and entry door. I thought she was upset to see it, but when I asked, she said it was just the mail. Later that night she told me she was behind on her rent and had to come up with it or find another place.

By then I was calling Beth to talk between our dates. Her situation ate at me. I'd been on the street, and I couldn't handle the thought of her being in such a predicament. I knew she didn't have a job, so it didn't seem likely she would have her rent paid on time. I wanted to help her. I couldn't give her money, but I was living in a two-bedroom basement apartment by myself. Beth and I hadn't even slept togeth-er—we'd barely kissed—but I told her she was welcome to stay with me until she could get something else. At that point we were friends, and a friend had helped me when I was down. I wanted to do the same for Beth. We moved her in right away.

I'd lived in the same apartment community for years. It wasn't a palace, but the rent was low and my landlord didn't bother me. I hadn't insisted on the usual periodic painting or other updates because I was afraid my rent would go up; thus, my walls were yellow with nicotine and my carpet had seen better days. It wasn't the first time I'd chosen a basement apartment; I did it so that Mike and Jay wouldn't disturb any neighbors, first as kids with their running and later as teenagers. Even though I had no need now that the boys had left, I was right at home. The windows, which were high and small, suited my lifestyle. I even had black curtains over them to help me sleep. My plant purchases were based on what grew best in dim light. I should have grown moss.

I did have one plant I loved. It was a fluffy fern that sat in a beauti-ful macramé hanger. It didn't get enough light inside the apartment. I had to take it outside to save it, so I hung it on a tree. One day it was gone. I suspected that someone had stolen it, hanger and all. I bought another fern and another hanger, but I couldn't afford to keep that up, so I also purchased a key ring with a separate locator, a popular choice for people who frequently misplaced their keys.

I stuck the locator on top of the dirt in the new planter and hung the whole works outside on the same tree as before. The leaves of the plant hid the device, which was sound activated by whistling. When the second plant went missing, I went after it. I walked up and down the halls of my building whistling, and sure enough, I heard beeps coming from one of the apartments. I knocked on the door and said to the guy who answered it, "I think you have my plant." He denied it, but I saw *both* of my ferns inside, and I walked right in and got them.

When I showed him how I'd found the one, there was nothing more he could say.

Beth and I got along well, and she worked hard keeping the apartment clean and cooking fantastic meals for us. Her domestic talents were great, but I had expected her to look for a job so that both of us could contribute financially to the household. She had been a stay-at-home mom during her marriage, and it was a role she liked, but I couldn't afford to be the sole breadwinner.

I hadn't been back at the kindergarten school long enough to get a raise. I'd taken a substantial pay cut to become a custodian, and I couldn't even earn extra with overtime, so I was worried about money. Jobs were hard to find, but I helped Beth get part-time work as an aide in my school district. By then our relationship was romantic; I really fell for her, but we were losing money. Beth worked only two hours a day, not enough to qualify for medical insurance, and she had prescriptions to fill. Both of us were trying to help our children, too. I felt the pressure. I wasn't capable of continuing to support both of us. I began acting different, and we both knew it, but I didn't tell her why.

Work was going great for me at the kindergarten school, but I was working third shift and sleeping during the day, which meant that Beth and I weren't seeing much of each other. Our lack of time together was bothering her. I was worried about money and she was worried about the relationship. I think Beth let me sleep sometimes just to avoid the growing tension between us.

Before we'd been together a year, a day-shift job came up in the district. Day jobs came along every five years or so, if that; anyone wanting one had to wait for someone to leave or retire, and most of the time it was retirement. The prevailing advice in custodial circles was: if you ever want a day job and one comes up, you'd better take it.

A day job had come up once before, but I hadn't put in for it because I knew that another applicant had some personal troubles and needed it worse than I did. If I'd really wanted it, I would have gone for it anyway, but I'd worked twenty years at night and loved it. I didn't want a day job, but everyone else seemed to, so I convinced myself that I was interested.

I asked Dave about the job. It was in an intermediate school, mostly fourth grade. I would be part of a team working during school hours, helping teachers and students in addition to keeping the school in shape. Dave knew the setup. He also knew the personnel at every school in the district, including my future boss. "It's a good job, Joe, with good people," he said, "but I would hate to lose you again. I know how you work, and I can trust you."

After Dave had given the job his okay, I mentioned it to Beth, and sure enough, she asked me to take it. I pursued that job because of her. It seemed that most of the reasons I changed jobs were for other people. I was always trying to make someone else happy. I could even say that about leaving the meat plant. That one definitely wasn't my choice.

I interviewed for the day job against a man I'd recommended for our school district. It was a close contest, but the tie breaker came in one question: "What do you know about computers?" The other guy said he didn't know anything, and I said I knew a little bit. That was the truth; I could e-mail, and that was about it. But I could learn, and I said so. Beth and I had a computer at home. It wasn't new, but one of my sons had rebuilt it. Beth used it most of the time. She was all over the Internet, but I had no need to get on the machine myself. That would be changing soon; I got the day job and started working at the intermediate school in the spring of 2004.

One day that summer I came home and found Beth packing. She'd rented her own place. If I'd known she was going to move out, I never would have changed jobs, but she didn't tell me until she was ready to leave. I found out later that she moved to another state and married a man she had met online. She must have been looking for something better than what she had with me.

Beth e-mailed me once in a while. It wasn't unusual for me to hear from my former lovers; I wasn't good at closing things out with people. Back when I left my wife, I thought I'd made my intentions very clear, but she didn't take the news well. After I was on my own she pursued me for years, hoping for reconciliation. A few e-mails from Beth were nothing compared to that.

My new job at the intermediate school was working out. I didn't have my good friends with me as I had in the past, but I was still Mr. Joe; the name had stuck. I found that working the day shift was complicated with students, teachers, and even the public coming and going. More people paid attention to me. I also had more to do, but I vowed to do the best job I could. I did little jobs for the teachers when they asked, and I helped the kids, who were now at school during my whole shift. Soon I became the greeter when people came in to evaluate our facilities for their events. It was different, but what was I going to do, quit? I liked cleaning and waxing, and that was still what I did most of the time.

Things took an ironic turn with Beth gone. I enjoyed my cleaning job and left my area spotless every day, but then I came home and didn't feel like doing anything. The apartment seemed particularly empty without Beth, and I went into a funk. I didn't even want to go into some of my rooms. After all my years of working alone, things had reversed. I was so busy at school that I hardly had a minute, but when I got home, there was no one—no one but me. I had my alone time, but now there was no joy in it.

I gave up my bedroom. The bed had been Beth's, and that had no appeal. I didn't even use the closet. I seldom did laundry because the coin-operated washer and dryer were three flights up. Most evenings it was too much trouble and too easy to put off. Every day I'd get home, have a few beers, and lie down on the couch to unwind. Sometimes I drank NyQuil or cough syrup to help me relax; and then I watched TV until I fell asleep. I rarely changed out of my uniforms after work, so by default they became my pajamas, too. I slept on my couch for two years.

My usable space continued to shrink as I avoided the realities of my life. I seldom ate at home. Nothing interested me. The next step down was ignoring my mail. I got it from the mailbox, but usually I threw it unopened into a trunk. I couldn't face it. Haunted at home, I kept busy at work and was thankful not to see anything scarier than dirty restrooms or vomit. Maybe the intermediate school didn't have any ghosts. That would be something positive.

32
Life of a Custodian

I liked the chance I was being given to help children again at the intermediate school, but the day shift sure was a hustle. All of the custodians were busy. Our uniform shirts were like flags waving an invitation; we used to say we couldn't walk from one end of a hall to the other without getting stopped and asked to help someone or take on a project. Half the time someone would interrupt our lunch to ask us to clean up vomit, or worse. I was often the one to do it. As the junior custodian, I thought my job description must be "Anything no one else wants to do."

Flu season in your house can be bad. Flu season in a school is hell for the custodians, especially the junior guy. How many times did someone say to me, "It's flu season," and how many times did I think, *Duh*, as I went from one classroom to the other cleaning up after sick students. It was nonstop.

Before reporting for duty I always had to ask the teacher if the mess was on tile or carpet, because there were two different procedures requiring different equipment. A mop isn't much use on a rug. On tile, we used a product aptly named VomitSorb. Either way, the kids would all turn around to watch me. One time I had to laugh when a kid hollered, "Cleanup on aisle three!"

One day my boss handed me a pair of gloves, some bleach, tongs, and a long scraper. "I have a good job for you today," he said. Well, it must be true that in the spring, a young man's fancy turns to love. Someone was having safe sex on the picnic tables outside our school. We knew this because, unfortunately, the evidence was left behind. Of course, we had to take care of that situation immediately and keep monitoring it for the protection of our young students. It was my job to go around to all the tables—including some that had been moved to the ball field for ticket-taking—and . . . well, I'll let you figure out why I called myself "the condom catcher" and "the prophylactic police." All I needed was a hazmat suit.

Another of my jobs was cleaning goose droppings off the paved maintenance road leading to the ball field. Geese ran wild in our area, and their poop was everywhere. In the spring, our school had a day of field events for the kids. Their parents came to watch. We had races, relays, slip-and-slides—all kinds of outdoor activities. Someone had to clean up the area before that event, and I was elected.

I sometimes cut the grass, too. The grounds were large enough that we used a riding mower. We could mow close to the building with it, too, but we had to be careful. The building was on one floor, and the classroom windows opened out from the top. If someone opened one of the lower windows at the wrong time, it could have decapitated one of us.

Once when I was mowing near the building, I got close to an air conditioning unit that hid a nest. I had no idea about the nest. Suddenly a huge goose flew out from behind the air conditioner, went straight for me, and hit me right in the chest. It almost knocked me off the seat.

Don't show me the movie, or even the poster; I'm scared of birds. It's because they dive at you, and it's so quick, but the whole thing started when I was a little boy. Our next-door neighbors in Glen Ferris bred and sold parakeets. They were the same neighbors who had the nice uncle. Because we lived in a duplex, we could hear Mrs. P. through our kitchen wall, cooing to the birds. One time she invited Jane and me over to see some newborns. We'd never been in her house, but she had been telling us they had some eggs that were about to hatch. First of all, I had no idea what a newborn bird would look like. They have no feathers—in a word, gross! Second, I went over expecting to see a couple of birds in a cage, but what I got was an entire room of cages the size of refrigerators, all filled with loudly chirping birds. They fluttered and flew inside the cages. I didn't like being around them, even though I knew they couldn't get out.

Birds got inside the school sometimes, and because of the way many rooms were built, they could fly from room to room above the ceiling tiles. We never knew where they were. We could get called to a classroom to remove a bird, pop the tile expecting the bird to attack, and not even find it. In warm weather, windows were open in the gym. They were up high. One time a bird flew in and got into the custodians' break area. It was diving at us. I was scared to death, but I didn't want to show it. We tried to shoo the bird out of our room and get it to a door. "Let's get a net," I said. All we could think of was a volleyball net, and the other custodian went to the gym and got one. We each grabbed a couple corners, but the spaces were too big and the bird flew through the net. Finally we chased it to a corner, and it found another way out.

Dogs occasionally got into our building, and I had to catch them and get them out. We even had coyotes come across the ball fields. They were hungry, coming out for food where our students played at recess. For those, we called Animal Control.

Periodically we had lockdown drills at our school so that everyone could be prepared in case of danger. A lockdown drill is similar to a fire drill, except that the purpose is to lock every door in the building. If someone who constituted a threat—for example, a terrorist or even an escapee from the nearby county correctional institution—were to get inside, we didn't want that person to have a place to hide. A lockdown would limit access to our spaces, forcing the intruder to stay in the hallways. Teachers had to lock their classrooms and closets, the office personnel had their assignments, and the custodians had theirs.

One day a supervisor told me, "If this happens, Joe, if we're expecting trouble, you stand outside."

"What do you want me to do," I said, "dust him to death?"

33
Limping Along

I was covering a lot of ground at the intermediate school. Our facility, one of two on the campus, was built in a "pod" configuration and surrounded by other buildings, rolling grounds, and ball fields. In particular, I felt the hectic pace of my job when I walked. I was developing a limp. I had no pain, so I assumed it was something temporary, not a problem. Maybe I'd pulled a muscle in my right leg. I figured it would heal by itself.

I didn't realize my limp was noticeable to others until I was walking down the hall at school one day and one of the other custodians started mocking me. He was hobbling. I knew he wasn't being mean. This guy and I were friends, so I didn't get angry. I was glad he did it. It opened my eyes and let me see that my limp was worse than I'd thought.

I made an appointment with my doctor and asked him, "Why am I limping when I don't have any pain?" He started doing reflex tests on my arms and legs. I sat on the end of the examining table and he tapped my knees with a hammer and tested different places on my right leg. Then he had me stand up. When he put me on the ball of my right foot, my leg started to shake—fast. It was hard for me to keep my balance. My leg shook at other times, too. When I was getting up from a sitting position, it would just go up and down.

Based on the office visit—a visit without X-rays or MRIs—the doctor wasn't sure what the problem was. He gave me a couple theories, but nothing conclusive. There was no prescription for medication and no follow-up appointment scheduled, but I came back on my own. I had to. I was worried about my limp and my leg, so I made another appointment. The doctor mostly talked to me.

My condition got worse. I hadn't had pain in the beginning, but now it was painful for me to walk. Both hips burned and my right leg ached. I was losing feeling, too. I had numbness in my right leg, arm, and hand. I was dropping things, and a couple times I even fell. I had no warning; just went down.

I went back for yet another checkup. The doctor took some blood to see if I'd suffered a minor stroke and hadn't known it. He also recommended an MRI that would tell the same thing. I'm a person who wants to know what I'm dealing with, so I had the MRI.

One night the phone rang at home. It was a Friday, and it must have been 8 or 9 p.m. It was the doctor, calling me with the results. "Joe, I don't want to upset you," he said, "but you have a brain tumor." He went on: "I don't know if it's malignant, but I'm going to set up an appointment as quickly as I can for you to see a neurosurgeon."

It was a thirty-second conversation. I didn't say much because I was in shock. I'd expected the doctor's office to call during the day, and it wouldn't be the doctor himself. I'd expected to learn whether I'd had a stroke, not that I had a brain tumor. Now my doctor was sending my MRI results to a specialist. I'd known I might need another appointment, but now I was waiting for an appointment about a brain tumor. And it was urgent. Doctors don't say "as quickly as I can" for nothing.

Without any other information, I couldn't keep my mind out of the dark places. I thought a diagnosis of a brain tumor meant that I was screwed, as good as dead. Even though all the facts weren't in, I thought a good ending wasn't possible.

The first thing I did after I hung up from the doctor was to call my sister. It had been years since Jane and I had talked—maybe the trip to the casino with Mom had been the last time—but she was the one I wanted to tell. I didn't want to tell my sons yet, not until I found out if I had a malignant tumor, which would be life threatening. In the meantime, being alone with my diagnosis was too much for me to handle. I needed to share it.

When I called Jane, I got a recording, so I had two choices: leave a message or hang up. How could I say I had a brain tumor on an answering machine? I left a short message: "This is Joe. Call me. I need to talk."

It was two days before Jane called me back. I told her what I'd learned, but I had no other news and wouldn't until I went back to the doctor. That would be in about a week. In the meantime, I was in a daze. Waiting was torture, and I still had to go to work. At least there, I wasn't alone. I ended up telling two of the teachers I felt close to, and both said they'd have their church congregations pray for me. That did it. I felt like I had no hope.

At home I smoked too much and knocked myself out at night with beer. I was so nervous, and I had to calm myself, to soothe what nerves I still had. I could barely sleep.

Finally I got my appointment. As I drove into the parking lot, walked into the building, and got on the elevator, all I could think about was how my life could change in the next few minutes. I could find out I had six months to live. I knew that either my tumor would kill me or I'd have to go through some extensive treatment. The best-case scenario to me was that I'd have to have my head cut open and maybe end up a basket case afterward.

It seemed like I spent an eternity in the waiting room. It was probably only fifteen or twenty minutes; I wasn't keeping track — besides, I didn't even own a watch. I was so preoccupied with my own thoughts that I don't remember if the room was full or empty. I don't know how many people went in before I did, but after a while a door opened and my name was called.

I wasn't going for an examination that time. It was a consultation, and it took place in an office. I sat on the other side of a desk from the doctor, like they do on TV when people get the bad news. From the minute I laid eyes on the doctor, I was watching his face to see any clue, negative or positive, about what he was going to tell me. I got nothing.

He stood up and pulled some slides out of an envelope. They were slides of my brain. There were hundreds, but he had only a few that he put up for viewing. Then he stood for three or four minutes with his hand at the bottom of his chin, saying nothing but "Mmm-hmmm," while I waited. It was agonizing. I just wanted it to be over, whatever he was going to say, good or bad.

He finally sat down on the edge of the desk and said my tumor wasn't malignant. "It's the least dangerous kind, and very slow growing." I had to look down to make sure I wasn't dancing! I was trying to be cool, but I'd just passed a huge hurdle: *not malignant.*

He told me the tumor was about the size of a marble, and that if I could deal with it remaining in my brain, he didn't think it would harm me. If I wanted it out, he'd remove it, but that offer came with a warning.

"The tumor is resting on your right eardrum," he said. "It's in a bony area, hard to reach with traditional surgery. If we cut to reach it, the results could be bad." The doctor gave me three possibilities: deafness; sagging facial muscles on my right side, similar to the effects of a stroke; or death. He told me about an alternative to traditional surgery called Gamma Knife surgery that involved the use of radiation.

It would stop the tumor from growing and would shrink it over time. I didn't necessarily think it would work, but it was sounding good to me — especially compared with the other choice.

By then I was relaxing. I was the calmest I'd been in a week. I told him that if the treatment didn't involve getting my head cut open, I'd like to start with the Gamma Knife surgery. The doctor said he'd contact the facility in Kettering, Ohio, and get back to me with a surgery date.

Walking out of the doctor's office that day, I realized how close I'd come to dying. Of course, I'd known it since the first phone call, but now that I had a chance to be cured, I could face it. The doctor visit had been life changing, but not in the terrible way I'd feared. When I walked outside, everything looked brighter and more intense. I was so relieved that I smiled at everyone I passed. Not a bad day so far.

All of it had started with a limp. My limp was still present and so was the pain, but those early problems had gone to the back burner during the weeks after my diagnosis. Were they related? I didn't know.

The Gamma Knife surgery was scheduled six weeks in advance. The date of mine happened to be on my birthday, and I couldn't help thinking how ironic it would be if I died on the same date I'd been born. I hadn't been thinking of dying all the time, but after all, I was having brain surgery. I wasn't out of the woods by any means.

34
Cars

I bought a red sports car a month before my brain surgery, but I couldn't blame it on the tumor. I'd wanted a Mazda Miata for a while and had been looking for just the right one. At first I'd hoped to buy it new, but I found out I couldn't swing a new sports car on my budget.

I asked the Mazda salesman to call me if a clean, used one came in. I knew I was getting a convertible—most Miatas are convertibles—and I made only one stipulation. If the car was red, it had to have a tan interior—not black—and a tan cloth top. I lucked out when the salesman found one that fit my request perfectly. The car was five years old and had about 21,000 miles on it. Because it was so clean, it was still being featured in the showroom. So, in June of 2006, I reached a milestone when I purchased a car from a showroom with my own credit.

By the time I bought the Miata, I'd worked in my school district for nine years and had allowed myself to feel some job security. My money problems were starting to disappear, and I could actually qualify for a loan. It was a turning point in my life. I hated to remember what my boys rode around in when they were small.

When Mary and I had split up, everything important that we owned was in my name, and she let some bills go unpaid—including the mortgage. The house went into foreclosure. Mary had responsibility for a few other bills that didn't even amount to much, but the result was that I had no credit. On my first visitation with the boys, I couldn't have someone take me to pick up my own kids. I needed a car, and the only way I could buy one was from someone like the man across the street.

He lived across from my apartment building. I knew that he fixed up cars to sell for three hundred to five hundred dollars. They weren't all pretty, but they were dependable. When I came home from work, I'd go over to see what he was selling. One day I saw an Opel Kadett, gold and black. It had a few minor dents and rust spots, but it was $350, and he said he'd let me make payments. I snapped it up.

The man said the Opel had been his daughter's car. I knew then that he'd taken good care of it. His daughter had broken some rule, and he was going to show her who was boss by selling her car. It was early summer when I bought it. I could smell perfume in the car, which I thought was from the daughter and would go away soon.

As the weather got warmer, I expected the smell to disappear when I rolled down the windows, but the hotter it got, the more overwhelming the perfume became. I found out that the girl had lost the car because she'd been drinking and driving. She'd tried to cover up the smell from that drinking episode by pouring a whole bottle of perfume on the floor of her car. It took over a year for the smell to go away; I got so sick of that perfume that I ended up selling the Opel to a friend for a hundred dollars. He was divorced, too.

Cars had been an embarrassment to me for most of my life. So many of mine were beaters—the kind you might buy for a second car—only the beater was always my first car. I told people I used them to drive to work; I didn't say that I used them to drive everywhere.

I had a Ford Maverick that I called the snowmobile car, because in winter snow and road salt would fly up at me though the hole in the floor, which was so wide I could put my foot through it. Going through a mud puddle was the same; I got splashed. I also froze my tail off. The car had a heater, but it wasn't a good one. Even the insides of the windows would freeze up. I felt like Fred Flintstone riding along in the Flintmobile with his feet sticking out the bottom of the car, so I asked a convenience store clerk to save cardboard boxes for me, and I used those to cover the hole and protect myself from the weather. I'd tape plastic garbage bags around the flattened boxes to keep the cardboard dry. I guess I got about fifty miles per box.

Several of my cars had been red. The one I had loved most was the 1966 Mustang I'd talked Dad into buying when I was eighteen. I think it cost $2,800, and it was candy apple red. What a car! Even though it was our family car, I was the one who benefited most from my parents' purchase. By then Jane was out of the house, Mom and Dad spent many hours in their bedroom, and I had a driver's license. That Mustang was the biggest miracle of my teenage life.

The Miata was a miracle, too, and not just because I'd been able to afford it after owning a long string of clunkers. It was a sign of hope for me. In the weeks before my surgery, I burned up the back roads between my place and the intermediate school. When the sun was high I drove with the top down and the heat on my face. Even the payments stretching out before me spoke of the future. I won't say I didn't worry about the outcome of my surgery, but I had to believe it would turn out well.

35
Under the Gamma Knife

"I'm going with you when you have your surgery," my sister said. "In fact, I'll take you. You shouldn't go to the hospital alone."

Her offer was a relief; I couldn't think of anything lonelier than driving myself to a medical facility for brain surgery. I'd relaxed after learning that my tumor was benign; but, as the date of my appointment approached, I became apprehensive again. Even though the surgery would be non-invasive—meaning no one was going to cut into my head with a saw—it *was* a medical procedure. To me, the patient, it was worrisome and full of unknowns, even though the neurosurgeon had explained it.

The Gamma Knife was developed in Sweden in 1967. It isn't really a knife; more like a beam of radiation that precisely targets the affected tissue. It allows the doctor to treat diseased brain tissue while leaving surrounding tissue intact. The procedure is state of the art. It's called radiosurgery, and by the time mine was scheduled, well over two hundred thousand patients worldwide had already had it.

The Wallace Kettering Neuroscience Institute in Ohio is one of eighty-eight Gamma Knife sites in the United States. I was lucky to live so close to it. Mine would be an outpatient procedure, requiring most of one day. I could go home afterward.

My brain tumor had reunited me with my sister and my mother—again. Jane was taking me to Kettering, and we would go to Mom's afterward. That was one time I did not question having my family back in my life; I was thankful.

Jane picked me up at my apartment early on the morning of July eleventh, my fifty-eighth birthday. When we got to the medical center, she was shown to a waiting room, and I had to get ready. I knew that the first step, once I'd changed into a hospital gown, would be the addition of a metal frame—to my head. The "What to Expect" information on the facility's website says, "A lightweight frame is placed on the patient's head." I guess that's a polite way of saying "A lightweight frame is screwed to the patient's skull in four places, two on the forehead and two in back."

Jane says she watched them wheel me to the first location, the place where I had the frame attached, but I didn't look over at her. Maybe I was already sedated. They told me I would take something so that I wouldn't remember that part, and it worked; but later I was very much aware of the frame I was wearing like a strange hat. I knew how precise my treatment had to be, and that it depended on that frame staying in place. I kept touching it the way you do a loose tooth when you're a kid, to see if it moves.

The next step was a measuring process to help the doctors determine the path and dosage of the radiation. The treatment plan for each individual is calculated using a computer after the measurements are taken. Someone placed a clear dome full of holes into the metal frame on my head. Then they measured angles and distances. I couldn't see what they were doing, but it involved some kind of stick going into the various holes in the plastic dome. Then we waited.

One of the nurses brought me a birthday cake, which was very thoughtful. I think they sang to me, too. I felt no pain as I sat up in bed and talked to my sister and the medical staff. They came and went as the doctors developed my treatment plan. When it was time for my surgery, I was taken into an adjoining room and a heavier dome was placed in the head frame. I lay back on a table called the treatment couch, which is a far cry from a sofa; it's more like an MRI imaging station. When I realized that, my claustrophobia kicked in.

I'd had MRI scans when the doctors were trying to diagnose my limp and other symptoms. My older son had driven me to the first one, taking time off from his job, and when I got into that tunnel I freaked out. I couldn't do it. I would have done fine in an open MRI, which offers a space that isn't completely enclosed, but that wasn't possible for me. My brain scans required imaging with the highest contrast possible, and that came from traditional scanners. I had to reschedule that first appointment. My doctor prescribed Valium, and that worked. I had to be medicated or have some part of my body outside the tube; otherwise, I couldn't breathe. One other time I asked if I could have my little finger out, and they said no. So, Valium it was.

The surgery required that more than 200 gamma rays be focused on a pinpoint area in my head. If I moved even a tiny bit, the rays could be misdirected; therefore, the heavy helmet I was wearing was screwed into the machine, restricting any possible movement of my head. I asked for medicine to help me remain calm through the procedure, but the doctors wouldn't sedate me. They needed me to be alert.

My claustrophobia turned out not to be a factor because I went into the tube only as far as my chest. It didn't bother me a bit. In fact, I remember saying that I could have spent the night in that machine. I even joked to the doctor, "Don't worry, Doc. It ain't exactly brain surgery. Oh, never mind." And, with that, I lay very still so that the gamma rays could find their target.

Gamma Knife surgery doesn't change the patient instantly. The doctor told me my tumor would shrink slowly, over a period of months or even longer. I wouldn't notice anything unusual, but I might have a headache immediately after the procedure.

They removed the frame and put some medicine on the areas affected by the attachment process. I don't remember that step at all, but in a little while I was free to leave. Jane and I went to Mom's, and I fell asleep awhile on my mother's living room floor as Jane told Mom about our day. For me, the sweetest part was the knowledge that my surgery was over.

The first miracle of Gamma Knife surgery was the fact that I had no memory of the worst aspect—the frame—and only traces of the wounds where it had been attached to me. After they removed the frame, the medical staff had told me my head would be numb for a month, and it was. That was a strange feeling. When I went back to work, I would occasionally walk into things at school, for instance a light fixture jutting out from a wall. My head would bleed, but I wouldn't know, because I wouldn't feel it.

The second miracle would be the gamma rays invisibly working on my brain tumor over time. Without the surgery, my tumor would have grown and displaced something else inside my head. Now, with every day that passed, I was being healed; but I would need follow-up visits to the doctor to be sure the rays were doing their job.

36
Mom's Operation

I wasn't the only one having surgery. That same summer, Mom had had an operation to correct hardening of the arteries; or, rather, to reroute her blood flow, which was not reaching her feet. She was eighty-eight. Her thin legs and her feet were bright red, and nurses could not detect a pulse from her ankles.

It was my job to take Mom to the hospital on the day of her operation. Jane drove separately, arriving before we did and getting a wheelchair ready for Mom at the curb. When Mom saw that Jane had already arrived, she thought we were late—my fault, of course. "I could choke you," she said, forgetting the favor I was doing her and swiftly stirring up memories of my frightening and frustrating boyhood. She was hell on wheels that day, complaining about everything, and by the time she threatened to choke me, the feeling was mutual. Mom had no idea what Jane and I had to endure to get her set up for surgery.

Mom's doctor had made it clear that no surgery would take place if her lungs weren't determined to be in shape to survive it. He had ordered her to stop smoking and had prescribed two inhalers to fortify her respiratory system. She couldn't work either one. It wasn't just that her hands were weak from arthritis; she couldn't follow the directions regarding how far from her mouth to hold the inhaler, when to squeeze it, and when to breathe in. Coordinating all of that was too much for her. It was puzzling; why was Mom having so much trouble with directions? She had never seemed helpless.

Jane had ordered a twin-sized sleep sofa for her den in anticipation of Mom's need for help after the operation. As it turned out, she had to bring Mom to her house before the surgery just to administer the medications. Mom was a passive participant.

After we got to the hospital and completed the paperwork, the three of us sat down to wait for Mom to be called. Jane and I were on either side of her in a quiet little area of chairs and tables. I picked up a magazine. Suddenly Mom burst forth with a loud pronouncement: "That woman sitting across from us can't be that fat just from eating!" Damn, I wished she would think before she spoke. I brought the magazine up in front of my face.

After all of our preparation and waiting, the surgery was put off that day because the anesthesiologist refused to put Mom to sleep. He thought she would not make it through the procedure. Mom had been given a chest X-ray to determine her fitness for the operation, and it had revealed a spot on one of her lungs. The surgeon, with a surprising lack of tact, said, "If I had three guesses, the first two would be lung cancer."

Suddenly a vascular problem turned into much more. Jane and I were shocked. However, even the words "lung cancer" hadn't rattled Mom; when her surgeon had spoken with us, she had looked completely detached from the conversation that was all about her and flowing around her.

A pulmonary expert was called in. Mom had a CT scan and spent the night in the hospital awaiting his explanation of the scan results. Jane and I left the hospital in a daze. The word "Hospice" crept into our conversations. The next morning we were at Mom's bedside before seven, as directed, to catch the doctors on rounds and lend our support to our mother when the results were announced.

Mom's surgeon and the pulmonary doctor arrived together. "Hello there, young lady!" the specialist boomed to the frail patient sitting up in her bed, as though Mom had come into a shop to try on shoes. The verdict was not at all what had been predicted the day before; the spot on Mom's lung, as determined by the specialist, was very small and couldn't even be identified as a tumor; in fact, it didn't seem to be cause for concern at all.

Naturally, we brightened at the prognosis, which took us from cancer to "home free" in an instant and put Mom's vascular operation back on the schedule. Even though both doctors believed she most likely had emphysema after sixty-five years of smoking, they cleared her for surgery. The pulmonary doctor glad-handed her like a politician and then continued on his rounds.

Hours later, Mom was once again in the pre-op lineup, sitting in bed in a curtained alcove, when an Indian doctor in a lab coat came in to ask her some questions. She spoke with an accent, and I could see Mom tuning out, so I helped with the exchange. A few minutes later, when the woman had barely cleared the privacy curtain to leave, Mom looked at Jane and me and said, "I don't know where the doctor is, but the maid just left."

"She is your new anesthesiologist," we said.

What was happening with Mom? Was she nervous about her operation? It didn't seem so, but she was testing Jane and me, whether she realized it or not. We couldn't predict what she would say, or when, but we did know the volume would be high. Maybe her hearing aid was failing. She had returned it when she couldn't work the volume control. She wanted a simpler instrument. After the hearing aid was adjusted and returned to her, she insisted it was broken. Maybe the battery was dead. Whatever the cause, she was embarrassing us with her yelling. "Help, help!" she would call out like a drowning victim when she thought she'd waited long enough for whatever was next.

The surgery was performed and declared successful, but Mom's recovery was slow. Sometimes she seemed out of her mind. According to Jane, Mom tried more than once to escape from the hospital. She would ask visitors to help her get dressed in street clothes so that she could leave. She pulled the IV out of her arm once and repeatedly got out of bed. When she fell in her room, the staff ordered twenty-four-hour "babysitting" for her. For a while, she and her assigned companion solved jigsaw puzzles meant for children. And then, just like that, the effects of the anesthesia wore off and Mom was her old self, to our relief. Well, maybe not her *old* self—I wouldn't have been relieved at that—but her mind cleared and her sense of humor returned.

Mom was moved to the care center of a nursing home for a few weeks to complete her recuperation. Jane said Mom couldn't wait to get out of there and go home to her apartment, which we saw as a good sign. When she was released, my sister picked her up and took her home, and then the reality set in. As soon as they arrived, Mom sat down in her familiar place on the end of the couch, but she was lost—just lost.

She seemed not to grasp the joy we expected her to feel at coming home. She would sit and worry about this thing or that. Jane, who was listed on Mom's bank accounts, began paying her bills. Mom was supposed to continue using her two inhalers at home, a process that would have required constant monitoring—which we could not do, as both Jane and I worked. An organization called Comfort Keepers sent four people over to give Mom her medications, administer physical therapy as she began walking again, and keep a general eye on her. After a few weeks, the services tapered off and then stopped.

Mom continued to see the doctor for follow-up appointments. One of those times, Jane was on a business trip, and I took Mom to her appointment. I got a taste of what my sister had been doing for weeks. The waiting room was crowded, the doctor was running late, and Mom was a patient with no patience. "Hell's bells!" she said in her best outdoor voice, "Joe, how *long* have we been here?" Of course, all eyes were on us. It would have been a good time to hide.

37
He's Back

Mom was on the mend. My brain tumor, which could have been life-threatening, was now shrinking, and I had a new sports car. It doesn't get better than that, except for some reason the scariest ghost of my life picked that time to return to my dreams.

I called my sister one night, years after the event, to tell her about seeing the ghost in the overcoat. "My nightmares are back," I said. "I'm afraid to go to sleep." It was dark outside, and quiet in a way that makes you wish somebody would do something—start a car, throw a pan, anything. I was sixty years old, and in my mind that's too old to be worried you're going to lose it over some dream about a ghost.

"What nightmares?" Jane knew nothing of the ghost I'd seen in the hall of the kindergarten school. Why would I tell her I'd seen a ghost? Why would I tell anyone? It had taken me years to tell Dave it hadn't been a prowler that had freaked me out the night I'd called him to rescue me. I finally told him it was a ghost. I thought I owed him that.

This time I hadn't actually seen the ghost again, but he was invading my sleep. It had been two years since I'd left the kindergarten school for the intermediate school. My new school had been built about a mile from a cemetery. Was that it? Was the location of a building behind my nightmares? What the hell possessed people to disturb the dead, anyway? Didn't they learn anything from movies like *Poltergeist*?

I didn't really know that bodies had been disturbed. I just hoped the man in the overcoat wasn't actually going to follow me to the intermediate school. At least I was working days; I couldn't have faced the possibility of seeing that bastard again at night, on the job. The dreams were enough. The way I felt the night I called Jane, scared to lie down and shut my eyes, it was time to share my story. I hoped she'd believe me, but at that point I just needed a friend. I was tired of facing that crap alone. I was isolated in my apartment. The light from the kitchen, where I stood, made shadows across the living room. The other rooms were dark. My eyes kept shifting to the hallway, the extra bedroom, the bathroom door, and my room with its sweaty sheets.

"I thought I was rid of him," I said. "I dreamed about that son of a bitch for five years, and then the dreams finally stopped. I thought I was free." And I told her my story.

"After I first saw him, I was a mess. I started having nightmares and had to knock myself out with beer or NyQuil just to fall asleep, and tonight I wish I had something to take. I can't go through this again."

Jane surprised me when she said, "I thought I saw a ghost once. It didn't jump out and say 'Boo,' but I don't know what else it could have been."

"Tell me about it."

"When I was living in Connecticut, I had a friend who'd come to America from Latvia, a little country in Northern Europe between Russia and the Baltic Sea. Her name was Leydia. She was a business acquaintance, but she really took to me; called me Janie. I only met her in person a couple times, but we would talk on the phone. We eventually lost touch, so I don't know if she was dead or alive when this happened.

"Anyway, one summer evening I went to the Brooklyn Fair. It's a country fair on fifteen acres with livestock, food, contests, and entertainment. After I'd looked around the main exhibit area, I walked away from the crowd toward a ride, a set of swings near the perimeter of the fair, out where people might try to sneak in. It was almost deserted there. The sun had set, but it wasn't dark. I remember an expanse of green grass all around me.

"Suddenly I saw Leydia coming toward me across the grass. She was wearing tan slacks and a plaid blouse. She seemed to be walking faster than I was, and her gait was smooth. As we closed the distance between us, I was ready with a greeting, but she wasn't looking at me. She passed me without speaking. It was so quick and strange that I whirled around to call her name, but I didn't make a sound, because no one was there.

"She couldn't have gotten lost in the crowd," Jane said. "There *was* no crowd. I still wonder what I saw. I wasn't scared, just puzzled. I know it was Leydia floating past me that evening, but was it a ghost?"

Jane's story made me feel better, but it didn't solve my problem. I couldn't believe my luck when the ghost in the overcoat went away on its own, and I could return to a halfway normal life.

38
Writing Out Loud

Jane and I began spending more time together. We got to know each other again and discovered that we liked one another's company. We had more in common than either of us would have guessed. Of course, our family of origin was a natural topic, as were our own families and our jobs as we shared how we had spent the last twenty-plus years.

We found that we laughed at many of the same things. Who else would remember Dad's corny jokes, told over and over, or appreciate Mom's quick, edgy wit like a sibling? We made our own jokes, too, and sometimes we laughed until we cried. Mom always said Jane lacked a sense of humor, but I think Jane lacked *Mom's* sense of humor, which isn't the same thing at all. I loved to hear my sister laugh.

Jane and I discovered that both of us were compulsively early. As our friendship bloomed, we met at restaurants or the movies, often pulling into adjacent parking spots within moments of one another, ten or fifteen minutes ahead of schedule. Over the months, we went to the gambling casino and the race track. The casino was Jane's greater interest, so she took a book to read at the track while I studied the racing form. It was all very companionable.

In good weather we sat together on my little back porch. Mom and I had done the same thing a few times at her place. Sitting side by side, looking out toward the trees, was good for talking. Jane and I started calling it porch time. After missing so many years of each other's lives, we had a lot to say.

"I've always thought you were Mom's golden child," Jane told me one day.

"I thought *you* were," I said. "You were smart and always had your act together."

"But you were popular. That's what Mom wanted for me. You were good-looking, and you dated in high school. I was a plain girl, a bookworm with no boyfriends."

"I didn't think I was good-looking at all. I had no self-confidence."

My sister and I had seen in each other what we envied, what we thought we lacked. We had missed so much by drifting apart, but had we ever known each other on the inside?

We tooled around in the Miata with the top down, talking above the wind and making plans. We became great friends. I learned that my sister had gone to Romania and was writing a memoir about her trip. When Jane had turned sixteen, she got a portable typewriter for her birthday. She wanted it because she had an idea for a book, a book about us, that she called *Jody and Me*. She didn't get very far with the writing—a few chapters—but I loved that book. Maybe it's a natural reaction when one is a subject of a story.

By the fall of 2006, Jane and I were talking about writing a book together. I had a story to tell, but I wasn't going to sit down and type it out. That would have been agonizing: I'm a slow typist, and I didn't have any desire to try what my sister could already do so much better. She was still writing her book about Romania, but we began work on *Mr. Joe* around Halloween. The idea of the book had taken hold, and the stories were pouring out of me. We could be anywhere, and I'd remember a tale from the kindergarten school, or the meat plant, or my childhood. I'd start talking enthusiastically about some experience, and Jane would stop me every time. "Don't tell me now," she would say. "I won't remember it."

"But *I will*." I didn't understand why the timing was such a big deal.

"You'll have to tell it again. Your words could change. The story might not come out exactly the same way." Jane was a stickler about capturing my stories as I told them. She knew we needed to record each one, but I couldn't always control when a story popped into my mind. That was a process we had to work out.

She had installed speech recognition software on her computer, so we spent a few evenings training it to recognize my voice. I didn't like talking to the computer. I felt self-conscious, and the program kept getting my words wrong. Jane would have to go in afterward and clean the piece up. That method was too slow and inaccurate for what we were doing. By the time both of us had tried to make readable passages out of what I said, we had lost the flavor of it.

We decided to meet on a regular basis and try something else. Once or twice a week we sat together in Jane's home office. I would talk, and she would type what I said. She could go into the documents later and make them fit together. If I thought of a story when we weren't working, I e-mailed her a reminder. The note could contain whole, coherent sentences: "Remind me to talk about the police demonstration next time" or just a few words: "Butterfly garden." When we met, we had those notes as starter subjects.

The files for *Mr. Joe* accumulated slowly, as Jane was busy with her own book, but each meeting gave us a chance to become reacquainted and share stories from our lives. Because we had been apart so long, the stories I was telling about my work, my family life—even my childhood—were new to her. My life began to unfold on her computer screen. I still couldn't picture a completed book. "After we're done," I said, "I won't be upset if we throw it in the fireplace." To me, the best part was the experience of writing a book with my sister.

One night we were on the phone. Jane had been watching a documentary about the Black Hills of South Dakota. "Do you know where I'd like to go?" she said. "I want to see Mount Rushmore."

"I've wanted to see it for twenty years," I said.

"Well, let's go." And that quickly, we were planning a road trip to a little town a few miles from Mount Rushmore National Memorial. The name of the town, Spearfish, made me smile every time we said it. I was beyond excited. My trip to Peggy's in 1998 had been my last vacation.

The drive from Ohio was over 1,200 miles and would take us eighteen and one-half hours, according to MapQuest. Those calculations didn't take stops into account, and for us there would be many stops. To paraphrase Will Rogers, I never met a rest area I didn't like.

Lately I'd been dealing with a new challenge: I didn't have a lot of notice when I had to go. I was traveling with my other best friend, Imodium, which is a drug used to control diarrhea. I had to take it for peace of mind. We could be driving twelve to thirteen hours a day.

On a June morning in 2007 we loaded Jane's PT Cruiser and set out for Spearfish. We took turns driving as we crossed Indiana, Illinois, and Iowa; dipped into Nebraska; and headed to the western edge of South Dakota. We stopped at every rest area from Cincinnati to Spearfish, just in case. We didn't miss one. Jane was patient with the stops, especially considering that they all turned out to be false alarms, thanks to the Imodium.

We ate at Cracker Barrels and then fought to stay awake. We gambled in Iowa; we stopped to tour the "World's Only Corn Palace"; but mostly we rode. The hours flew by as our trip became a talk-a-thon. We paid twenty dollars in the pouring rain to see the huge carving-in-progress of Chief Crazy Horse on a mountainside and later saw the same thing from the highway for free, minus the rain.

I saw Mount Rushmore with my heart. The minute I glimpsed those majestic carvings, I felt a surge of joy and patriotic pride. I could hardly believe I was standing there. By the time we walked the Avenue of Flags toward the memorial, I had to wipe my eyes. My legs wouldn't let me walk the path around the mountain, but the view from the visitor center was glorious. I could barely take my eyes off it.

The trip to South Dakota was everything I'd wanted and more. My sister and I had been compatible traveling companions. Our friendship was stronger than ever.

Jane finished her memoir, *It Started with Dracula*, in 2010. A year later it was published. In the meantime, we had accelerated our writing schedule, and in September 2011 we had a first draft of *Mr. Joe*. "We need to have some people read this," Jane said, "to get their reactions." We were thrilled to make copies for the volunteers, with one for me as well. After the others were distributed, I sat down to read Mr. Joe from start to finish for the first time. That reading threw me into a tailspin.

First of all, I was reading material that I had shared with Jane but had not expected to find in the book. Our work sessions had been great, but I didn't know when I was off the record and when I wasn't. Jane had told me about one author who told it like it was in her travel memoir because she didn't think anyone would read her book. I told Jane everything that came to mind for the same reason. The other lady's book became a best seller.

Now people we knew were reading things about me that I had kept secret for years, things I didn't intend to reveal, things that could embarrass me or hurt other people's feelings. Even the parts I had intended for print seemed larger, wilder, and more threatening than they had in Jane's office. People were going to read that I'd seen ghosts and make fun of me. My sons were going to read about my financial troubles and be embarrassed. My school administrators were going to realize I'd written about our district. I thought I might to have to move away and tell no one my destination.

I didn't need anything else to upset me, but my reading of *Mr. Joe* brought back the most painful times of my life, including my childhood. I felt like I was living through them again. Jane had told me I might experience some strong emotions as the book progressed. We couldn't stop the memories—I had to go through that part—but our writing process had to change.

I'd been writing out loud and had no idea what was ending up on the pages of *Mr. Joe.* Jane had been using her creative talents to fill gaps in the stories, and some of her statements by "me" were off base. As the second draft took shape, she added a signature line at the end of each chapter. I was officially going to approve the book at every stage. When she completed a chapter, she read it to me; later I would read them all for myself before anyone else saw the manuscript. If I had no corrections, I would sign on the line.

The approval process eliminated the risks inherent in merging our very different writing styles. My sister and I were learning to meet in the middle.

39
Mia

In my search for a romantic relationship, I'd never been able to find anyone who was considerate the way I was, and I was tired of trying. That summed up my feelings on love until I met Mia at age fifty-eight. We met through an online dating site I'd joined at my son Jay's urging. He thought I needed someone. Does this sound familiar? Does it sound like the beginning of the Beth story, or maybe the Peggy story, when my older son Mike did essentially the same thing?

My boys cared about me and wanted me to be happy. By then, both were involved in significant relationships. So, in the spring following my Gamma Knife surgery, I saw Mia's picture on the dating site and contacted her. I enjoyed "talking" to her—which actually meant that we were writing back and forth online—but it was a while until I even knew where she lived.

Mia was interested in subjects that appealed to me: heaven, the Universe, astrology, the life cycle, and the soul. The book about heaven I'd read on the plane in 1998 had kick-started my fascination. Early in our friendship, Mia mentioned another book to me: *The Seat of the Soul*, by Gary Zukav, but I didn't follow up.

Besides the fact that we hit it off so well, our online correspondence was a nice escape for me. My health was going downhill, and that was worrisome. Nearly a year after the discovery and subsequent treatment of my brain tumor, I was still limping and didn't know why. In addition to the limp, I was weak and had been losing feeling on my right side. At that point, I was trying to diagnose myself.

When I found out that Mia and I lived at opposite ends of the same state, it was good news. I knew I liked her, but I'd had such bad luck with women that I wanted someone far away so that I could control the pace of the relationship. I didn't want to be in a position to move in with anyone else, even though I was still in my basement apartment and hadn't owned a home since my marriage ended. Mia, a widow, had a house, but it was four hours away—inconvenient. I realized that if I went to see her, I'd be taking the long way home again—not as an avoidance tactic, but literally.

The first time I met Mia in person, I drove to her hometown. I couldn't wait to meet her. I was glad to see that she was attractive; her hair was fixed and she had on a flattering outfit. After all the time we'd spent online, I was comfortable around her right away. In fact, I liked everything about her. She was a good person, not at all demanding and very considerate of me. I could tell there wasn't a trace of Mom in her. That was a victory.

Our first meeting was such a success that every couple of months, when I had vacation time, I went back to Mia's. We fell into a pattern. We took turns cooking or ate out. We walked in the malls for exercise. Moneywise, we shared the costs of food and outings. Mia became a positive force in my life. She cared for me, and by that I mean that she liked me and she helped me to take care of myself.

I wanted to help her, too. Mia had been suffering from depression since losing her husband of thirty years. Being with me gave her a distraction and an outlet. In addition to our shared activities, we could talk about many things. When she spoke about herself, I was a good listener. I could make her laugh.

During one of our visits, she gave me a copy of *The Seat of the Soul*, which I started reading after I got home. It was like trying to read the phone book: nothing stuck. The words didn't even make sense to me, so after thirty or forty pages, I put it down. Mia said I just wasn't ready for it yet. "Don't force yourself," she said. "When you're ready, you'll read it."

In the meantime, I was a physical mess: I was limping more, losing strength, and hurting. Even though I was frightened by the possibilities, I had to find out what was wrong with me. My doctor kept ordering tests. They tested me for some badass diseases, like leukemia. It was nerve-racking to wait for the results, a relief when the worst ones came back negative, and ultimately disappointing when the tests failed to identify the source of my trouble.

In order to do my job, I had to go to a pain specialist for shots. Even then it seemed that my legs and hips hurt all the time. The pain got so bad that in August of 2007 I went on medical leave. The timing wasn't great—near the start of another school year—but I couldn't handle the physical work. Once my leave started, I was alone twenty-four hours a day. Being isolated for such long stretches of time amplified my worries about my health. I was so scared that I couldn't stand my own thoughts. Besides that, I was failing miserably at taking care of myself. I wasn't eating right, and I started drinking; when I went out for groceries, I'd get beer.

I didn't go to the store often because, by then, maneuvering my car seemed like a lot of trouble. I had to haul my right leg into the Miata with my hands, so right away you know that I wasn't very effective at using the gas pedal and brake. It was also hard to shift gears, with my right hand weak and going numb. I had no desire to negotiate busy store parking lots; however, the road to Mia's was almost straight interstate. I could handle that, and I didn't want to be lying on my couch alone with no groceries. I wanted to be with her.

Once I got in the car, I was fine. As summer passed into fall, I would have to watch the weather, because the Miata didn't perform well in snow. Otherwise, the drive was routine. I would leave early in the morning before rush hour, when traffic was light, and arrive four hours later at Mia's door. Being there was a great relief, because I was falling apart mentally. I still didn't know what was wrong with me, and neither did the doctor. Mia was a caretaker by nature. She had cared for her husband when he was ill, and now it gave her pleasure to have me there, even though I was in poor health.

I spent more and more time at Mia's. She talked to me about the afterlife, astrology, and the Universe. For my birthday that summer, she took me to a psychic. Mia did more to change my life than any other woman I'd ever been with. Sometimes I thought she was casual about maintaining her appearance, but maybe we both were.

I still hadn't read *The Seat of the Soul*. Between the book I'd found on the plane years before and Mia's influence, the seeds had been planted, but they hadn't sprouted. Every once in a while I'd sit down and read something from it, but I wasn't enjoying it and still didn't understand it. I liked Sylvia Browne's books, but *The Seat of the Soul* was difficult for me. I only kept trying because Mia thought it was so important.

Mia treated me well, but I couldn't escape the reality of my declining condition. It panicked me. I went home for doctor appointments, during which he and I would discuss my symptoms. The pain doctor gave me treatments on a limited basis, and after each treatment I headed right back to Mia's. Being with her was so much better than staying home, but even under Mia's watchful care, I didn't feel right. I wasn't just physically weak; I was depressed. I reached a low point during that time when I thought I was going to die. You can talk about not caring if you live, but I really thought that might be "it" for me. Thoughts of suicide entered my mind. I wouldn't have killed myself, but . . . if I'd been hit by a bus, I wouldn't have minded.

I knew something had to change. I was beyond desperate. I had to figure out whether to get busy dying or get busy living. Mia and the doctor were helping me on the outside, but I needed something to help me on the *inside*. I was ready for *The Seat of the Soul.*

40
Seat of My Soul

I was home from Mia's for yet another doctor appointment when I realized I didn't like my own life. That's a hell of a thing to face when you're already down, not to mention alone.

I still had *The Seat of the Soul*, and I picked it up and took it with me when I went back to Mia's. She had a part-time job, so sometimes I was in her house alone. I didn't have much to do when she was at work, so one day I started reading the book again. I had to start at the beginning; there was no way I could remember what I'd read before.

That time, *The Seat of the Soul* started making sense to me, and that was only the beginning of the miracle. There is no doubt in my mind that I'd been grasping for something to believe in, because I finally got it. I read the book straight through, staying up all night to finish it. It had a lot of credibility for me. The author, Gary Zukav, wasn't just somebody with a theory; he was a professor of quantum physics.

Before I embraced Zukav's book, I seemed to have one problem after another—debt, credit, loneliness, drinking. I would get through one crisis and something else would hit me. I thought I was destined for bad luck and misery. The truth is, I was afraid to face my problems. I always had to know what they were, but then I often decided to ignore them. During my divorce, I'd learned to put my problems out of my mind so they wouldn't depress me or drive me crazy. Putting them on the back burner worked for a while, but I let them go too long. Eventually my problems piled onto one another until I was overwhelmed.

The Seat of the Soul gave me hope for the first time in years. By answering every question I'd ever had about God and the afterlife, the book showed me there was something "out there" that was on my side. Mia called it my "aha" moment. All I knew was that from that moment on, even when I was by myself, I wasn't alone any more. I embraced that book completely, and it changed my life.

The Seat of the Soul taught me that I finally had an ally beyond the physical realm—a spiritual Universe that connected to me and would help me. This was something Mia already knew and practiced. She told me how to ask in a specific way, by saying "Thanks and praises" before—not after—my requests. I loved the idea that we can ask for help from the Universe for anything, large or small, and get it. Never in my life had I felt that assurance, not when I was attending revivals and learning to preach; not even the times I had found peace in the Catholic Church.

I started with small requests. For example, I asked the Universe to help me locate some lost papers. I asked it to help me find a rest area on the highway. When I misplaced my car keys, I asked the Universe to help me find them. I even asked for money, and the Universe always answered. I bet I did it fifty times, for little things, and it always worked. To finally feel that power was miraculous! I hesitated to ask for anything big, like winning the lottery; I was afraid that if it didn't work, I wouldn't believe, and I loved believing.

Mia taught me never to say, "What else can go wrong?" because the Universe answers every question. If I asked in a negative way, it might just show me what else could go wrong. I had gone through so much with Mom, and then in my marriage, and later trying to do the best I could with the boys, that I had developed a doomsday attitude, always thinking I couldn't get a break. Once I understood that, I began to change my thinking: I assumed something good was going to come my way. I'd always looked for the good in people, but this was even better. I knew I was not going to be let down.

The Seat of the Soul taught me about karma and accountability. *Karma* is our destiny in balance. It means that all of us are accountable for everything we do, large or small, good or bad. Every action will come back to us in kind, and every person's actions contribute to the karma of the Universe. When we make a decision, our choices affect others and ultimately come back to us. It makes sense to do what is right; if we do the wrong thing, we are held accountable, and that's karma.

According to the book, each person has a physical self and a soul. The physical self lasts one lifetime, but the soul can return in other bodies. Our physical selves are on earth to learn lessons that will ultimately help our souls to heal. If we intentionally do wrong, we will have to spend more time on earth learning our lessons.

After reading *The Seat of the Soul*, I'm not intimidated or unduly impressed by rich people or those in high positions. I learned by reading that anyone who is still here on earth, regardless of wealth or station, still has lessons to learn. The rich and mighty are no better than

I am; if they are still here, then they are still learning—just like the rest of us.

I realized through reading Zukav's book that we can face our troubles or run and hide. After I understood karma, I decided to face my problems so that my next life would be better. Running away had always been my main fault. Lately, with my health going down the tubes, I'd been consumed with thoughts of dying. A few times I'd even thought about willfully ending my life, and that would have been the ultimate act of running. Believing the theories in *The Seat of the Soul* gave me the courage I needed to pull out of it.

As I began to face my problems, I noticed a positive change in my outlook. Every time I saw even a small result, my belief grew and my pile of worries got smaller. If I had been bugged about a debt, I settled it. As I faced each challenge, I learned that people would work with me, and a weight lifted off me. My problems didn't go away as I got better, but they didn't seem so big or overwhelming.

The Seat of the Soul contained other ideas that I could relate to my life. I liked the idea that some people are five-sensory, believing only what their senses tell them, and others are multi-sensory—able to perceive what is beyond the physical world. The five-sensory people believe that this lifetime is all; there is no afterlife. I knew that I was multi-sensory, having seen ghosts and now talking to the cosmic Universe.

There's a chapter titled "Intuition" that intrigued me. The idea was this: if we are open to it, people on the Other Side can plant information in our minds. If heaven is similar to the world we know, and the people there are working on the same kinds of projects we are, then they can give us the gift of their experience and discoveries. It's called *intuition*, but we're actually being told. Once we recognize that possibility and allow it to happen, the Universe helps us learn how to use the information. Many people block such messages out or don't recognize their intuitive moments. After I read "Intuition," I had another "aha" moment remembering some of my hunches and how they had helped me—from the lights in the gambling examples to my premonition of the car crash in Glen Ferris that would have killed me, had I not recognized the scene from a dream and pulled off the road.

The Seat of the Soul taught me to be positive and to love myself. Because of that book, I realized that I could control my destiny, and I wanted to live. Once I implemented the choice to be positive, it all went uphill. I started being nicer and wishing good thoughts for other people. What a feeling to know that the more good I put out, the more good would come to me. I was helping everybody!

As a result of reading *The Seat of the Soul*, I decided to hang around this planet for a while and get better. Now that my mind was going in the right direction, I wanted to get my body into shape. I believed that my physical self was out of alignment with my soul. Mia had given me the care I needed, and *The Seat of the Soul* had given me the incentive to love myself and to take care of myself, so I returned home.

A week before my medical leave ended—the doctor had already signed my note to go back to work—I went in for an epidural, which is an injection of drugs to block pain in a particular area of the body. I had to have somebody drive me, and I had to agree to wait thirty minutes after the treatment before leaving, or they wouldn't give me the shot. My friend Bob drove me to the appointment. He told me he was scared when he saw me, because he thought I was dying. Well, in spite of my newfound beliefs, I scared myself.

My right side had been weak for months, and I had been falling. I had crutches and a cane, but even with that support, my right side would collapse and down I'd go. I could be anywhere—the grocery store, a mall, or out on the sidewalk. Every curb, step, or incline was a danger zone to me, because my right foot wouldn't go up when it was supposed to. Once I lost my balance, I couldn't correct myself; if there was nothing solid to grab, I was going down. I had to learn how to fall in order to minimize my injuries. I would try to hit the ground and roll, much as I had when bailing out of cars in my hitchhiking days.

People would see me fall and think I was drunk. That hurt. Instead of helping me, they judged me. They would mutter that I was disgusting, noting the time of day: "Drunk already! It's only ten in the morning!" Some would tell their children to stay away from me. I remember falling inside a mall in Middletown, Ohio. A little girl eight or nine years old came over to help me, and suddenly I heard, "Get away from him! What's wrong with you?" It was her mother. Imagine the humiliation of falling in a public place and then hearing, "Don't get near him," or "Don't touch him." I quit going out.

The epidural didn't seem to help at all. I could barely walk, even after the thirty minutes were up. When the pain doctor saw that, he told me I needed to contact a specialist, so I made an appointment with a neurologist. He was pretty sure he knew what my trouble was: a spinal disease called cervical myelopathy. The discs in my back were closing in on my nerves and were going to sever them if I didn't have an operation very soon. "You'll be paralyzed from the neck down," was what he said. "Once that happens, Joe, I can't fix you."

It was November when I was finally diagnosed. I was relieved to have a name for my disease and even more relieved that it could be fixed; but then the neurologist delivered a blow: "You aren't in shape right now to survive the surgery."

Now I had something very big to ask the Universe.

41
Moving Mom

While I was trying to get a grip on my declining health, Mom had been losing ground, too, in a different way. She'd recovered from her vascular surgery but, after all, she was eighty-eight. She was frail even before the surgery; she weighed about ninety pounds, couldn't walk far, and carried her groceries from the car one or two items at a time. She took frequent naps and, according to Jane, was giving up activities she had enjoyed. But weren't those normal signs of aging?

Most recently, Mom had had trouble working the simplest appliances. Jane had given her a low-end tape player so that she could play some old cassettes of big band music. The instructions were basic, but Jane wrote them out anyway: Put the tape in. Push Play. When the tape finishes, push Eject. Mom couldn't do it. She also began to obsess about clocks.

Mom had an old alarm clock on her coffee table that she loved. It had no electronic parts; she wound it manually and flipped one button to set the alarm. The numbers and hands were easy to see. When that clock wore out, finding a replacement was a challenge. Jane and I bought one clock after another, some digital, and Mom hated them all. We didn't realize why. We thought she should get with the times.

One day Mom called my sister because her microwave was beeping and she didn't know how to shut it off. Even though Mom kept to herself and was not well acquainted with her neighbors, she also ran next door in a panic. The microwave incident provoked the neighbor to say to her, "You should not be living alone." Another neighbor took her a casserole. Mom was seen as helpless and in need of attention, even though my sister stopped by often.

Mom started saying after making a mistake, "You know, I used to be smarter than both of you." She knew she was losing her mental faculties, and that hurt her more than anything. It destroyed her.

Jane took Mom to the doctor for an Alzheimer's test. There were thirty items on it, and Mom got twenty-five right, a score too high to classify her as an Alzheimer's patient. Jane and I still thought it was time Mom moved to a safer environment, and we knew just the one: an independent living facility where she'd played bridge for years. It was nearby and familiar. She wouldn't have to leave the part of town she knew best. When an apartment opened up, we took her to see it. My sister was particularly interested in what the woman who showed us around would think of Mom. Would she notice anything? Jane even asked her, "Do you think our mother will fit in here?" We both gave a sigh of relief when she said yes, and we took the apartment.

They told us during our tour that a cat had the run of the place. Cute, unless you hated cats, as Mom did. The cat was a concern because we had discussed getting Mom an electric scooter. The distance to the dining hall was prohibitive for her, and we didn't want her to skip meals. Jane made a crack about the cat. I kept quiet, but we were thinking the same thing. If Mom had a scooter and Fluffy was in the wrong place at the wrong time, well, I wouldn't want to be that cat. Neither of us knew enough about cats to realize that the more likely scenario would have the cat way ahead of Mom.

The facility had a nonsmoking rule, and the penalty was eviction if an employee even smelled smoke in one of the units. It was harsh, especially now that Mom was back to smoking. Had we convinced her that she could only have a cigarette outside on her patio? It was just another thing to make us cross our fingers. If Mom didn't smoke in her room or murder the cat, maybe we would be all right.

We decided to involve Mom as little as possible in her own move. She knew she was moving, but she seemed detached. Jane made the preparations. It turned out that some of Mom's furniture was falling apart and had to be replaced. Jane bought her a new couch. She got Mom's favorite lamps rewired and bought new shades for them. She bought Mom new sheets and towels. We wanted everything to be nice.

On moving day, we settled Mom in Jane's living room in front of the TV. She was more likely to fall asleep than to go around my sister's condo getting into any trouble. We directed the movers at Mom's old place and then unpacked her boxes in the new apartment, putting everything away. We filled her drawers and closet, made her bed, got her bathroom ready, and set out some framed pictures. By evening, the apartment glowed with warm light. The manager sent a plate of freshly baked cookies that we put out on the dining room table. When everything was ready, we went to get Mom. We wanted her to walk in, love her new apartment, and have no work to do.

You might wonder why, after all the grief and sadness of our childhood, we tried so hard to give Mom a perfect transition to her new home. It's a valid question; after all, what kind of home did she give us? Maybe it was our training kicking in: appearances are everything. Or maybe we knew we'd pulled a fast one by getting Mom into independent living before her mind crumbled away.

Mom wasn't a threat to me any longer. She had a short temper sometimes and occasionally blurted out embarrassing remarks, but drinking wasn't a factor. Jane dealt with her more than I did, so her point of view was different. I could see that Jane was tired. We needed this arrangement to work.

Mom's place looked like a movie set when we finished. It was perfect. When we brought her in, she looked around as if she didn't recognize her own furniture—and, to be fair, she hadn't seen some of it before, or the arrangement. After Jane and I had worked so hard, I was disappointed in Mom's reaction, which I thought was neutral at best. A few people stopped in to welcome her that evening. She didn't say a lot, but she smiled. We noticed that instead of offering the cookies to her visitors, Mom moved the whole plate into her bedroom, where it would sit on the bottom shelf of the night table until every crumb was gone.

I was practically delirious with joy to get home that night. I was so glad to be alone that I could have rooted like a hog on the living room rug. Surely Jane felt the same way.

After a period of confusion, Mom began to blend into the fabric of life in the independent living facility. Though she was not the most social person or the smoothest talker, she made friends, which was the best outcome we could have hoped for. One day she saw a woman get out of a car and thought she was seeing someone she knew from Glen Ferris. "Mildred!" she exclaimed happily to the woman from England, and they became fast friends in spite of the mistaken identity. One day we went over to take Mom to lunch and saw a look on her face of almost childlike happiness to be sitting on the sofa beside her new best friend.

The receptionist was protective of Mom. When I came to visit, I was given the third degree. They liked her there. It was only later that things turned chilly.

Mom had a hard time. She couldn't always find her way to and from her living quarters. She had a phone in her new apartment, but she didn't know how to use it. She'd call the desk and have the receptionist put her outgoing calls through. Mom called Jane a lot, and the first thing my sister heard was our mother shouting her name: "JANE!" That can wear you out.

Sometimes Mom and "Mildred" would go outside looking for Mom's car with an outing in mind. Fortunately, they never found it, but their adventures kept the staff on its collective toes. Mom began to dream of the past, when Jane and I were children, and she would wake up disoriented. She would then go to the front desk to ask if anyone had seen her little boy—me. She began to ask that her meals be brought to her, and then she would store them in her refrigerator, barely touched. "I think I'd like to go home," she'd say from time to time.

"Where is home?" Jane or I would ask. Once she said, "The Glen Ferris Inn."

Mom was evicted after seven months. It wasn't from cigarettes or a dead cat; the deciding moment came when she fell and was taken to the hospital in an ambulance. The facility asked us to hire someone to watch her twenty-four-hours a day. Once Jane and I realized what the hourly rate would be, we did the math: hiring a sitter for Mom would increase her monthly fees by *ten thousand dollars*! We couldn't do it. We wouldn't do it, so one day Jane received an official letter giving us a date to have Mom moved out.

We had about a month to find Mom another place. We had discovered that being in her former neighborhood wasn't a plus for her: she was always inside, so location didn't matter except to those of us going back and forth. We found a suitable retirement home a few miles away, but Mom failed the interview, which included questions such as "What season is it?" She couldn't answer that one without looking out her patio door. Mom could no longer qualify for independent living, and we were desperate to find her a home.

All that summer I was suffering. I knew that Jane needed help with Mom, but I was also worried about myself, my own health. Running around to retirement homes didn't help my legs any. When it came to moving, I cleaned because I was too weak to lift boxes and slide furniture around.

It was time to strategize. How many times could we move Mom? We'd been trying to get her into "normal" places when we suspected she wasn't normal at all. Jane decided to have Mom tested again for Alzheimer's. That time, the doctor said she had a mild case. It was progressing.

With an official diagnosis, we were able to get Mom into a facility for Alzheimer patients. They could take her in assisted living within the short time frame we needed. This time the staff understood Mom's condition going in, and they assured Jane and me that they intended to keep her. We were so relieved we nearly cried. The monthly cost was three times that of the previous place, which in turn had been triple the cost of her original apartment. She had some money invested, enough to last a year and a half, and we just had to go ahead.

The Alzheimer center advised us not to tell Mom she was moving again, but to bring her ahead of her belongings. The staff would watch Mom while we brought her things into her new studio apartment. After all, she was now unlikely to put all of the facts together.

On the day of the move, I took Mom to lunch at a pancake house, and then I dropped her off at the Alzheimer facility. That was how she left independent living—unaware that she would never return to it. Jane was watching from the parking lot as I helped Mom into the Miata. As soon as we left for lunch, Jane went in and began packing Mom's things for the movers.

The plan worked, and Mom settled into the Alois Alzheimer Center. We had again moved her favorite possessions, though the quantity had shrunk to fit the available space. Mom seemed unconcerned about having her own things around her; did she still know they were hers? We didn't bother with a television, because the lounge was steps from her door. At last she had no phone, a relief to Jane.

Mom was well cared for and as happy as she could have been, but she didn't understand her disease. She thought she was in a mental institution. We used to take her out for a ride sometimes, and when we brought her home she would see the sign and say, "Are we back at the crazy house?" One day a resident had gotten out the door—which had a delayed lock—and was running away with his relatives chasing him down the road. All they needed was a butterfly net to complete the stereotype.

42
Going to Health

My neurologist prescribed a month of steroids so that by December I would be strong enough to have the back operation I needed. I'd known a few guys who'd taken them, and I wondered about the side effects. The doctor said I might notice "flushing color" after I started taking the pills, so after I'd taken a dose I looked in the mirror. From my chest up, I was bright red! The line was so distinct that I looked like a section of Neapolitan ice cream: vanilla on the bottom and bright strawberry on top.

I didn't have much company where I lived. My sister worked. Mom spent her days and nights in the Alzheimer center. Only my younger son saw me during that time, and Jay was worried to death about me.

The first week I was on the steroids was the way I could imagine being on crack. I had so much energy that I was staying up thirty hours at a time. I hadn't wanted to help with the heavy work during Mom's moves, but now I was moving the refrigerator to clean behind it, moving furniture around, and scrubbing everything in my apartment. I even cleaned out my bedroom closet. I knew it had been a long time when I found some clothing Beth had left behind years earlier.

My personality began to change as a result of the steroids, but I didn't notice it at first. Being alone, I had no one to tell me what I was like. If I went out, I usually went on short errands by myself. I noticed that, if I was at a stoplight and it didn't turn green right away, I had no patience. If I was standing in line at the market and someone ahead of me didn't move along, I'd be furious. I was developing a steroid-induced rage. Everything had to move fast for me. When I realized I was not just physically messed up, but also out of control and paranoid, I was seriously worried.

I began to have dreams about our old Mustang, the red car I had loved back in Glen Ferris when I was in my teens. In every dream I was looking at that car. It was okay in the first few dreams, but then the car got dirty, and its body began to rust. The car was getting worse in every dream.

I went to Mia's. Between doctor appointments, I stayed with her. By then I was eating again. I loved ham, and I'd been eating a lot of it in ham-salad sandwiches. When my right foot swelled up to twice its normal size one night at Mia's house, I freaked out. I had so many things wrong with me at once, and I didn't know what most of them were. It helped that I wasn't alone, but that night I was so scared about my foot that I got up in the middle of the night and went to the drugstore. I asked the pharmacist to look at my swollen foot. He said I was retaining salt and that the only way I could get rid of it was through my urine. He told me to start drinking lots of water. Even though I followed his advice, my foot stayed swollen. I went home and called my doctor.

Every time I had a medical appointment, I weighed in. I was conscious about my weight, because my eating habits had been so bad. Normally I weighed in the low 160s, but one day on the doctor's scale I was at 152. I'd lost ten pounds!

"Look at me," I said to the doctor. "Do I look too skinny?"

"You look fine to me."

When I went home that night, I started worrying again. I took my shirt off and stood in front of the mirror, feeling my ribs with my hands. My legs were thin, too; everything seemed bad. I needed to start gaining weight. I got in the car and drove straight to Walmart to buy some of those drinks for old people who might not be getting all their nutrition. It was the same product Mom had been drinking to gain weight. When I got to the store, it was closed. I had picked the one night—Sunday—when Walmart was not open! When I realized I had to wait to buy my drinks, the steroids kicked in and I felt a familiar rush of anger. It was hard to be positive during moments like that.

When I went back to the doctor about my foot, I weighed in again, and the scale said 133 pounds. I seemed to be wasting away—everywhere but my swollen foot; nothing was helping it. The doctor said my circulation seemed all right, but I possibly had a blood clot. He called two emergency facilities to get me in quickly for an ultrasound, and then sent me directly to the one that could take me. The results of the ultrasound would determine whether I was going to the hospital for surgery. Yes! Another operation could be in my future—the *near* future. I felt like a crash-test dummy.

"Be careful," he said as I left to drive myself with a stick shift I could barely operate. "If you do have a clot, it could break loose and go to one of your lungs." *Thanks*.

When I got to the emergency clinic, they weighed me in, and I was 172 pounds. I couldn't get over the change in my weight. My doctor wanted to see me when I was done, so when I came back to his office, I told the nurse I'd been freaking out every time I stepped on the scale. "Oh," she said, "that scale hasn't worked for weeks." Since they were still using it, the staff must have known how to read the scale, but I sure didn't. I thought I was losing twenty pounds a week! I hadn't lost anything; in fact, I'd gained.

I didn't need the emergency surgery, so I went back to Mia's. Even with her part-time job, she could be with me. Mia was good company, but I felt lousy,and my dreams of the Mustang continued. Mia said that a vehicle in a dream represents the dreamer's body. The Mustang was me! I kept getting worse, and so did the car.

I was still taking the steroids and feeling crazy. One day we'd been out and were going back to her place. I was driving. Mia and I usually went to the same places, but sometimes weeks or months apart, and I didn't always remember the directions. We got to her neighborhood, and I recognized her street, but probably because I'd been lost so often, she told me where to turn. I was livid. "You're telling me to turn?" I yelled. "This is the only street I do know!"

Luckily, at one point in her life Mia had been on similar medication. She understood, but I couldn't stand myself. I wanted to stop taking the steroids before the month was up. My dosage was two pills, three times a day, and a half hour after I took a dose I was an ass again. On one of my trips back for doctor appointments, I told the neurologist what I was thinking: "I want to quit the steroids. I almost did."

"If you had stopped taking them," he said, "the consequences would have been catastrophic. You have to taper off. That's withdrawal, and it can be very dangerous." After that conversation, I knew I had to keep taking the pills until the month was up, so I tried to time it so that I took a dose just before bedtime. Maybe I would be less rude that way.

I was gaining weight on the steroids. The pills were supposed to rebuild muscle mass, and water retention was a side effect. I blew right up. My head actually got wider. My right foot swelled up so badly it looked like a giant potato. I couldn't see any trace of my ankle. It was impossible to get any of my socks on, let alone a shoe, so I had to buy a different kind of sock. It was wintertime, and when I went out I had only a sock on that foot. I walked with a cane, and I was a bastard because of the steroids.

Mia felt sorry for me. She knew I hated being mean and that I couldn't help it. My steroid dosage was mild compared to what athletes take. The next chance I got, I told my doctor, "Don't ever put me on those things again."

On one of my last appointments before my back surgery, I met with another doctor who said, "We have to get you in sooner." I was getting worse fast. He gave me a neck brace to wear all the time until the surgery.

In my last dream before my surgery, the Mustang was riddled with bullet holes. There were so many holes—hundreds—and they weren't regular bullet holes. These holes were large, like they had been made by a shotgun slug. I couldn't find three inches over the whole body of that car that hadn't been shot up by a gun.

The operation was performed in December 2007, just before Christmas. While I was on the operating table, something unusual happened. I woke up. They'd already put me out, and in the middle of the operation I heard the surgical staff panicking because I was awake. I jumped and couldn't catch my breath. For a while I was gasping for air and jerking around the table. Then I was out again.

Later I read that sometimes, in severe circumstances, the soul can actually jump out of the body. The soul is allowed to leave—to take a break—so that the person won't suffer so much. It re-enters the body later, and sometimes the re-entry is rough. I wondered what had caused my experience on the operating table: Had my soul left my body and then returned? It would validate what I'd been reading.

I spent Christmas that year recuperating at my son Jay's house. He picked me up from the hospital and took care of me for a week. I went with his girlfriend every morning and afternoon when she walked their dogs, because the doctor told me I had to get out every day.

When I returned home, I was still off work for several weeks. Between the pain and the surgery, I'd been off almost six months, but only six weeks of it came after my back operation. I could have used another two or three weeks, but I counted my blessings and went back to work. I was finally feeling better! I kept dreaming of the Mustang, too, and it was nice and shiny.

43
More School Ghosts

I heard stories at the intermediate school. They were ghost stories, and I just groaned to myself. Was I ever going to be free of ghosts? Nothing had happened to me there, maybe because I was working days, but other people had seen or heard things.

Pete was a custodian who worked third shift. There was only one other person in the building with him—at the other end. One night he had finished dust-mopping a hall. He left for a moment, and when he came back he saw something on the floor—the floor he'd just cleaned. It was a magnetic nametag. They're used to identify the kids' lockers. He picked it up and read it: "Barry." The kids always had their first names on their locker tags, but Barry could be a last name, too. In fact, it was Pete's last name.

He started looking for a locker with no nametag so that he could put it back. Of 250 lockers in his area, none was missing a nametag. Pete knew the tag had fallen off a locker, so he kept searching and finally found that locker in a distant area. That magnetic tag might have fallen off the locker somehow, but it could not have made it to Pete's work area on its own, in the time he wasn't looking.

Pete was primed to believe ghosts inhabited the intermediate school. He had experienced the TVs and printers going on and off while he was cleaning, a phenomenon also common at the kindergarten school. When the locker tag showed up in his area, he didn't keep it a secret. "I talked to someone who believed in the supernatural," Pete told us. "He said this *being* was letting me know that it knew who I was."

Our head custodian—my new boss—told us that he was changing light bulbs on a ladder one day when the ladder starting shaking so badly he almost fell off. He turned around to yell at whoever was messing with him, and no one was there.

Several of the stories we heard involved strange occurrences in the gymnasium. Another custodian, Stan, said he was going through the gym once and a voice clearly said his name: "Stanley." Of course, no one was there. This didn't happen to me, but others would hear a ball bouncing in the gym, like someone was dribbling it. They'd go in, and a basketball would be in the center of the floor, moving as if someone had just dropped it.

The custodians worked events on weekends, and those events were opportunities to earn overtime pay. The pay was good, because each event lasted several hours. With the setup and cleanup, a guy could earn an extra two hundred dollars in a day, but we had one custodian who wouldn't go into the building alone for weekend duty. He paid his teenaged kids five dollars an hour to go with him.

The community events we hosted were often sporting events held in the gym. We had a large space, and the fees from renting out the facilities helped our school district. It was good for community relations, too, but most of those events ran the hell out of me.

When I worked an event, I was usually alone; one custodian was the norm. The drill was this: I had to open the building, do the setup—for example, set up tables and pull the bleachers out from the wall—and then clean up after the event was over. In between setup and cleanup, I had to resupply the bathrooms every few hours and be available in case the people managing or attending the event needed something.

One Saturday I was working a karate tournament. It was my last chance until fall to earn overtime pay. The karate tournament was an annual event involving five hundred people in our gym—one hundred of them competing. I had to open out the bleachers and set up fifty to a hundred chairs and thirty heavy tables. That translated to a three-hour setup before the people arrived, and then they were in the school for another eight hours.

There was an order to the events, and the last ones were competitions among students breaking boards with their hands. When they break boards in karate, they use a soft wood. It's very good for kindling, so weeks before the tournament people try to get dibs on the broken wood for their fireplaces. We had a big rolling Dumpster called a gondola that we kept in the gym. The karate people put their used wood in the trash and I dumped it into the gondola.

After the tournament was over, the students helped me with the take-down before they left. They were great; they saved my tired butt. My next order of business was to get all the wood and trash outside. First I pushed the gondola with the used wood out the back door, into the receiving area. When I was sure the last people had left, I locked the main doors. Then I cleaned the gym.

I went over all the bleachers, checking for drinks and food, and then collapsed them. I dust-mopped the floor and then damp-mopped the sticky places to get the spills up. When I was done, I turned the lights off. By then it was getting dark, but some light was still coming in through the windows.

I took the gondola full of wood outdoors, boxed up the firewood orders, and threw the rest in our big Dumpster. When I came back in, the door locked automatically behind me.

I walked back into the gym and stopped cold. My heart started to hammer. There on the floor was a pile of wood scraps, big enough that I knew I hadn't missed it when I was cleaning. I couldn't have. Maybe these weren't the exact pieces I'd just taken outside, but they were from the karate tournament—no doubt about it—and they hadn't been there when I'd left a few minutes earlier. I knew no one could have gotten into the school. Everyone associated with the tournament had been gone for an hour and a half, and I'd just locked the wood scraps outside and myself inside.

I looked around the gym, which was dark and quiet. I was quickly going from uncomfortable to afraid. I was alone in the school with something—whatever had moved the wood—and now I had to clean it up. There was no getting around it. As much as I wanted to forget the mess, turn around, and head for my car, I couldn't.

The rule for custodians was that we worked an event until everything was done. I thought about coming back the next day to finish cleaning in the daylight, but I wanted to get it done. If I came back, I'd still be alone. I sighed and got my broom again, hoping I could at least take the stuff back outside in one trip and then get the hell out of there. The pieces were hard to sweep up, and I was nervous, but finally I could see the end of it. Just as I finished, I heard footsteps on the bleachers. They were loud, echoing in the empty gym.

I straightened up and turned to where the noise was coming from, but I couldn't see anything. Someone was walking back and forth across the bleachers, and it wasn't just a couple steps; it didn't seem to end—only that was impossible. The bleachers were collapsed; I'd already pushed them back against the wall. I looked all around. A shiver started on the backs of my arms and fanned out between my shoulder blades. I would have given anything to see another human being— say, a karate student accidentally left behind—but I knew I was alone.

That's when I heard the voice. It belonged to a boy about twelve or thirteen. His voice hadn't changed yet, and it was crystal clear. It called out in the friendliest way, like he was glad to see me. It rang out from one end of the gym to the other: "Hello."

I wasn't the least bit interested in being friendly, because I was hearing a boy's voice that *did not come from a boy*. I was alone in a dimly lit gymnasium, and it spoke to me out of the deep quiet. I was frightened.

I hadn't been afraid of the woman I saw crossing the office doorway at the kindergarten school. I knew she was a ghost, but she was going about her business. Like the ghost in the overcoat, this child was aware of me.

After my time at the kindergarten school, I didn't think I could ever be more afraid, but I was wrong. I got out of that gym fast and went to another area of the building where I still had a bit of work to do. The building had to be ready for school again on Monday, but I could not go back into that gym. It could wait until Monday morning.

44
One Loving Smile

Considering the illness she was battling, Mom was doing well at the Alois Alzheimer Center. Until the side effects became too troublesome, she took the drug Aricept. Its strong benefit is to slow the progress of the disease. Many days Mom seemed fine.

She always looked sharp. Jane knew her taste and bought her clothes. Institutional laundries can be hard on clothing, so Jane stuck with no-iron shirts and slacks. Occasionally something of Mom's was beaten to death in the wash or mixed in with other people's garments, so Jane regularly went through Mom's closet, weeded out the mistakes, and hung the coordinating outfits together. I don't know who dressed Mom every day, but her clothes always matched. We made sure she got her hair done regularly at the center, too.

One day Jane and I went to see Mom and she held out her hands. Her nails were shaped and painted pink. In all the years of scrubbing my cuticles raw with that cursed brush, I had never seen Mom's nails done. She was like a kid with those pink nails, looking at her hands and turning them this way and that.

Maybe it was the same day, maybe another day; that isn't important, but something important happened. Jane and I were sitting in Mom's room. Mom was on her couch and Jane was next to her in a side chair. I was sitting directly across from Mom. Sometimes there are long silences with old people, especially those attempting to converse around memory loss. Topics can seem to come out of the blue.

"Isn't he handsome?" Mom suddenly asked no one in particular. Jane turned to look at me and missed what happened next.

Mom smiled at me, and I will go to my grave remembering that smile. It was amazing, so soft and sweet that it almost glowed. I didn't say a word, but I'd never seen a prettier smile on anybody in my life. I knew it was meant for me. If Mom had been given one or two seconds to make up for everything she'd ever done to me, she couldn't have done any better than that smile. After nearly sixty years, I knew that my mother loved me.

Mom started slacking off on her meals. She just wasn't interested in food. Jane went by once or twice at dinnertime, sat by Mom at the table, and tried to get her to eat; but Mom would manage only a few bites. She still liked dessert—had always wanted to eat it first—but getting nutritious food into her became a challenge. One day they told us that Mom had to be moved to the nursing unit because she wouldn't feed herself. Her disease was progressing.

In the nursing unit Mom's own furniture became secondary to the bed that was already in the room, and we needed to dispose of most of her pieces. My sons came and loaded the dining room table and chairs, the china cabinet, and other items into a pickup truck for storage in Mike's garage. No one in the family needed a couch, so we left Mom's in the assisted living apartment for the next occupant.

Mom's space had continued to shrink; she now had a roommate and a shared bathroom. Jane and I felt sorry for the roommate because we knew from experience that Mom might treat her like a stick of furniture unless she had a reason to be friendly. Then one day we were asked to wait in the lobby while the room aired out. Mom's roommate was well into the adult diaper phase, and she'd had a major accident. That day I felt sorry for Mom, too.

We began asking Mom to sign important papers. With one of those, she relinquished the Ford Crown Victoria she hadn't used in years, the one she used to look for in vain with her friend "Mildred." She signed that car over to me. I'd had to scrape for nearly every car I'd ever owned. Now Mom's Ford joined the Miata at my place, making me a "two-car family" for the first time in my life.

I was planning a trip to Mia's when Mom was put in the hospital with pneumonia. I asked Jane whether I should go. Mom's mind wasn't what it had been, but she didn't seem unhealthy. Had I ever seen her ill? I couldn't remember that I had. She'd had the vascular surgery the year before and had come out fine. Jane said, "Go ahead."

Mom was eighty-nine, her ninetieth birthday less than two months away. In the years since we'd been reunited, she had told me several times that she didn't want to reach age ninety. She was done living; I know that for a fact.

I didn't ask her what was significant about age ninety; maybe nothing was, but later that number made me think of the day Jane and I worked the Ouija board for her and Grandmama.

Mom had also told us she was having nightly dreams about Grandpop, Grandmama, and even my great-grandmother, Granny Petty. During the dreams, they were in Mom's room with her, standing at the foot of her bed. I'd read enough of Sylvia Browne's books to know that Mom's dreams meant our family members were preparing her to meet them in the afterlife.

I had just gotten to Mia's the morning Jane called to say that Mom had passed away, and I left right away for the long ride home. I don't remember that I cried in the car—I was numb about the news—but I did think about how glad I'd been to have Mom for a while after all the years of misery. At least we had been a family for the last twenty-one months.

I felt lonely driving down Interstate 71 and couldn't wait to get to Jane's place. She was the only one who would understand how I was feeling.

Jane told me what had happened. She had gone to the hospital to visit Mom, who was awake and trying to talk. Mom's speech was impossible to understand. She had a lunch tray, but couldn't eat. One of the things that can happen to Alzheimer's patients is that they forget how to swallow. Jane asked the nurse to give Mom a swallow test, which Mom failed. Jane left for home, intending to come back later. She was going to make a quick trip to the grocery store.

My sister tripped on a concrete step outside her house and fell onto her left foot. "I knew it was broken," she told me. "I heard it crack." She drove herself to the emergency room and came home several hours later with pain pills and a set of crutches. She hadn't made it to the store or back to the hospital.

During the night a nurse called, but Jane slept through the ringing of the phone. In the morning she called the hospital and found out that Mom had passed away the previous night from aspiration pneumonia (foreign matter entering the lungs) and dysphagia (difficulty swallowing). The hospital nurse described Mom's death as peaceful, noting that she had become extremely calm just before she passed on. Neither Jane nor I had seen Mom to say good-bye.

I was a mess after I got home. In my family, I'm the emotional one. I couldn't even go to Kroger's for food; I'd be shopping, and I'd start crying like crazy in the store. I never knew when it was coming, so I didn't want to go out.

Luckily we were on spring break from school. I had intended to go in to work and catch up on a couple things, but I didn't. I stayed home by myself so that no one would see me. Jane's son, daughter-in-law, and granddaughter were at her house, and I didn't want to upset

Annie, who was five. I was thinking ahead to the service, too, worried that I'd burst out crying in the funeral home. If ever there was an appropriate place to shed tears, a funeral would be it; but I was embarrassed to be so out of control. I would have to greet people and hold it together, so I asked the Universe to help me.

While I was hiding from the world, a song came to me. I'd always liked music and had even made up a few poems, but I wasn't a songwriter. I was sitting at the computer, and words started coming to me as fast as I could type them, which wasn't all that fast. They weren't even my words; I knew they weren't. I was taking notes. I think the song was whispered to me from somewhere.

"One Loving Smile"
Some times should be forgotten; some things should go untold,
The pain that scars a little boy who's only five years old.
The memories never left me; they're burned into my soul,
And the dreams, they still remind me of when I was five years old.

I can't think of any reason why a child should feel such pain;
Why any life begins like this; what can there be to gain?
What lessons are we being taught? What debt is being paid?
Why we're left so helpless, so lonely and betrayed.

I wish I knew the answer; I wish I knew a way
To help the many children who go through this each day;
To help them know a loving home, to stop what they've been through;
To stop the pain that they have felt for what their parents do.

One loving smile, one loving smile;
All I wanted was to see one loving smile.
It almost took a lifetime; I waited quite a while,
By God's grace, my mother gave me one loving smile.

"One Loving Smile" got me through the funeral service because, as soon as I wrote it, my feelings toward Mom changed. All the negative feelings left me, and I had good memories instead of bad. I hadn't forgotten anything she did, but after that song I had only good feelings about her. I haven't had a bit of trouble since. I can't say it any better; "One Loving Smile" said it all. Even though I hadn't been with

Mom when she died, I felt that things were settled between us. I was all right.

Even though I was clear in my mind and heart about Mom, I didn't want to identify her body. Jane and her son and I went to the funeral home one evening, and the director asked who would officially identify Mom. Right away, Greg and I declined. Jane asked me to do it, but I didn't want to; I was afraid to see her. Then I thought: *Here we go again. Jane is doing everything, and I'm not helping.* So after they brought the body up on a gurney, I went over and stood by my sister. I knew that I could never redo that moment. I had to step up to the plate.

If I hadn't changed my mind, I wouldn't have had the closure I felt about my role as a son. Jane had gone through so much with Mom, and I had to be with her then. It was *our* mother. I'll always remember what Jane said as we stood looking at Mom one last time: "It's finally over."

Mom had decided years before to be cremated. The cremation would take place before the funeral service, so we picked out an urn for her ashes that night. Jane had brought an outfit for Mom to wear. It was one of Mom's favorites: a striped blouse, blue pants, and a jacket she had worn nearly every day. That jacket was good looking, and so soft that I thought it was a sweater. Jane had bought it for her in Santa Fe. It had a pattern of galloping horses.

Before we left, my sister wanted a five-dollar bill, but none of us had one. "Mom didn't have money at the Alzheimer's center," Jane said. "They didn't allow the residents to keep cash. Mom always asked me for five dollars. That was all she wanted, just five dollars for walking-around money, and now I'm going to put a five-dollar bill in her pocket for this journey."

The funeral director contributed the five, and Jane paid him back before the service. "Five Dollars and a Sweater" turned out to be another song that I wrote. I loved what Jane had done and couldn't get it out of my mind. Aside from the fact that Mom might have been the first person ever to wear a sweater to a cremation, it was the kindest, most thoughtful thing I ever saw anybody do.

45
Exit Points

Mom was gone. The service was nice, if you can say that about a funeral. Two of the big bosses from work came to pay their respects. Both of my sons were there, two of my grandchildren, our friends, and Jane's son and his family. Her daughter-in-law, Amy, corralled the little kids and helped them color pictures in coloring books while the rest of us took our places on folded chairs to hear the minister we'd hired through the funeral home.

Jane, Greg, and Amy had made a display of family photos for the occasion. The pictures gave our Cincinnati friends a perspective, and I found myself explaining them several times. I enjoyed it. Not that long ago, I'd sat with Mom and looked at the old photo albums she'd brought from Glen Ferris. I'd never thought about it before, but we didn't have family pictures displayed in our house. Aside from a couple in Mom and Dad's bedroom, most of ours were closed away in albums. I never saw my parents with a camera. How do you go your whole life and just realize that? I remembered other people's houses with framed photos on the TV or on the wall going up the stairs. I remembered Grandmama's dresser with our school pictures stuck in the mirror frame, but our walls were bare of people. Mom decorated with china plates and a couple of my sister's college paintings. She was in a retirement home by the time Jane and I learned that she didn't like looking at pictures because they made her sad.

Mom's ashes were sealed in a beautiful white urn with a rose design. It sat on a pedestal among the flowers at the front of the room, a subtle reminder to those who noticed. We were trying to keep it from the little kids, who knew that their great-grandma had died but would have been confused by the display. We succeeded until it was time to leave. As we headed for the parking lot loaded down with plants and flower bouquets, one of Jane's friends called to her, "Do you want me to grab your mom and carry her to the car?"

Cremation is the way to go, in my opinion. Besides the fact that it's quick and clean compared to the route a body takes underground, burial is hell for a claustrophobic.

I won't be put in a coffin. It doesn't even matter that I'll be dead. The minute I realized I wouldn't be able to stick a finger out, I decided to be cremated. I don't even want my ashes put in an urn. I told Jane, "If you do it, I'll haunt you. You can scatter my ashes, but carry them with the lid off and pour them out quickly."

I knew from my reading that death is only the end of our physical selves. The soul goes on. I also had read that we all have times in our lives called *exit points* when the soul can decide whether or not to leave the body. These are the times when an individual can exit his or her life. It was the psychic Sylvia Browne who said that before we are born, each of us designs five exit points—times of choice—for our life on earth. I hoped there was some wiggle room in Sylvia's theory because, according to my calculations, I'd already used at least three of mine.

When I dreamed of the car accident in Glen Ferris years ago, I had no idea the actual scenario would take place, but that accident was an exit point for me. By pulling off the road, I decided not to take it. My getting so sick and depressed before my back surgery offered up another exit point that I declined, thanks to *The Seat of the Soul*. Was the third one the time my car was totaled and I spilled chocolate milk on myself? What about when I was jolted on the operating table?

If I understood it correctly, exit points are part of karma. Each time we return to earth, reincarnated, to learn our lessons, we choose what our life will be. As one example, we might be poor in one lifetime and then choose to be rich in the next. Sometimes our choices prove too much for us to handle. Exit points are built in for the times when our earthly life gets too tough. I'd had suicidal thoughts from time to time when things got rough for me, when I thought nothing positive was going to happen, but that was before I realized I was putting out negative karma.

The important thing about my exit points is this: each time I reached an exit point, I chose living instead of dying.

I had to believe that Mom had picked her exit point and was now happier on the Other Side. When I thought of her that way, my sadness lifted and I was at peace. Now that I was on the mend physically, mentally, and spiritually, I felt like I could get back to living my life. It felt good.

Over the next few months, I began to think about the future. When the new school year began, Mr. Joe would be sixty years old. Medically speaking, I had been through a lot, and my body was not strong the way it had been in 1997 when I started working at the kindergarten school. My job at the intermediate school was challenging, and I wondered how long I would be able to work. How long did I *want* to work?

It was nearly 2009; time was flying, the way people always said it would when I got older. I would turn sixty-two in 2010. Was that too early to retire? I ran the numbers over and over again. Mom had left Jane and me some money—not a lot, but certainly a cushion. As a retiree, I would have a pension and could collect Social Security. The insurance side of things would be a challenge, but I thought I could live well enough on my projected income. My needs were simple; I hadn't been much of a shopper since my college days, and I had no interest in collecting possessions at my age. To me, most "things" were clutter. I watched my spending—a habit from the lean times—and I didn't see that changing in retirement.

I had earned the right to stop working. I deserved it. If I set a goal to retire at the end of 2010, I had two years to put the details to my plans. Even thinking about it brought feelings of relief and joy that told me I was on the right track. If I could hold out physically until my benefits kicked in, I'd be home free. Retirement would be a different kind of exit point, definitely better than the other kind.

46
In with the New

The doctors had fixed me, and my friendship with Mia had saved me just as surely as they had. Between her loving care and *The Seat of the Soul*, I was a new man, beginning a new life. She and I started talking about something more permanent. To me, "permanent" wasn't necessarily marriage. I was thinking we could live together. My idea was that we would take that step after I retired, but Mia didn't want to wait. For me, it was a two-year comfort zone; for her, it was just a long time.

I'd been pushed in every relationship I'd ever had. There was always some sense of urgency, and it seemed I was the one who needed to act. I'd never gotten to take my time on anything, so I didn't welcome it when Mia began to push for us to move in together. I did have an agenda that I didn't share with Mia. I thought that waiting two years would give me time to help her get over her depression, so that she would feel better about herself. I had no point of reference for the mourning period of a widow, but I didn't like to see her sad.

I also wished she would take better care of herself. Mia was a pretty woman, but her clothes and grooming didn't always reflect the beautiful person inside. I started dropping hints, always in a positive context, because I wanted to help her. When I saw a nice outfit in a store or catalog, I'd tell her, "That would look great on you." One day she showed me a photo of herself as a secretary. The photo had been taken several years before, and in it she looked happy. She was well dressed and attractive. "I know how to dress," she said. "When I was working, I had a closet full of clothes." She had seen right through me.

Mia was an important part of my life, and I was tired of the four-hour commute to her house. She had never been to mine. We decided that she should come and stay for a couple of weeks, get to know my city, meet my family, and decide how she felt about possibly moving three hundred miles from her hometown.

I hadn't changed my mind since leaving Marilyn twenty years earlier: I would not move into another woman's house. I didn't want to move Mia into my little basement apartment, but she would have to consider relocating. How could I leave my job, my children, and now my grandchildren? Besides Adrianna, there were Mike's children, Jacob and Janie, to consider, as well as their half-brother, John. The answer was simple: I couldn't. I hoped that Mia would come to me.

Mia came to visit in October of 2008, around Halloween. The apartment looked as nice as it could. Jay had painted my kitchen. I'd cleaned the place when I was on steroids and thought it still passed inspection. I'd replaced Beth's bed with a new one. Mia didn't need my ghosts.

I was working at the intermediate school. Mia didn't have a car at my place—I'd gone to get her—so during the week she was alone in the apartment until I got home. She didn't seem to mind. When we were together we visited family, did errands, or went out to eat, much as we had at her house. It was everyday life.

We got along well together, and during her visit we decided that she would move in the spring. It wasn't my first choice, but I agreed to it, and that led to another decision. Now I needed to find a better apartment.

After Mia left, Jane and I began to look for a place near my work, which also meant that I would be living closer to her. We found the perfect apartment, a one-bedroom with a den and a small covered porch. "I'm like a cicada, finally moving after seventeen years," I said to my sister—and we did know what cicadas were like after experiencing multiple cycles that released the buzzing insects all over Cincinnati. I hadn't wanted to move in all that time. I said it was because of the low rent, but maybe inertia had played a role. I hadn't had any reason to move, but now I did; and once I had committed to moving Mia in, I wanted everything to be just right.

Jane was replacing some of her furniture, and I decided to round out my collection as well. Well, maybe "round out" isn't the right term. None of my old pieces would work in my new home. The upholstery reeked of nicotine, and I didn't plan to smoke in my new place. I ordered some beautiful pieces for my—Mia's and my—apartment: in addition to the dinette set and bedroom furniture I'd already bought, I got a couch and a chair and two end tables. Now that I would have washer and dryer hookups, I also needed those appliances. Out with the old; in with the new.

I had banked most of the money Mom had left me, but having a small inheritance helped when I was buying furniture. Jane and I even went shopping for bathroom accessories. I wanted every room to be attractive for Mia. She hadn't minded that my sister and I were picking out decorations for her new home; she said she liked our taste.

Mia and I had worked out the details of our new arrangement. We would split the rent, which was nearly twice what I'd paid for my previous apartment. Her move-in date would be in April 2009, though she didn't have a great deal to move in. After I had everything ready, she would arrive with her suitcases and her dog. I had mixed feelings about a dog joining us in a new, expensive apartment with all of my new furniture, but I'd agreed because I loved Mia. Her pet, a small dachshund, was a fact of life. The dog was sweet, but old. We never knew when he was going to pee. All of a sudden we'd see a puddle underneath him and grab the paper towels. I guess it could have been worse.

I wasn't worried about having enough money; I was still at the intermediate school. Mia already had a job here, thanks to a transfer from her current employer. Of course, she'd never seen the place where she'd be working, didn't know how to get there, and knew no one. But does anybody when they start out?

I had continued to make clothing suggestions to Mia. As we moved closer to our move-in date, I had passed the hinting stage. When I was young, I had done something similar for Dad, and he had appreciated it, but Mia let me know that she wasn't going to change for anyone but herself. After I thought about it, why would she want my "help"? There was no difference between what I was offering and Hannah coming up the hall to "help" me clean the kindergarten school.

I moved in March, and what a difference! I was so excited to be in a clean, beautiful place, and I realized what I'd been missing by stubbornly holding onto my other apartment for so long. I ordered curtains. I put up pictures. I hung my clothes in my bedroom closet for the first time and thought about my previous closet—the one I didn't use for years after Beth left because it was full of stuff—hers and mine. Having a walk-in closet is great when you're not afraid to walk in.

Soon I'd be sharing that closet. I wanted to feel good about it. I liked Mia so much, but that thing of mine about loving clothes, and knowing clothes, kept rearing its head. Should I bring it up again? Was it really that important? I saw it as part of the larger issue, the matter of Mia's depression.

I had been hoping to see her become more like the happy person she had showed me in the picture of herself. I had always been honest with Mia, and now wasn't the time to stop, but I hated the thought of overstepping my bounds and losing the good relationship she and I had developed during our two years of dating. Mia had been my salvation during one of my darkest times. She had taught me about astrology and the Universe. She had given me hope for this earthly life and what lay beyond it.

I asked the Universe to help me. The Universe doesn't always give us the answer we want or expect, but it always answers.

I had to admit that this was about what I could live with. I had been dragging my feet in the relationship, and it was time to tell Mia why. She and I always talked online, typing our conversations on chat instead of talking on the phone. I left her a message: "There are things I can't handle. A better man might not be bothered by them, but I can't get past them." There it was. Mia would know what I meant.

I thought she would respond. I thought we would talk it through; that had been our way. I didn't know we'd written our last words to one another until she changed her password to the dating site and cut off all communication.

As usual, the aftermath for me was a mixture of regret and relief.. Mia had been my best friend. I had grown during our relationship. My communication skills in particular had improved: with her, I had learned how to trust, As a result, I opened up. It was a brand-new feeling for me. I began to see that I had not helped my previous relationships by hiding my feelings.

I would miss many things about being with Mia. At the same time, I knew that I could not take the relationship where she wanted it to go. I couldn't commit, not in her time frame. If she hadn't pushed me, maybe I'd still be with her, but moving her to Cincinnati was a game-changer. When it came down to that, I hadn't been able to seal the deal. Were commitment phobia and claustrophobia related? They must be. Even with Mia, I'd had to keep one foot out of the covers.

Breaking up had not been pleasant, but I knew it was for the best. Life went on, and I enjoyed my new place. Living above ground, close to work, surrounded by the furniture I'd chosen was a treat. I continued to develop my relationship with the Universe, the only one that *didn't* seem to trigger my commitment issues.

Something inside me shifted after that. All my life, I'd been wondering if was ever going to have the partner and home life I'd dreamed about. Now I had to ask: *Will I ever be ready*? Prospects were looking dim, and I wasn't getting any younger.

Did I even want the kind of life I had craved in my youth? I couldn't shake the specters of my failed relationships. My marriage still topped them all; would I ever be done with the guilt? With Mia I'd gotten close to a commitment, but I was afraid of being hurt again, afraid it wouldn't work out. The one redeeming thing about it was that I'd broken my pattern. When I was pushed, I had pushed back. When I did, I had pushed her away.

47
Back to the Drawing Board

I retired at the end of 2010 as planned, after fourteen years as Mr. Joe. The boy in the gym turned out to be my last school ghost.

All was well in my world until the spring of 2012, when I began having acute pain in my legs. It kept me awake at night, so I slept during the day, glad to escape the unrelenting agony. I had put off going to the doctor because of the $3,000 annual insurance deductible that was a consequence of my retirement, but I couldn't stand hurting all the time. I went.

My doctor gave me two prescriptions that worked well together, but instead of curing my pain, they were masking it. Relief was a temporary solution, and I needed to know if this latest problem could be fixed. My doctor sent me to the local hospital for a new MRI, a brain scan, and a nerve test. At least this time my medical history was there to guide the process. Would the path lead again to cervical myelopathy?

My history of being partial to enclosed spaces has never extended to forty-five minutes in a closed imaging device. I took my prescribed dose of Valium at the hospital. Half an hour later, once the drug had taken effect, I got on the table and settled in for the MRI. In a while I had to scratch my head. I knew I was supposed to hold still, but I couldn't. I moved my hand, and then heard through my earphones, "We have to start over."

I didn't know what a nerve test was, so I hadn't worried about having one, but after my MRI and brain scan, I reported to another room to be stuck repeatedly with a pin until I bled. The target areas were my right hand, arm, and shoulder. After the pinpricks, blood dotted my hand and arm for as far as I could see. If I'd taken a drink of water, I'd have looked like a lawn sprinkler.

For the next phase, the woman administering the nerve test shocked me with electricity. The first time she did it I thought—no, I desperately hoped—she'd given me too much by mistake; but it was the same every time, like being hit twenty times with a cattle prod.

I had to keep apologizing for my profanity. "I can't help it," I said through gritted teeth. Do other people feel what I did? I could barely stand the shocks, and I have a high pain threshold. Even the doctor told me I was the last one to bitch. That was the worst experience I've ever had in a doctor's office.

In the thirty seconds I saw the doctor, we agreed on a follow-up appointment so that he could explain my test results. For the meantime, he prescribed physical therapy, which I could take at my community center. "You're in my book," I said, and I liked his answer: "Maybe we can write a better ending this time."

My first physical therapy session was an evaluation. The therapist was great; she did a lot of stretching on my right side because it was unusually tight. She also gave me some exercises I could do at home.

When I met with the doctor for my test results, he said my back operation in 2007 had improved some of the areas impaired by cervical myelopathy. However, other areas were getting worse. I needed further surgery, which would be scheduled in the next few weeks. "This time we'll go in through your back, Joe, instead of your neck. Your first surgery was routine; we expect this one to be more complicated."

He ordered two more MRIs for me prior to any scheduling of surgery. "We need to see what's going on in your lower back and determine whether the affected nerves are in your spinal column." Before he left, he called in the nurse who was completing the insurance paperwork and rattled off the justification for coverage. *Whew.*

This time I was in shape for the surgery. I had quit smoking in September, 2009. I didn't do it for the usual reason—to improve my health; I did it to save money. I quit by using a prescription drug. The pills were expensive, but it was a short-term expense. Every day I put the six dollars I would have spent on cigarettes into a jar, and at the end of six months I had enough for a flat-screen TV and a Blu-ray media player. I gained a bit of weight after I kicked the habit, and that was another challenge I would meet in good time.

When I retired, the intermediate school staff threw a party for me and presented me with a framed memento. Everybody signed it. The school district gave me a set of luggage. Jane's present was two sessions with her personal trainer, and those sessions marked the beginning of positive physical changes for me. I began working with our trainer to rebuild the atrophied muscles on the right side of my body and restore the balance I'd lost when I began to limp. It took many months, but the results were amazing. My whole right side, including my hand, was stronger. Though I hadn't lost my limp, my two legs looked the same.

After I'd worked out for more than a year, my trainer began to talk to me about food. She even cooked for me sometimes, using nutritious recipes. Her goal was to change my thinking so that I would start eating better. Most of my life I'd eaten what I wanted, because I worked so hard that I didn't gain weight. I used to think nothing of eating a whole pizza by myself. At work, a group of custodians would go out to a restaurant every Friday and stuff ourselves until we wanted nothing more than to fall asleep. When the teachers gave us leftovers from their parties, we'd scarf them down. Portion control was not part of it. Calorie-counting did not enter our minds. It was only when I wasn't smoking that my appetite came back to bite me. Nutrition was a tough sell, but I finally got it.

I had cooked when the kids were growing up, but after they left home I wasn't that interested. Once I had a kitchen I liked and began learning about healthy eating, I started to cook again and to fix up my kitchen. I bought a new set of dishes. My son Mike gave me a set of cookware. I got a crock-pot, a grill, and the first coffee maker of my life. I began making soups from scratch. I bought vegetables I'd thought I hated for sixty years because I wouldn't taste them. I even traded recipes with my cooking friends. I discovered fiber and restored my body rhythms. The Universe was sending me what I needed, when I needed it.

Next I cut back on drinking beer. I did it to eliminate the calories, not the alcohol. As with the cigarettes, I did the right thing for the wrong reason. It was a good decision. I wasn't an alcoholic, but there were many times when I drank to escape. As my life came together, I didn't need to drink that way. I had gained courage to face life's challenges and had developed a positive attitude toward myself and others. I could no longer abide negativity. That isn't to say I was rid of it, only that now it took a greater toll.

In June, while I was waiting for my surgery date, I went to West Virginia with Jane. My sister was signing books at an outdoor festival. "It will be a distraction," I said, figuring the trip would keep my mind off my medical situation. I was taking pain medicine, but I had a hard time. Walking was involved, in addition to long sessions of sitting in one position; and the temperature that day was ninety-one degrees.

Mr. Joe

The festival coordinators had set up long tables for us, and because we'd be sitting in the sun in the extreme heat of the day, someone brought the authors large umbrellas on wooden poles. Ours kept falling over, maybe because I tied it to a folding chair with a bungee cord. I'd tried to stick it in the ground, but the dirt was so dry and hard that I couldn't have scratched "Help" with the point. Between the heat, the unstable umbrella, and the few customers interested in buying books, I thought a better name for the event was the Hades Festival.

My surgery was scheduled for July 24. I was glad, but concerned that I would wake up in the middle of it as I had the first time. I had weeks to ruminate on that black thought, which buzzed around my mind like a horsefly. The thought of waking up on the operating table wasn't the only thing that worried me. "What if this is another exit point?" I said to Jane. "I mean, how many do we get?" The dark thoughts swirled and I sought my favorite distraction, but the heat warnings kept me from the racetrack. Finally it was time for my last pre-op appointments.

I was told to report to the hospital at five-thirty on the morning of my surgery. Two hours later, I would be under and the surgery would be underway. I just wanted it over. I wanted to wake up at the end and see my friend and trainer, Anita, administering healing touch in the recovery room. My workout sessions had delivered a bonus when she and I had become good friends. A couple years earlier, I would not have dreamed I'd even be using the term *healing touch*, which is the name for energy therapy given to balance a person's physical, mental, emotional, and spiritual well-being. As it turned out, Anita did that for me before my surgery, removing a boatload of accumulated negativity. I felt the difference as soon as she was done. I'd been anxious for days, and the healing touch left me with a sense of well-being.

I was already hooked up to an IV. Before the nurse had put that needle in my arm, she had asked if I wanted Lidocaine to numb the area. "It's like what the dentist does before he gives you Novocaine," she said. I was sick of needles and said yes. What she hadn't told me was that the Lidocaine was a shot.

Nervousness brings out my sense of humor. When the anesthesiologist came in to talk to me, at one point he said, "You will not remember this." I said, "Could you also block out the years between 1972 and 1980?" Those were the years of my marriage. I quickly amended my request: "Leave in the years my sons were born."

I remember nothing after I was wheeled into surgery. The operation took two and a half hours, according to Jane and Anita, who were waiting. The important thing was that I slept through the whole procedure. After another hour and a half in recovery, I was assigned a room.

Being in the hospital overnight was a positive experience with so many people taking care of me, but still embarrassing at times. To prevent blood clots, I had to wear tight white stockings that came up to my thighs. At one point there were three women at the foot of my bed trying to remove them. "You'll have to lift your leg higher," they kept saying. I told them, "It would be easier if I was wearing underwear." I also had to start walking, which meant toddling up and down the hall outside my room with the back of my gown open. Those situations were personal to me, but the hospital staff had no doubt "seen it all."

I had both a walker and a neck brace. My doctor had deemed the operation a success, but my convalescence would take an entire month. It began in the hospital as I learned new ways of moving. I had to wear the neck brace 24/7, and thus could not look down. I had to back up to furniture and feel it with my legs before sitting. I even had to practice sitting on the toilet. I couldn't resist asking the two physical therapists, "Do you want me to grunt?"

I started reading another book in the hospital: *Blessings from the Other Side*, by Sylvia Browne. When I read the section on exit points, I realized I'd been remembering incorrectly. Exit points are "opportunities to head home again" when we know our work on earth is done. They have nothing to do with committing suicide, as I'd thought during the dark months of 2006 before my illness was diagnosed.

I stayed with Jane after my release from the hospital. She dressed my incision, ran errands, and helped me when my movements were restricted. On August 6, nearly two weeks after my surgery, I moved back home. I was still wearing my neck brace and could not drive, but I felt good. I had one remaining appointment with the doctor on August 24.

I had to depend on others for a few weeks to take me anywhere I needed to go. Because I didn't like to ask, I felt trapped. The time dragged. By August 24 I was ready to fling my neck brace into the nearest Dumpster and wrap up the whole episode of my surgery.

The doctor gave me a good report. I was not yet pain free, but he expected that I would be. I would still need months of physical therapy, but I could drive myself to the appointments. Wheels again!

Epilogue
Home

I still live in the apartment I rented in 2009. I live alone. That could change one day; but, as I get older, I doubt it will. I've dated some, but I still love my alone time.

On any given day I feel like I'm in *The Wizard of Oz*, clicking my heels together. After a huge storm, I've landed in a happy place. Sometimes I think about all the times I bought or arranged furniture, cleaned, and moved, looking for a home. I have one now. I have a home, and I am back with my family—people who were there all along. We all just got better. My sister and my sons and their families are close by, and we see each other, but we have our boundaries in place, too.

Mom has been gone nearly five years. Because of that one loving smile she gave me, I'm in a good place with my memories of her and my childhood. It took a lifetime, but I know that she loved me. I talk to her sometimes, and I think she answers. I've found unexplained pennies in my apartment that I believe are pennies from heaven—signs from Mom. For instance, more than once I've cleaned my bathtub and later found a shiny penny lying in it. A few times the paper hand-towels on my bathroom vanity have left their holder and landed in the sink while I was asleep. The bathroom doesn't have an air vent, so it wasn't a breeze that caused those towels to move.

I think Mom looks out for me now. One day I was in a gambling casino, not having much luck, so I asked her to help me. A few minutes later, as I was walking through the casino, I spotted a very shiny penny on the floor next to a slot machine with "Knights" in the name. Mom's maiden name was Knight, so I sat down and played that machine. I won more than a hundred dollars.

By the time Jane went through Mom's papers, I was expecting the one meant for me. Mom had kept her important documents in one of those fireproof metal boxes with a lock. The box was light enough for her to carry, and she kept the key on a string tied to the handle. So much for subterfuge; in her later years, Mom kept anything important in plain sight. When I went to her place, I always saw that metal box with its key on a brown string sitting on the floor by the couch, and it reminded me.

"There's something with your name on it," Jane said, handing me an envelope. I didn't tell her what it was, but I knew. It was that I.O.U. I'd given Mom when I was twenty-two years old. I still thought it was unbelievable that my mother wanted to hold forty dollars over my head from the grave—especially when I knew I'd paid it—but time had helped. I knew myself by then. I knew that I'd always done the best I could. I also had the memory of Mom's smile in the Alzheimer's center to help me forget the I.O.U. I tore it up and threw it away.

I still battle my old guilt feelings about marriage and fatherhood. I've wondered many times whether I've been a success or a failure. I made some wrong turns. Sometimes I get down on myself, thinking I flubbed my life and the lives of others. When that happens, the Universe sends me a message. Maybe it's one of the boys, or a friend, showing me what I find so difficult to see myself.

Jane says I saved my children. I never thought of it that way, but she tells me, "When you took custody of those little boys, you *saved* them. You cared for them all those years without a support system, and that took love and courage." I know I learned how to be a dad the hard way. Sometimes I think of that word from the custodian's creed: *entrusted.* That's the way I felt when the responsibility of raising my sons fell to me.

My boys are in their thirties now, and I couldn't be prouder of them. Mike supervises a production crew—a job similar to my last one at the meat plant, but in a different setting—and he's better at it than his father was. Jay has a talent for working with computers and will soon complete a degree program in technology.

Watching my sons live their lives, sometimes making the same mistakes I made, is like dreaming about the ghost in the overcoat: I have to stand aside, as some sleeping man, and let it happen, good or bad. I still want to make everything right for everyone I love—some habits are hard to break—but I know I can't. Whatever happens with my kids, it's out of my hands. I just try to be a positive influence in their lives. Sometimes we have disagreements in our family, and it kills me, but I speak up. I do my part to make up, too. It's important. We aren't perfect, but we're as normal as I've ever been.

I wonder about my dad. Did he want a family? He didn't seem to hunger after it like I did. Did Dad think he was a success as a father? He and I made some of the same mistakes, as hard as I worked to avoid them.

Mia took me to an astrologer for a reading once for my birthday. The astrologer said that Dad was waiting in line to talk to me. He was in some spiritual equivalent of a halfway house, a place where the dead go to learn the lessons they should have learned on earth. This was back when Jane was taking care of Mom. Dad's message was that he was worried about my sister, but not about me. His ghost had told me years before not to worry about him, so I guess that made us even.

On a recent summer day Jane and I met our two Indiana cousins and their dad—Mom's brother—for lunch. Uncle Bob told us stories about Mom and other members of our family. It was liberating to hear him talk openly. He knew the suffering Jane and I had endured with Mom's drinking. Our cousins knew it. We always thought we were keeping a secret, but Uncle Bob told us that alcoholism and insanity ran in our family. That was negative, but I could laugh about it. If we had a family crest, what would be on it—someone in a straitjacket?

Happy stories are the ones that make me emotional, because they represent things I didn't have. Maybe that won't change, but I feel better about life now. Once I got my head together, I knew I could be okay without necessarily having a woman in my life. I know I can't make something out of nothing. I can't make someone else care about me if it isn't meant to happen. I have my beliefs now. I have grand-kids, my sister, and good friends. I get out. I'm better health-wise and financially; the pressure from my days of struggling is over.

Telling my story in *Mr. Joe* was a different kind of struggle, with points of victory and defeat. In particular, it was tough acknowledging and explaining all the mistakes I've made. I felt guilty all over again. To do this book, I relived my life without the cushion of time. It took me more than sixty years to get through it the first time, so the acceler-ated pace for the book threw my emotions to the winds as I went over every fear, screw-up, and mistake I'd ever made. It's the hardest thing I've ever done, but my great reward for hindsight has been insight.

The survival skills I developed as a boy to insulate myself from the negativity in our home had continued to serve me in adulthood--but those skills did not always serve me well. Hiding my feelings and running away had made me a poor communicator in my relation-ships. Issues from my childhood had sabotaged my pursuit of a nor-mal family life. My survival mode of behavior—my reluctance to face unpleasantness--was a reason I was so haunted by my past. Someone said that ghosts appear to us because they have unfinished business.

So did I until I found the courage to face my problems and improve my life.

I wish I had known the power of the Universe as a boy. I remember all the lonely times I hid and felt that I had no one on my side. I think I would have done better all my life if I had known what I learned at sixty from *The Seat of the Soul*: that I was never alone.

As this book went to press, I had benefited from physical therapy. The therapist knew exactly what to do: she stretched the muscles in my right leg so that I would relearn to walk by putting my heel down first instead of my toes. In between sessions I walked on the treadmill at my apartment complex. I improved every week, and by the time my postoperative X rays were taken, my spine had healed perfectly. The nerves in my legs had not settled down from the surgery, but that would come in time.

I recently took my sister to see the kindergarten school, scene of so many of my ghost encounters. It is now an administrative building. Inside, we passed a set of stairs that led down to the old boys' locker rooms. That was an area the custodians had hated to clean. The whole lower level was smelly and dark. Custodians had felt cold spots there, and even Dave had sensed a presence in the gloom. No students had used those rooms in a long time, but I hadn't forgotten.

"I don't want to go down there," I said.

We came to another set of stairs like the first one, with an old sign that said "Girls" and an arrow pointing down to more lockers. A gate had been pulled across at the top to block access to the steps. I recognized the spot I'd heard about. "This is where the Shadow Man is," I said.

"What do you mean?"

"They say he's always here. This is where he's seen." We couldn't see anything right then but a jacket and a hat thrown over a post. It was late morning. We were steps from the exit, and light poured in the windows.

"Where are you, Shadow Man?" my sister asked the empty space, and nothing happened. Nothing at all.

My ghosts are gone. I recently came into possession of the oval mirror that hung over the console table by our front door back in Glen Ferris, the mirror where I saw Grandpop's ghost when I was twelve. Jane had it stored away, and I had a place for it over the loveseat in my den. At sixty-four, I am no longer afraid to look in the mirror.

Book Club Discussion Questions

- Joe's response to ghosts changed with his own experiences. What factor did he identify as a measure of his fear? Have you ever seen a ghost? How did you react?

- Joe was reluctant to tell others about his experiences with ghosts. What was he afraid of? Would you have felt the same way? Have you kept a secret about yourself because of what others might think or do if they knew?

- Joe had a premonition about driving that saved his life. Have you ever "seen" events occur before they actually happened? Did you have an opportunity to change the outcome, as Joe did?

- Have you faced addiction in your family? Have you ever been afraid of a family member? What did you do?

- What is a normal family? Do you believe you had a normal family as a child? Are you part of a normal family now? Explain your answer.

- Do you believe in coincidences? Was Mr. Joe's life a series of coincidences or serendipitous events, as when he found the book on the plane? What role did his choices have in determining his life path?

- How do you define a great dad? What was your dad's role in your life? If you are a father, what forces shaped your behavior toward your children?

- Do you think single fathers have the same struggles as single mothers? How are we influenced by the roles assigned to each sex by society? What is the difference between the perceived role and the actual role of a parent, in your experience?

- Have you ever been homeless? Down to your last few dollars? Have you struggled to feed your family? What sacrifices did you make? Joe sometimes stretched the truth, as when he claimed not to be afraid of heights in order to accept a house painting job. Could you compromise your beliefs or face one of your worst fears to earn a living?

- What did Joe discover about his behavior in relationships? How did his family history influence his dreams for the future? Did his childhood influence reality as well?

- Life can turn on a dime. What events, both positive and negative, made the greatest impact on Joe's life? What events have determined the direction of your life and shaped your goals? Do you think life is ever what we expect?

- Many of us, including Mr. Joe, have tried to change someone else. Do you think we act to help the other person, or to make life better for ourselves? Does our motive change the process? Does it change the outcome?

- Do you believe that we were put on earth to learn lessons? If so, what lessons did Joe learn? What might your lessons be?

- Mr. Joe's medical issues had a positive side. What was it? It is hard to imagine anyone emerging from a medical crisis unchanged. Have you, or has someone close to you, faced such a challenge?

About the Authors

Joseph Barnett grew up in Glen Ferris, a small town in the mountains of West Virginia. He attended West Virginia University and in 1970 settled in Cincinnati, Ohio, where he still lives. Contact: mr.joe2013@gmail.com; Publicist: www.randeegfeldman.com.

Jane Barnett Congdon, Joseph's sister, shared his early background in Glen Ferris. She went on to graduate from Concord University, Athens, West Virginia, and made a career of words. She retired in 2009 after thirty years as a textbook editor in Cincinnati. Jane is the author of the memoir *It Started with Dracula: The Count, My Mother, and Me* (Bettie Youngs Books www.BettieYoungsBooks.com). Contact: www.janecongdon.com, or www.randeegfeldman.com.

Other Books by Bettie Youngs Book Publishers

On Toby's Terms

Charmaine Hammond

On Toby's Terms is an endearing story of a beguiling creature who teaches his owners that, despite their trying to teach him how to be the dog they want, he is the one to lay out the terms of being the dog he needs to be. This insight would change their lives forever.

"This is a captivating, heartwarming story and we are very excited about bringing it to film." —**Steve Hudis, Producer**

ISBN: 978-0-9843081-4-9 • ePub: 978-1-936332-15-1

The Maybelline Story
And the Spirited Family Dynasty Behind It

Sharrie Williams

A fascinating and inspiring story, a tale both epic and intimate, alive with the clash, the hustle, the music, and dance of American enterprise.

"A richly told story of a forty-year, white-hot love triangle that fans the flames of a major worldwide conglomerate." —**Neil Shulman, Associate Producer,** *Doc Hollywood*

"Salacious! Engrossing! There are certain stories so dramatic, so sordid, that they seem positively destined for film; this is one of them." —*New York Post*

ISBN: 978-0-9843081-1-8 • ePub: 978-1-936332-17-5

It Started with Dracula
The Count, My Mother, and Me

Jane Congdon

The terrifying legend of Count Dracula silently skulking through the Transylvania night may have terrified generations of filmgoers, but the tall, elegant vampire captivated and electrified a young Jane Congdon, igniting a dream to one day see his mysterious land of ancient castles and misty hollows. Four decades later she finally takes her long-awaited trip—never dreaming that it would unearth decades-buried memories, and trigger a life-changing inner journey. A memoir full of surprises, Jane's story is one of hope, love—and second chances.

"An elegantly written and cleverly told story. An electrifying read." —**Diane Bruno, CISION Media**

ISBN: 978-1-936332-10-6 • ePub: 978-1-936332-11-3

The Rebirth of Suzzan Blac

Suzzan Blac

A horrific upbringing and then abduction into the sex slave industry would all but kill Suzzan's spirit to live. But a happy marriage and two children brought love—and forty-two stunning paintings, art so raw that it initially frightened even the artist. "I hid the pieces for 15 years," says Suzzan, "but just as with the secrets in this book, I am slowing sneaking them out, one by one by one." Now a renowned artist, her work is exhibited world-wide. A story of inspiration, truth and victory.

"A solid memoir about a life reconstructed. Chilling, thrilling, and thought provoking." **—Pearry Teo, Producer,** *The Gene Generation*

ISBN: 978-1-936332-22-9 • ePub: 978-1-936332-23-6

Blackbird Singing in the Dead of Night
What to Do When God Won't Answer

Gregory L. Hunt

Pastor Greg Hunt had devoted nearly thirty years to congregational ministry, helping people experience God and find their way in life. Then came his own crisis of faith and calling. While turning to God for guidance, he finds nothing. Neither his education nor his religious involvements could prepare him for the disorienting impact of the experience. Alarmed, he tries an experiment. The result is startling—and changes his life entirely.

"Compelling. If you have ever longed to hear God whispering a love song into your life, read this book." **—Gary Chapman,** *NY Times* **bestselling author,** *The Love Languages of God*

ISBN: 978-1-936332-07-6 • ePub: 978-1-936332-18-2

Fastest Man in the World
The Tony Volpentest Story

Tony Volpentest
Foreword by Ross Perot

Tony Volpentest, a four-time Paralympic gold medalist and five-time world champion sprinter, is a 2012 nominee for the Olympic Hall of Fame. This inspirational story details his being born without feet, to holding records as the fastest sprinter in the world.

"This inspiring story is about the thrill of victory to be sure—winning gold—but it is also a reminder about human potential: the willingness to push ourselves beyond the ledge of our own imagination. A powerfully inspirational story." **—Charlie Huebner, United States Olympic Committee**

ISBN: 978-1-936332-00-7 • ePub: 978-1-936332-01-4

DON CARINA: *WWII Mafia Heroine*

Ron Russell

A father's death in Southern Italy in the 1930s—a place where women who can read are considered unfit for marriage—thrusts seventeen-year-old Carina into servitude as a "black widow," a legal head of the household who cares for her twelve siblings. A scandal forces her into a marriage to Russo, the "Prince of Naples." By cunning force, Carina seizes control of Russo's organization and disguising herself as a man, controls the most powerful of Mafia groups for nearly a decade.

"A woman as the head of the Mafia who shows her family her resourcefulness, strength and survival techniques. Unique, creative and powerful! This exciting book blends history, intrigue and power into one delicious epic adventure that you will not want to put down!"
—Linda Gray, Actress, *Dallas*

ISBN: 978-0-9843081-9-4 • ePub: 978-1-936332-49-6

Living with Multiple Personalities
The Christine Ducommun Story

Christine Ducommun

Christine Ducommun was a happily married wife and mother of two, when—after moving back into her childhood home—she began to experience panic attacks and bizarre flashbacks. Eventually diagnosed with Dissociative Identity Disorder (DID), Christine's story details an extraordinary twelve-year ordeal unraveling the buried trauma of her forgotten past.

"Reminiscent of the Academy Award-winning *A Beautiful Mind,* this true story will have you on the edge of your seat. Spellbinding!" **—Josh Miller, Producer**

ISBN: 978-0-9843081-5-6 • ePub: 978-1-936332-06-9

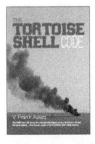

The Tortoise Shell Code

V Frank Asaro

Off the coast of Southern California, the Sea Diva, a tuna boat, sinks. Members of the crew are missing and what happened remains a mystery. Anthony Darren, a renowned and wealthy lawyer at the top of his game, knows the boat's owner and soon becomes involved in the case. As the case goes to trial, a missing crew member is believed to be at fault, but new evidence comes to light and the finger of guilt points in a completely unanticipated direction. An action-packed thriller.

ISBN: 978-1-936332-60-1 • ePub: 978-1-936332-61-8

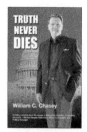

Truth Never Dies

William C. Chasey

A lobbyist for some 40 years, William C. Chasey represented some of the world's most prestigious business clients and twenty-three foreign governments before the US Congress. His integrity never questioned. All that changed when Chasey was hired to forge communications between Libya and the US Congress. A trip he took with a US Congressman for discussions with then Libyan leader Muammar Qadhafi forever changed Chasey's life. Upon his return, his bank accounts were frozen, clients and friends had been advised not to take his calls.

Things got worse: the CIA, FBI, IRS, and the Federal Judiciary attempted to coerce him into using his unique Libyan access to participate in a CIA-sponsored assassination plot of the two Libyans indicted for the bombing of Pan Am flight 103. Chasey's refusal to cooperate resulted in a six-year FBI investigation and sting operation, financial ruin, criminal charges, and incarceration in federal prison.

ISBN: 978-1-936332-46-5 • ePub: 978-1-936332-47-2

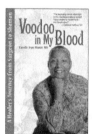

Voodoo in My Blood
A Healer's Journey from Surgeon to Shaman

Carolle Jean-Murat, M.D.

Born and raised in Haiti to a family of healers, US trained physician Carolle Jean-Murat came to be regarded as a world-class surgeon. But her success harbored a secret: in the operating room, she could quickly intuit the root cause of her patient's illness, often times knowing she could help the patient without surgery. Carolle knew that to fellow surgeons, her intuition was best left unmentioned. But when the devastating earthquake hit Haiti and Carolle returned to help, she had to acknowledge the shaman she had become.

"This fascinating memoir sheds light on the importance of asking yourself, 'Have I created for myself the life I've meant to live?'" —**Christiane Northrup, M.D., author of the New York Times bestsellers:** *Women's Bodies, Women's Wisdom*

ISBN: 978-1-936332-05-2 • ePub: 978-1-936332-04-5

Electric Living
The Science behind the Law of Attraction

Kolie Crutcher

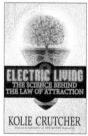

An electrical engineer by training, Crutcher applies his in-depth knowledge of electrical engineering principles and practical engineering experience detailing the scientific explanation of why human beings become what they think. A practical, step-by-step guide to help you harness your thoughts and emotions so that the Law of Attraction will benefit you.

ISBN: 978-1-936332-58-8 • ePub: 978-1-936332-59-5

Hostage of Paradox: A Qualmish Disclosure

John Rixey Moore

Few people then or now know about the clandestine war that the CIA ran in Vietnam, using the Green Berets for secret operations throughout Southeast Asia. This was not the Vietnam War of the newsreels, the body counts, rice paddy footage, and men smoking cigarettes on the sandbag bunkers. This was a shadow directive of deep-penetration interdiction, reconnaissance, and assassination missions conducted by a selected few Special Forces units, deployed quietly from forward operations bases to prowl through agendas that, for security reasons, were seldom understood by the men themselves.

Hostage of Paradox is the first-hand account by one of these elite team leaders.

"Deserving of a place in the upper ranks of Vietnam War memoirs." —**Kirkus Review**

"Read this book, you'll be, as John Moore puts it, 'transfixed, like kittens in a box.'" —**David Willson, Book Review, The VVA Veteran**

ISBN: 978-1-936332-37-3 • ePub: 978-1-936332-33-5

Amazing Adventures of a Nobody

Leon Logothetis

From the Hit Television Series Aired in 100 Countries!

Tired of his disconnected life and uninspiring job, Leon Logothetis leaves it all behind—job, money, home, even his cell phone—and hits the road with nothing but the clothes on his back and five dollars in his pocket, relying on the kindness of strangers and the serendipity of the open road for his daily keep. Masterful storytelling!

"A gem of a book; endearing, engaging and inspiring." —**Catharine Hamm, Los Angeles Times Travel Editor**

ISBN: 978-0-9843081-3-2 • ePub: 978-1-936332-51-9

Universal Co-opetition
Nature's Fusion of Co-operation and Competition

V Frank Asaro

A key ingredient in personal and business success is competition—and co-operation. Too much of one or the other can erode personal and organizational goals. This book identifies and explains the natural, fundamental law that unifies the apparently opposing forces of cooperation and competition.

ISBN: 978-1-936332-08-3 • ePub: 978-1-936332-09-0

Out of the Transylvania Night

Aura Imbarus
A Pulitzer-Prize entry

"I'd grown up in the land of Transylvania, homeland to Dracula, Vlad the Impaler, and worse, dictator Nicolae Ceausescu," writes the author. "Under his rule, like vampires, we came to life after sundown, hiding our heirloom jewels and documents deep in the earth." Fleeing to the US to rebuild her life, she discovers a startling truth about straddling two cultures and striking a balance between one's dreams and the sacrifices that allow a sense of "home."

"Aura's courage shows the degree to which we are all willing to live lives centered on freedom, hope, and an authentic sense of self. Truly a love story!" —**Nadia Comaneci, Olympic Champion**

ISBN: 978-0-9843081-2-5 • ePub: 978-1-936332-20-5

Crashers
A Tale of "Cappers" and "Hammers"

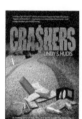

Lindy S. Hudis

The illegal business of fraudulent car accidents is a multi-million dollar racket, involving unscrupulous medical providers, personal injury attorneys, and the cooperating passengers involved in the accidents. Innocent people are often swept into it. Newly engaged Nathan and Shari, who are swimming in mounting debt, were easy prey: seduced by an offer from a stranger to move from hard times to good times in no time, Shari finds herself the "victim" in a staged auto accident. Shari gets her payday, but breaking free of this dark underworld will take nothing short of a miracle.

"A riveting story of love, life—and limits. A non-stop thrill ride." —**Dennis "Danger" Madalone, stunt coordinator, *Castle***

ISBN: 978-1-936332-27-4 • ePub: 978-1-936332-28-1

The Ten Commandments for Travelers

Nancy Chappie

Traveling can be an overwhelming experience fraught with delays, tension, and unexpected complications. But whether you're traveling for business or pleasure, alone or with family or friends, there are things you can do to make your travels more enjoyable—even during the most challenging experiences. Easy to implement tips for hassle-free travel, and guidance for those moments that threaten to turn your voyage into an unpleasant experience. You'll learn how to avoid extra costs and aggravations, save time, and stay safe; how to keep your cool under the worst of circumstances, how to embrace new cultures, and how to fully enjoy each moment you're on the road.

ISBN: 978-1-936332-74-8 • ePub: 978-1-936332-75-5

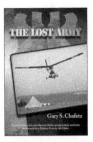

The Search for the Lost Army
The National Geographic and Harvard University Expedition

Gary S. Chafetz

In one of history's greatest ancient disasters, a Persian army of 50,000 soldiers was suffocated by a hurricane-force sandstorm in 525 BC in Egypt's Western Desert. No trace of this conquering army, hauling huge quantities of looted gold and silver, has ever surfaced.

Gary Chafetz, referred to as "one of the ten best journalists of the past twenty-five years," is a former Boston Globe correspondent and was twice nominated for a Pulitzer Prize by the Globe.

ISBN: 978-1-936332-98-4 • ePub: 978-1-936332-99-1

A World Torn Asunder
The Life and Triumph of Constantin C. Giurescu

Marina Giurescu, M.D.

Constantin C. Giurescu was Romania's leading historian and author. His granddaughter's fascinating story of this remarkable man and his family follows their struggles in war-torn Romania from 1900 to the fall of the Soviet Union. An "enlightened" society is dismantled with the 1946 Communist takeover of Romania, and Constantin is confined to the notorious Sighet penitentiary. Drawing on her grandfather's prison diary (which was put in a glass jar, buried in a yard, then smuggled out of the country by Dr. Paul E. Michelson—who does the FOREWORD for this book), private letters and her own research, Dr. Giurescu writes of the legacy from the turn of the century to the fall of Communism.

We see the rise of modern Romania, the misery of World War I, the blossoming of its culture between the wars, and then the sellout of Eastern Europe to Russia after World War II. In this sweeping account, we see not only its effects socially and culturally, but the triumph in its wake: a man and his people who reclaim better lives for themselves, and in the process, teach us a lesson in endurance, patience, and will—not only to survive, but to thrive.

"The inspirational story of a quiet man and his silent defiance in the face of tyranny."
—**Dr. Connie Mariano, author of** *The White House Doctor*

ISBN: 978-1-936332-76-2 • ePub: 978-1-936332-77-9

Diary of a Beverly Hills Matchmaker

Marla Martenson

Quick-witted Marla takes her readers for a hilarious romp through her days as an LA matchmaker where looks are everything and money talks. The Cupid of Beverly Hills has introduced countless couples who lived happily ever-after, but for every success story there are hysterically funny dating disasters with high-maintenance, out of touch clients. Marla writes with charm and self-effacement about the universal struggle to love and be loved.

ISBN 978-0-9843081-0-1 • ePub: 978-1-936332-03-8

Thank You for Leaving Me
Finding Divinity and Healing in Divorce

Farhana Dhalla
Foreword by Neale Donald Walsch

The end of any relationship, especially divorce, can leave us bereft, feeling unmoored, empty. Speaking to that part of our hearts that knows you must find your way to a new and different place, this compassionate book of words of wisdom helps grow this glimmering knowledge—and offers hope and healing for turning this painful time into one of renewal and rediscovery. This book is balm for your wounded heart, and can help you turn your fragility to endurable coping, and will you rediscover your inner strengths. Best of all, this book will help you realize the transformative power inherent in this transition.

ISBN: 978-1-936332-85-4 • ePub: 978-1-936332-86-1

GPS YOUR BEST LIFE
Charting Your Destination and Getting There in Style

Charmaine Hammond and Debra Kasowski
Foreword by Jack Canfield

A most useful guide to charting and traversing the many options that lay before you.

"A perfect book for servicing your most important vehicle: yourself. No matter where you are in your life, the concepts and direction provided in this book will help you get to a better place. It's a must read." —**Ken Kragen, author of** *Life Is a Contact Sport*, **and organizer of** *We Are the World*, **and** *Hands Across America*, **and other historic humanitarian events**

ISBN: 978-1-936332-26-7 • ePub: 978-1-936332-41-0

The Morphine Dream

Don Brown with *Pulitzer nominated Gary S. Chafetz*

At 36, high-school dropout and a failed semi-professional ballplayer Donald Brown hit bottom when an industrial accident left him immobilized. But Brown had a dream while on a morphine drip after surgery: he imagined himself graduating from Harvard Law School (he was a classmate of Barack Obama) and walking across America. Brown realizes both seemingly unreachable goals, and achieves national recognition as a legal crusader for minority homeowners. An intriguing tale of his long walk—both physical and metaphorical. A story of perseverance and second chances. Sheer inspiration for those wishing to reboot their lives.

"An incredibly inspirational memoir." —**Alan M. Dershowitz, professor, Harvard Law School**

ISBN: 978-1-936332-25-0 • ePub: 978-1-936332-39-6

Cinderella and the Carpetbagger

Grace Robbins

Harold Robbins's steamy books were once more widely read than the Bible. His novels sold more than 750 million copies and created the sex-power-glamour genre of popular literature that would go on to influence authors from Jackie Collins and Jacqueline Susann to TV shows like Dallas and Dynasty. What readers don't know is that Robbins—whom the media had dubbed the "prince of sex and scandal"—actually "researched" the free-wheeling escapades depicted in his books himself . . . along with his drop-dead, gorgeous wife, Grace. Now, in this revealing tell-all, for the first time ever, Grace Robbins rips the covers off the real life of the international best-selling author.

The 1960s and '70s were decades like no others—radical, experimental, libertine. Grace Robbins chronicles the rollicking good times, peppering her memoir with anecdotes of her encounters with luminaries from the world of entertainment and the arts—not to mention most of Hollywood. The couple was at the center of a globetrotting jet set, with mansions in Beverly Hills, villas and yachts on the French Riviera and Acapulco. Their life rivaled—and often surpassed—that of the characters in his books. Champagne flowed, cocaine was abundant, and sex in the pre-AIDS era was embraced with abandon. Along the way, the couple agreed to a "modern marriage," that Harold insisted upon. With charm, introspection, and humor, Grace lays open her fascinating, provocative roller-coaster ride of a life—her own true Cinderella tale.

"This sweet little memoir's getting a movie deal. It will not grab the Vatican's blessing."
—**New York Post**

"I gulped down every juicy minute of this funny, outrageous memoir. Do not take a pill before you go to bed with this book, because you will not be able to put it down until the sun comes up." —**Rex Reed**

"Grace Robbins has written an explosive tell-all. Sexy fun." —**Jackie Collins**

"You have been warned. This book is VERY HOT!" —**Robin Leach, Lifestyles of the Rich & Famous**

ISBN: 978-0-9882848-2-1 • ePub: 978-0-9882848-4-5

The Girl Who Gave Her Wish Away

Sharon Babineau
Foreword by Craig Kielburger

The Children's Wish Foundation approached lovely thirteen-year-old Maddison Babineau just after she received her cancer diagnosis. "You can have anything," they told her, "a Disney cruise? The chance to meet your favorite movie star? A five thousand dollar shopping spree?"

Maddie knew exactly what she wanted. She had recently been moved to tears after watching a television program about the plight of orphaned children. Maddie's wish? To ease the suffering of these children half-way across the world. Despite the ravishing cancer, she became an indefatigable fundraiser for "her children." In The Girl Who Gave Wish Away, her mother reveals Maddie's remarkable journey of providing hope and future to the village children who had filled her heart.

A special story, heartwarming and reassuring.

ISBN: 978-1-936332-96-0 • ePub: 978-1-936332-97-7

Company of Stone

John Rixey Moore

With yet unhealed wounds from recent combat, John Moore undertook an unexpected walking tour in the rugged Scottish highlands. With the approach of a season of freezing rainstorms he took shelter in a remote monastery—a chance encounter that would change his future, his beliefs about blind chance, and the unexpected courses by which the best in human nature can smuggle its way into the life of a stranger. He did not anticipate the brotherhood's easy hospitality or the surprising variety of personalities and guarded backgrounds that soon emerged through their silent community.

Afterwards, a chance conversation overheard in a village pub steered him to Canada, where he took a job as a rock drill operator in a large industrial gold mine. The dangers he encountered among the lost men in that dangerous other world, secretive men who sought permanent anonymity in the perils of work deep underground—a brutal kind of monasticism itself—challenged both his endurance and his sense of humanity.

With sensitivity and delightful good humor, Moore explores the surprising lessons learned in these strangely rich fraternities of forgotten men—a brotherhood housed in crumbling medieval masonry, and one shared in the unforgiving depths of the gold mine.

ISBN: 978-1-936332-44-1 • ePub: 978-1-936332-45-8

Trafficking the Good Life

Jennifer Myers

Jennifer Myers had worked hard toward a successful career as a dancer in Chicago. But just as her star was rising, she fell for the kingpin of a drug trafficking operation. Drawn to his life of excitement, she soon acquiesced to driving marijuana across the country, making easy money she stacked in shoeboxes and spent like an heiress. Only time in a federal prison made her face up to and understand her choices. It was there, at rock bottom, that she discovered that her real prison was the one she had unwittingly made inside herself and where she could start rebuilding a life of purpose and ethical pursuit.

"In her gripping memoir Jennifer Myers offers a startling account of how the pursuit of an elusive American Dream can lead us to the depths of the American criminal underbelly. Her book is as much about being human in a hyper-materialistic society as it is about drug culture. When the DEA finally knocks on Myers' door, she and the reader both see the moment for what it truly is—not so much an arrest as a rescue." —**Tony D'Souza, author of** ***Whiteman and Mule***

ISBN: 978-1-936332-67-0 • ePub: 978-1-936332-68-7

Bettie Youngs Books

We specialize in MEMOIRS

. . . books that celebrate

fascinating people and

remarkable journeys

In bookstores everywhere, online, Espresso,
or from the publisher, Bettie Youngs Books
VISIT OUR WEBSITE AT
www.BettieYoungsBooks.com
To contact:
info@BettieYoungsBooks.com